THE POWER OF THE HEART

ANGELO THOMAS CRAPANZANO

ISBN: 978-1-961017-48-1 (sc)
ISBN: 978-1-961017-49-8 (e)

Rev. date: 06/13/2023

DEDICATION

I dedicate this novel to all my brothers and sisters in Jesus Christ.

CONTENTS

CHAPTER ONE

First Step to the Future

Mike, after his last class that day, returned to his University state room. Mike was a student at the Ohio State University in Columbus. His goal was to become a Medical Surgeon. When he settled in he decided to call his parents. His father was a carpenter for a large construction company. Most of his work was on large Business office buildings. He did more than carpentry work for the company. He also did a lot of the planning. He had been assigned a large job in San Leandro California. Mike dialed his mother's cell phone number. His Mother answered.

"Hello, this is Nicola Costello. How can I help you?" This was her normal answering since most of the calls were to hire her husband Joseph for carpenter business.

"This is your son, Mike. How are you doing down there? When are you coming back to Ohio?"

"That is a very interesting question," said his mother. "The job was calculated to take about two months. But your dad, with his wisdom, made a special arrangement so that it only took one month."

"What was the arrangement that Dad did that cut the time in half?"

"Well you know that it rains most of the time here in the San Francisco area. So, it is hard for the workers to work in heavy rain. Your father, using good common sense, built the outer wall first and used each floor as the roof as the workers worked in the area under each floor as the building went up so that most of the time they did not work in the rain."

"That is great," said Mike. "So, when are you going home?"

"That is the problem," said Mike's mother. "They are so

impressed with you father, that they offered him a job as Construction Manager. His salary is almost double. So, we are planning on moving here. We are looking to buy a house here just south of the city in the country."

"What are you going to do with the house here in Ohio?" asked Mike.

"We are going to keep it until the time when your father retires. We are going to rent a truck next week and move everything down here. We will move all your things too. This we will do of course if we buy the house where we made an offer. We will probably put the house in Ohio for rent."

"Wow mom, after I graduate will I have to live in California?"

"I would like that," said his mother. "There are a few good hospitals here."

"But I was accepted at the Medical University in Toledo Ohio. That will make it a long way for me to come home during my college years."

"Call me next week and I'll tell you what our final decision is. You may have to live with whatever we do."

"Alright Mon," said Mike. "I will call you next week. Love you, goodbye."

"I love you too, goodbye". With that said Mike hung up and went into his bedroom to change clothes. He just entered the room when he heard a knock on the door. He walked to the door and opened it.

"Hi Carol" said Mike before she could speak. "What can I do for you?"

"Oh Mike, did you forget our plans for today? It is Friday. Don't you remember that you promised to take me to the PlayHouse Restaurant? There we can have dinner and dance all night. I am looking forward to having your arms around me."

"I'm sorry," said Mike with a sad look on his face. "I was so worried about my mom and dad that I forgot that it is Friday. Come on in and give me a minute to change my shirt. I will only be a minute." He was out in less than five minutes. "Let go."

"What is the problem with you, your family?" asked Carol as they left.

"Let's go to the restaurant," said Mike. "I will tell you all about it while we are eating."

Mike originally met Carol in the first week of his final year. She had just started her first year. Mike went down to the University cafeteria for dinner. In all the first three years he had not made close friends with the other students. He had decided that he was going to work hard all week. On weekends he would drive down to Fairlawn to spend the weekend with his parents and his sister. When he walked into the cafeteria he saw this pretty girl sitting alone at a table. Without thinking he walked up to her table and asked if he could join her. He told her he hated to eat alone. She said that she would like him to join her. She told him that she also hated to eat alone. She told him she felt like a sore thumb in front of an audience. From that day on they went out every Friday. What made them so attracted to each other was that during their conversations getting to know each other, they found that they were both Born-Again-Christians. Soon they found themselves in love.

When Mike and Carol got to the PlayHouse Restaurant, they sat down at a table and were given the menu. After they ordered Carol turned to Mike.

"Now," she said, "Tell me what is going on with your parents. I know that since we met that you have not gone home on weekends to see them. Are they angry with you?"

"No," said Mike, "In fact they are happy for us. The problem is that, as you know, my father was given a small job in California. He did such a great job that they offered him a high position there in California. So they are planning to buy a house there and move there permanently."

"Oh Mike," said Carol with a sad look on her face. "That puts a stumbling block in our relationship."

"Why do you say that?" asked mike.

"Well I have three more years to go for my graduation,"

answered Carol. "If you were here in Ohio I could see you once in a while. If you are in California, I don't see how we could ever be together again."

"But I will be in Toledo for four years. That is not too far away."

"But after you graduate you will probably find a job at one of the California Hospitals."

"Well" said Mike, "let's not try to guess the future. Let's finish our dinner and start dancing." They did just that. They danced all night. It was eleven thirty when they went to their rooms at the university. However, they spent ten minutes at her door saying goodbye mostly with kisses.

They spent every Friday together during the next three weeks. They went to dinner and once to a movie. The other day after dinner they spent time together in Mike's room, where they just watched TV. Mike was very careful so that the kissing did not get out of hand. Mike made sure to remember that they both were strong Christians. After the last class and the final tests Mike went to Carol's room. She was just getting there.

"Hi Mike. I was hoping to see you before I left."

"When are you leaving?" asked Mike.

"My parents surprised me. They are waiting in the parking lot. I am going to leave as soon as I finish packing. I did most of my packing last night but I want to change my clothes to traveling clothes. That is why I'm so glad to see you here. I want to say goodbye and make plans for our next get together."

"I was hoping we could spend some time together before you left," said Mike. "I was hoping you could stay for the graduation."

"My parents want to be on the way home," said Carol sadly. "They have plans for the weekend. I have no choice."

"Let's stop this talking," said Mike. "Let's keep in contact through the phone. We can make plans later." Mike then grabbed Carol and started kissing her. She loved the action and gave in to the kissing. About ten minutes later, Carol's cell phone rang. It was her Mother.

"Where are you?" asked Carol's mother. Mike heard it since his head was next to Carol's head. "We have to be going before it gets dark."

"I just got to my room. I want to change my clothes and I will be right down. I have already packed all my belongings. I will only be there for about five minutes." With that said Carol gave Mike one last kiss and went inside. Mike went sadly to his room.

The graduation took place in the University auditorium. Mike's mother and father attended but Mike's sister had final exams and could not make it. Before Mike went to the auditorium he packed up all his possessions and placed them in the trunk of his car. He didn't want to stay in his college room. He wanted to stay in the motel with his parents. Mike then went to the auditorium. Until it was his row of graduation students turn to go to the stage he sat and waited. Soon his row was called. The student then in single file walked up the steps and across the stage to the professor who handed out the diplomas. Mike finally walked across the stage to get his diploma. His mind however was on Carol. He worried that he would not see her again. After receiving the diploma he sat in the aisle with the other student that had received their diploma. It took one and a half hours to give out all the diplomas. After they were dismissed, Mike went into the hallway where he met his parents.

"Mike," asked his mother. "Do you want to stay through the graduation party? I would like to start on our way home."

"No," said Mike. "I am ready to leave here, but isn't it too late to travel?"

"We have a reservation at a hotel about a two hour drive from here which is on the way home. We can have dinner there and spend the night there. Tomorrow they will start to travel to get home. They are not there yet."

"Let's go then," said Mike. "Where is your car?"

"We came in a truck," said Mike's father. "I will get into it and turn on the lights and blow my horn. You come and find it. When you get where we are, blow your horn. I will pull out and you follow me to the hotel."

"Why are you driving your truck?" asked Mike. "It would have been easier if you would have come by plane and I then drove us all home."

"We came yesterday," said Mike's dad. "We had a few things to pick up at the house before we rented it out."

"All right then," said Mike. "Lead the way."

"Just in case you get separated from us along the way, let me tell you what our plans are," said Mike's dad. "First we are going to Findlay for dinner. Then we will take Route 75 to Toledo where we will connect with route 80. Route 80 will take you directly to San Francisco with only two stops along the way. Here is my card with the address of our new home."

"I will follow you all the way," said Mike. Mike then went into the parking lot and got into his car and searched for his father's car. Since it was a truck it was easy to find. From there on it all worked out as planned.

Two hours later they pulled into Findlay. They found a motel, ate dinner in their restaurant and then went to bed. The next morning, they took Route 75 to Toledo. They soon found route 80 and headed south. It was early afternoon when they stopped at the city of Davenport. They had lunch there and then proceeded towards Omaha. Omaha was located on the border of Iowa and Nebraska. It was about six in the evening when they got to Omaha. They found a hotel that had a restaurant and after dinner they went to sleep. The next day after breakfast they headed west. That evening about seven they reached Salt Lake City Utah. At Salt Lake City they repeated what they had done the last two days. The next morning, they proceeded west on Route 80. When it was about noon, Mike got a call from his father on his cell phone.

"Mike," said his father. "I don't think we should stop for lunch. I would like to go straight home."

"I agree dad. I would like this trip to be over as soon as

possible." It was about four in the afternoon when they arrived at the home in San Leandro. Mike was amazed at the house. It was a beautiful ranch house with a double car garage attached on the left side. It had a very wide driveway into the double car garage. It also had another drive way that went on the side of the garage. Mike's dad backed into his drive so that he could remove all that was in the truck into his garage. Mike pulled in behind him. Mike's dad then came out of the truck and walked to Mike's car.

"Please come and help me unload the truck. After it is unloaded, pull out and let me park my truck on that drive on the side of the garage. Then you can pull up behind me so that the garage drive will not be blocked." This was done according to Mike's father's request. After they parked the car they went inside and Mike helped his father bring all the furniture they had taken out of the truck and brought them to the house where Mike's mother wanted them. They then took Mike to the bedroom they had prepared for him.

"Wow," said Mike as he entered the room. "This is twice as big as I had in Ohio and twice as nice. I would love to live here."

"I'm so glad that you like it," said Mike's mother. "I will leave you here to unpack. I have to go into the kitchen to start dinner." With that said she left. Mike then hung his shirts, pants, and suit in the closet and stored all his other clothes in the dresser drawers. He then laid down on the bed to rest. It was about an hour later that he awoke at the sound of his name.

"Michel, Michel," said a young woman entering the room. I'm sorry that I woke you but I need to hug you."

"Cathy," said Mike as he got up and was suddenly hugged by his young sister. It's so nice to see you. I have missed seeing you grow up these last four years. How are you doing?"

"I'm doing great. I just finished my first year at Golden Gate University."

"Have you decided what you want to study?" asked mike.

"I'm not too sure," said Kathy. "I think I want to be a corporate

Attorney. I don't want to be a lawyer who takes on small cases for the general public."

"Hey you guys," yelled Mike's mother from down states. "Dinner is ready." Mike and Kathy both went down to the kitchen. They all sat around the table. Mike's mother had set a large baked chicken in the center of the table.

"This is a day to remember," said Mike's father. "We are all together once more."

"Say a prayer Joseph," said Mike's mother. "Then cut the chicken."

"Thank you Lord for all the blessings you have given us," started Mike's father. "Thank you for bringing us all together. We Thank you lord for this food. We ask that you bless it and let it be a blessing to our body." Mike's father then reached over and cut the chicken. Kathy liked the chicken wings. Mike took a chicken leg. Mike's parents both liked the chicken breast. They all ate joyfully. When they had finished the chicken they all ate the salad last. It is the Sicilian custom to eat the salad last. After the salad Mike's mother brought out an apple pie.

"Well Kathy," asked Mike, "what are you going to do until you have to go back to school?"

"I have a job at the city mall downtown," said Kathy. "I am a sales lady in the Belden women's clothing store. I will work in the women's shoes department. I don't start until Monday. I suggest that you and Mike take the next two days to see San Francisco." That evening they all sat around and talked about the possible future. At about eleven they all went to bed. The next morning Kathy got Mike up and they both had breakfast and set out for San Francisco. The trip was very exciting. They saw buildings they never saw before. They stopped at a restaurant and had a quick lunch. They then proceeded in their viewing of the city. On the way back as they entered San Leandro city they passed a sign that said Fairmont Hospital.

"Do you have a hospital right here in your hometown?" asked Mike.

"Yes," said Kathy. "It is the best around here. It has an emergency area, a surgery area. And a nurse's area that takes care of patients that are there from accidents. Mostly come through the emergency room."

"That is great," said Mike. When I get my Doctor's degree I can perhaps come here to practice."

"That's right," said Kathy. "You want to be a surgeon. I guess that you will never want a private office."

"Even if I didn't want to be a surgeon, I don't like the idea of treating a patient just in an office with minimal equipment. I would rather work in a hospital where a lab is nearby."

"Would you like to go and check out the hospital where someday you may be working there?" said Kathy.

"Do you think it would be OK?" asked Mike.

"It would be fine," said Kathy. "We have a lot of time. If anyone asks you what you are doing there tell them you are checking out the place you could be working someday."

"Let's go," said Mike eagerly. They followed the arrow on the sign and were soon in the hospital parking lot.

"You go on in," said Kathy after she parked the car. "I don't want to go inside. I don't like hospitals. They give me a fearful feeling. You go I will wait for you here in the car. It shouldn't take you more than fifteen minutes."

"I won't be long," said Mike as he left the car. He entered what looked like the main entrance. He was on the first floor. There was a hallway that went deep into the building. On his right off the hallway was the entrance to the hospital cafeteria. Located opposite the entrance to the cafeteria were the elevators. As he walked down the hallway a few steps he could see from the signs that the first floor was mainly offices. One of the signs said that the lab was at the end of the hallway. Mike retreated to the elevators and went up to the second floor. As he walked down the main corridor he noticed that most of the patients had casts on their arms, feet and other places on their body. It was obvious that most patients were recovering from an accident. When he got half way down the hall he came to the nurse's counter.

"Can I help you find someone?" asked the nurse.

"No," answered Mike. "I am here to get acquainted with the hospital. I hope that someday I will be working here." Mike then proceeded down the hall. At the end he found steps that took him to the third floor. As he walked down the hall he noticed that most patients were connected to life preserving equipment. Just as he got to the third floor nurse's counter a gentleman walked up to him.

"Can I help you with anything?" asked the man. "Were you sent here to evaluate the hospital? I am Gary Cromer, the head of this hospital"

"I'm so sorry sir," said Mike with a sorrowful look on his face. "My name is Mike Costello. I just graduated from Ohio State University. I graduated with a pre-medical degree. This fall I will go to Toledo's Medical University. I would like to become a Surgeon. This hospital is only ten minutes from my home. I would like to work here after I graduate."

"Will you follow me to my office?" said Mr. Cromer.

"Of course," answered Mike. They then walked down to the other end of the hall to the manager's office

"Come on in and have a seat," said Mr. Cromer. Mike walked in and took a seat across from the desk."So, you would like to work here after you graduate?" asked Mr. Cromer.

"Yes sir," answered Mike, feeling a little uneasy.

"Well what do you think of this hospital now that you have reviewed it?"

"I think it is fantastic," said Mike. "It is so well organized."

"I am glad that you like it. Do you have any plans for the summer   months before you go to school?"

"I just got here so I didn't get a chance to seek a job," said Mike.

"What kind of a job are you looking for," asked Mr. Cromer.

"I have not given it any thought," said Mike

"How would you like to work here in this hospital?" asked Mr. Cromer.

"Are you kidding," said Mike. "I couldn't ask for anything more even if it is a janitor's job."

"We have a job available as a nurse's assistant," said Mr. Cromer. "Are you interested?"

"When do I start?" said Mike.

"First I want you to read this employment agreement document," said Mr. Cromer. "I have to go and get an employee hiring document. It is usually the job of Danna, the Employee coordinator who handles new hiring. However, she has taken a week's vacation. So, it will be up to me to hire you."

"I will read this document while you are gone," said Mike. Mike started to read the document. It was just some simple rules employees had to follow. He had no problem with it. Five minutes later Mr. Cromer returned to his office. Well," he said. "Was there anything in the document you read that you were opposed to?"

"It was all fine," said Mike. I agree with it all."

"All right then," said Mr. Comer. "I have the paper I need you to sign," He then laid a sheet in front of Mike. "Write your full name, your address, your phone number and Email if you have one in the space provided. Then at the bottom of the page you will see what your starting salary will be. You understand that a lot of your work in assisting the nurse will be to clean up the hospital room after the patients leave their room to go home. If you agree please sign at the bottom of the page." Mike joyfully filled in the required information and then signed at the bottom where it said signature.

"All done," said Mike. "When will I start?"

"How does eight o'clock Monday morning sound to you? You will work eight hours a day. You will work Saturday only if needed in an emergency. How does that sound to you?"

"That is perfect," said Mike happily. "Who do I see when I get here?"

"You will report to head Nurse Debra Miles on the second floor. I'm sure that you will be needed occasionally on the third floor. If you do, you will report to head Nurse Tammy O'Gara. Do you have any questions?"

"No," said Mike, everything is perfectly clear. I promise that I will do my best in anything that comes along in the job."

"See you Monday," said Mr. Cromer. Mike took that as a signal to leave. He got up and went down to the car where Kathy was waiting for him.

"What in the world took you so long?" asked Kathy with a questioning look on her face. "You have been gone for over an hour. What held you up?"

"You will never believe it," started Mike. "I started just to walk down each floor aisle that ran down the center of the floor. The first floor had mostly offices on each side. So I took the elevator to the second floor. There it had mostly rooms for accident victims. The hospital seemed to be excellently organized. On my right there was a sign that said Holland Medical center. I realized it was a location for family doctors. We had one very similar in Ohio if you remember. I didn't want to go there so I walked to the other end of the aisle. On the way I passed the nurse that was behind the nurse's counter. She asked me if she could help me. I told her that I was just reviewing the hospital. Now that I think about it she must have called the hospital manager. Anyway, when I got to the end of the aisle there were steps that took me to the third floor. On the one side there were mostly patients that were recovering from surgery. I didn't make it to the nurse's counter when I man walked up to me. He said that he was Gary Cromer, the head of the hospital. He asked me what he could do for me. To make the story short, I told him who I was and he then took me to his office and after much conversation he offered me a job for the summer. I start this Monday."

"Wow," said Kathy, being surprised by all that Mike told her.

"That is great. What kind of a job did he offer you? Was it some kind of a janitor job?"

"Not at all," said Mike with a joyful voice. "It was as a Nurse's assistant. I'm sure a lot of my work will be cleaning the hospital rooms after a patient has left and getting it ready for the next patient. However, when my work is done and I have some free time I can go into a hospital room and try to cheer up a patient."

"Sounds great," said Kathy. "But we had better get home. Mom probably has dinner ready." Kathy then started the car and they drove home. When they entered the house Mike's mother met them at the door.

"I guess you have seen and been everywhere," said the mother. "Did you have a good time?"

"You will not believe all that we have experienced," said Kathy. "However, I will let Mike tell you all about it."

"Did something exciting happen to you on your trip?" asked their mom.

You will not believe what took place," said Mike. "Let me hold off telling you until we are all at the table."

"All right," said Mike's mother. "If that is the way you want. I can hardly wait. Let go and sit down. The food is ready." After they all settled down Mike's mother brought the food to the table. They all got served and started to eat. After a few minutes Mike's mother turned to her husband. "I understand that something exciting happened to your kids as they toured the San Francisco city.

"Actually, it all happened in San Leandro," said Mike. Mike then related to his parents his time at the Fairmont Hospital. After he was finished both his parents showed their delight. They were especially delighted that Mike not only got a job but that it could mean that after he graduated he could get a permanent job there in San Leandro.

"That is fantastic," said Mike's father. "That is a gift from God."

"Dad," said Mike. "The job is an assistant job. It is only for three months. It is not such a big deal."

"It is to us," said Mike's mother. "You will be here for three months and if God answers my prayer it will be the same for the summers you will have till you graduate. And after you graduate you would be a fool if you didn't come back here."

"Well I just want to get through this summer," said Mike. "I will worry about next summer when it comes. There is so much that could happen before then."

"I can dream, can't I," said Mike's mother. After that Mike's mother brought a Strawberry Pie for dessert. After they finished the desert they all sat around and talked small talk about the news.

The next two days went by as usual. Mike's parents went to work and Kathy spent most of her time with Mike discussing their past experiences and watching TV. Mike told her all about his romance with Carol and how they promised to contact each other by phone at least once a week. Kathy told Mike that she had not yet met anyone that could be her one and only. Sunday they all went to church and after church Mike's mother made a wonderful Cavatelli dinner. After dinner Mike got his father to tell about his job experience. Once he started they could not shut him off. Soon it was time to go to bed. Mike wanted to go early so that he could have some time with his boss, nurse Debra Miles. The next morning Mike and Kathy had breakfast together. Not much was said until they were at the door to leave for their new jobs.

"Mike, I wish you a lot of luck at your job. Have a great day."

"You too Kathy," said Mike. "I hope that we both enjoy our job. I will see you tonight. I'm sure we will have a lot to talk about." They then got into their cars and left for the beginning of a new experience. Mike got to the Hospital at a quarter to eight. He walked down the hall to the nurse's counter. Debra was there already.

"I'm so glad that you came early," said head nurse Debra. "You are Mike, I hope."

"Yes," said Mike. "And I'm ready to go Miss Miles."

"Good, but please call me Debbie. Come and follow me please" She then took him to a room about ten feet down the hall from her counter. "This is the equipment room that has all that you will need to prepare the hospital rooms for the next patient"

"There is a lot of stuff in here," said Mike. "I'm not sure that I know what to do with some of it."

"I will show you what to do," said Debbie. "I'm sure you will get the feel of it all. Anyway you will only have to do this several times during the day. The rest of the time you will visit the patients and try to encourage them and cheer them up a little. Come, there is a room ready to be prepared for a new patient. One just got released." She then grabbed a few items, showed them to Mike and explained what they were for and proceeded to the room that needed cleaning. She showed Mike what to do. When that was done she took him back to the equipment room to get different equipment. They did these two times. At the final visit they got new sheets and pillows that they placed on the bed. The job was then completed. "Well Mike, do you think you can handle the job from here on?"

"It all makes sense and is so simple. I will have no problems. You have equipment that I didn't know existed. That makes the job so much easier. Don't worry; I have it all under my hat."

"Good," said Debbie. "A patient is just leaving. It is room 216. After you finish please let me know so I can make a final check. I think you will do fine. It will be my final check." Mike did go to room 316. The patient was just being placed in a wheelchair. Mike walked past them and after they got on the elevator Mike went into the room. Since it was a woman who had occupied the room Mike could see and smell the result of her being there. Mike quickly started to clean the room. He had no problem. A little after an hour Mike called Debbie. She came and just looked from the doorway. Mike then realized it was just a required routine.

"Great job Mike," said Debbie. "There are no more rooms to be cleaned, so if you like, go and meet some of the patients on this floor." Mike was happy to do just that. He went into the first room on the floor. It was a middle aged man that occupied the room. He looked like he had a broken shoulder and arm. He also looked very sad.

"Hi Mr. Muller," said Mike after looking at the patient's chart. "How are you doing? I am Mike. I am a nurse's assistant."

"I'm in a very sad and unhappy situation," said Mr. Muller, "and please call Mr. Joe."

"I thought you would be thanking God,' said Mike, "for surviving your fall. You only have a sore shoulder and a broken arm. You could have hit your head and broken your neck. I know of a man who was cleaning his gutters and fell, breaking his neck. He died in this hospital. He was in a room not too far from this room."

"I never thought of that," said Joe. "I should thank God. It could have been much worse."

"How come you are alone," asked Mike.

"We run a clothing store," said Joe. "We are just making ends meet. We just can't close the store. When she found that I was going to be Ok she left to open the store. She will be here around five or six." Mike then remembered a humorous story about a hardware store problem. He told it to Joe. Joe couldn't stop laughing. It was just what he needed.

"Well I need to leave now," said Mike. "I have other patients to see. Keep up the good cheer. I will see you later."

"Thank you for your time here with me," said Joe, still with a smile on his face. You have brightened my day." Mike then left the room. It was about eleven-thirty. Mike decided to go to lunch before checking another room. He had a sandwich and a cup of coffee. After he ate he went into the room next to the one he had been to before. In the room there was a woman with a man sitting next to her bed. They were both very happy looking and slowly talking to each other.

"I see you two have realized how lucky you are to be here alive," said mike.

"We are Born-Again-Christians," said the man. "We thank the lord that we got through the accident with only minor injuries."

"My name is Mike. I am Nurse Debra's assistance," started Mike.

"I am Carl Longo," said the man. "This is my wife Ashley Longo.

"Nice to meet you," said Mike. Then after a little small talk Mike told them about the humorous story he had told Joseph in the next room. They all laughed joyfully.

"I have to go now," said Mike. "I will keep in touch."

"And when you come please bring another funny story," said the woman.

"I will try," said Mike. "See you later." Mike then left. He decided to go and see Debbie to see if there was anything she wanted him to do. As he pasted one of the rooms he heard a woman crying. He walked into the room and looked at the patient's chart. He found her name.

"Dear Ellen" started Mike. "Whatever happened to you is over. You should thank God that you are still alive."

"I am not crying for myself," said Ellen, hardly getting the words out. "I am worried about the health of my fiancé. I don't see how he could have survived. I asked the nurse and the doctor and they couldn't tell me what happened to David"

"My name is Mike. I am Debra's assistant. Can you tell me what happened, perhaps I could help you."

"Dave and I were going to a meeting with our wedding planner." said Ellen between tears, "A car came through from the left and hit our car right on the driver's side. I don't remember anything else. I just remember waking up here."

"Well listen to me," said Mike. "I am going to find out what happened to your fiancé. I will be right back. I don't know if you are a Christian. If you are, just trust in God. I am a Born-Again-Christian. Have faith." Mike then left and went directly to the emergence room. He found that Dave was rushed to the third floor operating room. He was told that a part of the car had stabbed him in his chest and was still in him. Mike then ran up to the third floor to see what happened. He went directly to Head Nurse Tammy.

"Hi nurse O' Grady," said Mike. He introduced himself and told her what he wanted to know about the victim of the auto accident.

"Please call me Tammy," started Tammy. "He was in surgery for about two hours. It was a touch and go situation. I think the surgery went well. He is now in the rehab room. The surgery assistant nurse is keeping him sedated. If you want to talk with him he will not be awake until possibly tomorrow afternoon." Mike thanked her and quickly went down to the second floor to the room Ellen was in. As he entered the room he shouted to Ellen.

"Ellen honey," he shouted. "He survived the car crash. He is alive." Mike then walked up to the bed and grabbed her hand. He is in the recovery room. He was in surgery for about two hours. They had to remove a piece of the auto door that was driven into his ribs. They removed it and closed a bleeding vein. They are going to keep him drugged until tomorrow afternoon. So, he will not be awake until then." When he saw Ellen crying harder he stopped talking. "Do you understand what I just said?"

"I'm not crying because I'm unhappy," said Ellen with a smile on her face. "I am crying because I am so happy and because I love you for all that you have done."

"I will keep watch over him," said Mike. "I will keep you informed of his healing. When he is transferred to a regular hospital room and he is awake I will get a wheelchair and take you to him. Don't hold your breath. It may be awhile."

"I will be here waiting for you," said Ellen. "I'm not going anywhere."

"Stay cheerful," said Mike. "I will see you soon." That said Mike left for another room. Mike spent the rest of the day visiting other patients. He brought cheer to all of them. Most of them he told them the funny story he had told Joseph Muller. They all enjoyed it. Seeing how much they enjoyed humor Mike remembered that he had a booklet that gave many funny stories. He decided that when he got home he would look up the book and to bring it with him the next day. The next day Mike went directly to Dave's room. The nurse was there getting him ready to move to a regular hospital room.

"How is he doing?" asked Mike.

"And good morning to you," said Nurse Tammy O'Gara.

"I'm sorry Tammy," said Mike "Good morning to you. I am just worried about Dave."

"He has improved better than we expected. I am just about to move him to a regular room."

"I would like to put his fiancé in a wheelchair," said Mike, "and bring her up to be with him."

"That is a great idea," said Nurse Tammy. "He will be sedated till about two this afternoon. Come up about then and we will try to wake him up then. I will help you bring Ellen up to see him."

"You know who his fiancé is?" asked Mike.

"What you have been doing," said Tammy "is known by everyone in this hospital."

"I had better watch what I am doing," said Mike. Then seeing that Tammy was trying to move David to the bed that would move David to the other room Mike asked. "While I'm here can I help you?"

"Yes," said Tammy. "That would be very kind of you. Help me get him on this other bed and if you have time help me get him in the bed in the other room."

"I'd be glad to," said Mike. Mike grabbed David by his feet while Tammy grabbed him by his shoulders and they moved him onto the movable bed. Then they moved him to the other room and Mike helped her move David to the room bed.

"Thank you so much," said Tammy. "You made moving him so much easier. Thank you so much."

"It was my pleasure," said Mike. "See you at about two. Mike then left to go down to the second floor. There he had two rooms to clean. When he was done he went to two rooms and after telling them the funny story he left and went to Ellen's room.

"Hi Mike," Ellen said when she saw Mike. She was laying there waiting for Mike to come.

"Hi Ellen," said Mike. "I just came from the third floor where David was. We just moved him to a regular hospital room. The nurse there told me that David has made a fantastic improvement. At about two they are going to let him wake up. I will go there and if they say it would be alright I will get a wheelchair and take you there."

"May God bless you with all his love," said Ellen. "My love will not be enough."

"I am only doing my job," said Mike. "I am going to go to lunch now. See you later." After lunch Mike went and visited some of the other patients. Two were new. After introducing himself he did all he could do to cheer them up. Before he left he told them a funny story. He left them all laughing. When he left the last one it was almost two. Mike then went to the third floor to the room David was in.

"You are just in time," said Tammy. "I just injected him with a prescription that will wake him up." While they were talking, they heard David moan. Tammy went up to him and asked him to wake up.

"Ellen where is Ellen?" he moaned before completely waking up "Ellen" he repeated, "Where are you?"

"Hi David," said Tammy. How do you feel?" It took a little while before David answered.

"I am worried about Ellen, my fiancée" Mike then stepped up to David. She is fine," said Mike. "I have been taking care of her. When you wake up and feel like it, I will bring her up to see you."

"How is she?" asked David, not being satisfied with Mike's answer.

"She has a badly bruised shoulder, a broken arm and a scraped leg. She will be well."

"Please go and get her right now," said David. "I gotta see her." Mike and Tammy then went to the supply room and got a wheelchair. They then took the elevator and went down to the room where Ellen was. They rolled the wheelchair into the room. Ellen was surprised to see them.

"Good morning Ellen," said Mike. "Would you like a ride to the third floor to see your fiancée?"

"Stop talking and start putting me on the wheel chair and take me upstairs," said Ellen with excitement. Tammy and Mike gently lifted Ellen out of the bed and placed her in the wheelchair. Bending to fit the wheel chair caused her to give out a small moaning sound. They quickly took her to the elevator and wheeled her into David's room. As soon as David saw the wheel chair as it entered the doorway David yelled out

"Ellie, sweet heart, is it you?"

"Dave honey, are you all right?" said Ellen. "I didn't think you could make it"

"What makes you think that?" asked David.

The car hit us right on your side," said Ellen as she grabbed David's hand and tried to get up.

"I'm sorry Ellen," said Tammy. "You cannot get up. Please don't try. If you do, you will fall and I will have to take you back to your room, and not bring you back until you are discharged. I don't want the responsibility."

"God forbid," said Ellen. "I will be good. Please let me stay here for a little while."

"I will let you stay until noon. You and David will have very different lunches. If all goes well I may bring you back in the late afternoon."

"Let us go and leave the lovers alone so that they can have private time together," said Mike.

Alright," said Tammy. "I will check on you every once in a while." Mike and Tammy then left. Mike took the elevator to the second floor. He was so delighted that he could help the young lovers.

The rest of the day Mike cleaned two rooms and visited two other patients on the second floor. After small talk in which he tried to bring a cheerful atmosphere in the room, he told them the story he had told Joe. It did bring laughter to the patients.

When Mike got to the second floor he went to the first room where he had met Joe Muller.

"Hi Joe," said Mike as he walked into the room.

"Hi Mike," said Joe. "I thought you would not come back to see me once you cheered me up. It is so good to see you."

"I have been very busy with patients that need me more than you do," said Mike. "Is there anything you need?"

"Yes," said Joe. "I need another joke to keep me entertained until my wife comes tonight."

"Well," said Mike. "I don't have another joke but an interesting thing happened in a hotel room not far from here.

"What happened?" asked Joe, becoming interested.

"I walked into the room of a middle aged French man I had talked to before. He was getting dressed and packing his hospital gown," started Mike. "I asked him if he was getting discharged"

"Going home," he said in his foreign accent, "I'm going home to die." I was surprised because his chart said that he was cured of his problem. What is the problem I asked him? He answered me as follows.

"I was to go home yesterday but now I am going home to die" Joe hesitated for a while until the whole thing sunk in. Then he started to laugh out loud.

"You are sneaking in a joke," said Joe, still laughing.

"Well I have to leave now," said Mike and left. Mike then spent the rest of the day going into other rooms. In each room he started with small talk that was meant to bring some cheer to them. He always ended up with the humorous story he had told Joe. After cleaning some rooms on the second floor Mike was asked to clean a room on the third floor. Before he went up he talked with Nurse Debbie and told her the joke. She found it very funny. When he went to the third floor he told Tammy the same joke. She also laughed at the story. After cleaning the room on the third floor Mike went home. When he got home his mother was cooking dinner. He found that he was the only one there.

"Hi mom," said Mike. "Where is everyone?"

"Hi sweetheart," said Mike's mother. "Your dad is working a little late. But he will be home soon. I have no idea where Kathy is."

"I'm here," said Kathy as she entered the door. "I had a customer that kept me after closing. He was a good customer so we were willing to satisfy his needs." Just then Mike's father walked in the door.

"Is dinner ready?" he inquired. "I am very hungry."

"If you all will sit around the table," said Mike's mother. "The food is ready. I will bring it right away." They all sat around the table and each filled his dish with the amount of food they wanted. After a few minutes Mike turned to his dad.

"How was your day dad?"

"It was as good as usual. We were on the third floor so we were not protected by the next upper floor since there was none. However, thank God it didn't rain today. That is why we worked until we were finished with that floor. How about you Mike. How was your first day at the hospital?" Mike told them about all the patients he had met. He told them how thrilled he was to be able to help Ellen and her husband. He then told them about their problem. He then told them the story about the man who was going home to die. Mike's mom and Kathy laughed heartily. Mike's father only smiled. Mike wondered if his father had heard the joke before. However, Mike decided not to ask. Soon they finished eating and spent the rest of the evening with small talk. Before Mike went to sleep he checked his book of jokes. He found several that he liked. He rewrote them so they would look like they occurred around a hospital. Mike then went to sleep feeling satisfied with his effort for the day.

The next morning Mike ate breakfast with his sister. His father had long gone. His mother was somewhere in the bedroom cleaning. She had breakfast with her husband. After breakfast Mike went directly to the hospital second floor. There were three rooms that needed cleaning. After he finished the three rooms he went to the third floor to see David. He found that Ellen was already there.

"Hi," said Mike as he entered the room. "I see that you two are together again. How did you accomplish that?"

"Nurse Tammy came down and got me," said Ellen. "She promised that as long as our health allowed, she would give us two hours a day to be together."

"That is great," said Mike. "I will stop in once in a while to say hello. Right now, I came up to see how David was doing. Since it seems like he is fine I will say goodbye and go and do my other jobs."

"It will always be nice to see you," said David as Mike left. Mike then went into the other second floor rooms to cheer up the patients. Some of the rooms had new patients. His story about how lucky they were always worked. After they brightened up a little he told them a humorous story. He always left them with a smile. The rooms where there were patients that he had met before always had a smile as he entered the room. After some small talk he gave them a joke they had not heard. He left them with laughter. At about twelve thirty he went to lunch. After lunch he was asked by Debra the second floor head nurse to clean up three rooms that had just emptied. One was on the third floor. After that was done it was time to go home. That evening was like the evening before. They asked the same questions and what they had gone through that day. This was the same for the next several days. Nothing new was happening.

The days that Mike spent in the hospital soon became the same every day. He would brighten up the lives of new patients and tell new jokes to patients he had seen before. Although each day seemed the same, the challenge with each new patient made each day different and special. He was always successful in brightening up the hospital atmosphere. He loved his job. It was really never the same. At home he and his parents and sister all became a standard family like they were back in Ohio. Life together was very loving. They didn't think of the time things would change. However, the days slipped by. Too soon it was the last week of August. Mike's plan was to leave for Toledo the following Monday. That evening at the dinner table Mike turned to his father.

"Dad," he started. "You know that I am leaving next Monday for Toledo. I love my job here so much that I hate to leave it"

"I try not to think of it," said his father. "Life here with all of you has been so wonderful. I hate to see you go."

"You know dad," said Mike. "Several years ago, I remember you describing your effort to become a building designer and carpenter, as the power of the heart. What did you mean by that dad?"

"That is a human characteristic, at least it is mine," started Mike's father. "What it means is that if in your mind you find something you like or a profession you would like to join but you find something that makes it difficult to get, you can drop it and go for some other trade. You tried but it was too hard to obtain. You will forget it and move on. It was a good Idea but it didn't work out. That is because it all was from the mind. However, if the desire comes from the heart you will not give it up. You will go after it and work as hard as you can to get it. The heart's desire cannot be erased. It will drive you till you accomplish what the heart desires.

"I know what you mean," said Mike. "I feel that way about becoming a hospital surgeon. I think that as a doctor I can not only brighten the life of a patient, but I can also cure them of their problem."

"I have no doubt that you will be a great surgeon," said Mike's father.

Friday came up too soon. At four thirty at the end of Mike's work day he stopped at nurse Debbie's counter.

"Hi Debbie," said Mike. "This was my last day. I come to say goodbye. I have enjoyed working here so much I hate to leave. But my desire to be a doctor is unbeatable. I hope to be back next summer if the job is available."

"I hope you will be successful in all that you desire. We will miss you more than I can tell you. You have been such a blessing to this hospital floor. I suspect Tammy will feel the same. You have brought so much life and good feelings to the patients. I will pray that you come back next summer."

"Have a great life this winter," said Mike as he headed Out into the hallway.

"You too said," Debbie as Mike headed for the elevator. Mike was soon on the third floor. He found Tammy just coming out of a patient's room.

"Hi Tammy," said Mike. "I came up to say goodbye. This is my last day."

"I don't know what Debbie and I are going to do without you. You have been such a help to both of us. The patients on this floor ask about you every time I go into their room. It is going to be so hard without you. You have brought some joyful times for all of us. We are going to miss you terribly. I hope you are successful and return to us."

"Thank you," said Mike as he headed to the other end of the floor towards the main office. He knocked on the door and a man's voice asked him to come to it.

"Hi, Mister Cromer," said Mike. "I came here to say goodbye and to thank you for the job here. I enjoyed it very much."

"We are so thankful that you were willing to be a nurse's assistant. It is very hard to get someone to take that job. Also, I would like you to call me Gary. Mr. Cromer was my father."

"The best part of the job was not the cleaning of the rooms but the relationships with the patients," said Mike ignoring Gary's statement. The everyday contact with the patients was not only very interesting and educational but helping patients accept their situation was very joyful."

"I'm glad you enjoyed your time here," said Mr. Cromer. "Check with us when you finish the first year at the Medical University."

"Thank you Sir," said Mike. "Goodbye." After Mike left Gary Cromer called Nurse Debbie and Nurse Tammy to come to his office.

"Hi Chief," said Tammy. She had arrived first just down the hall from his office. "What do you want from me?"

"I wish to know how Mr. Michel Costello performed," said Gary. "I would like to write a record of his performance."

"I think that we could not have gotten a better assistant," said Tammy. "He has such a wonderful personality. Even when his mouth is serious his eyes are always smiling. He has done an excellent job preparing the hospital rooms for the next patient. He brought such a cheerful atmosphere to each patient that he visited. He has such a good nature that the patients all reacted to his cheerfulness. They are still asking for him." As they were talking, Debbie walked into the room doorway.

"Come on in," said Gary, seeing her there. "Come and have a seat. I am asking about Mike's performance. When Tammy is finished I want your input. I am making a record of his time with us." Debbie did as Gary said.

"I think that I have covered all that he has accomplished."

"Thank you," said Gary. "Just sit here and listen to Debbie's input." Then he turned to Debbie. "How about you Debbie, what do you think of Mike's job he has done here?"

"Well," said Debbie, "Tammy has covered it well. He has done a fantastic job. He has encouraged my patients and has made many of them cheerful when he was with them. He convinced many that they should thank God that they survived their accident. He told them how it could have been worse. After he got them more relaxed he told them a funny story about a patient in the hospital. He always left them laughing. I don't know how we are going to get along without him"

"Well thank you ladies for your input," said Gary.

When Mike got home his mother was cooking dinner.

"Hi mom," said Mike as he walked into the kitchen. "What are we having today?"

"I am cooking your favorite dinner," said Mike's mother. "I am making you a Cavatelli dinner with pork neck bones. I want you to remember me when you are away from school."

"Mom," said Mike with a tender smile on his face. "Thank you so much, but you don't need anything to help me remember you."

"Well anyway," said his mother. "It will tell you how much I love you."

"I love you too mom," said Mike. Just then Kathy walked in.

"Wow," said Kathy. "I smell something good."

"It is my going away present," said Mike with a large smile on his face. "But you are welcome to have some too."

"Thank you," said Kathy. "I'm going to school also on Monday. So, it could be my present too."

"Yes," said Mike. "You will be living at home."

"You will be welcome here too," said Kathy with a little laughter. "It is your choice."

"Very funny," said Mike. As they were kissing each other Mike's father came home. Mike's mother served the dinner. They all enjoyed it very much. After they ate, Mike's mother brought in a cherry pie. From that moment on everyone was very silent. Saturday for dinner they ate leftover food. Mike's mother had made too much Cavatelli. Sunday they all went to church. They all prayed that all would go well for both Mike and Kathy. After church Mike's mother made a steak dinner. They ate as if nothing was different. That evening they all huddled together and expressed how they were all going to miss each other. Time went by too fast. Soon they went to bed. The next morning, they all got up at seven. They ate breakfast together. Mike got ready to leave. He had packed all that he needed the day before and had all in his car.

"Please keep in touch," said his mother. She then hugged him. Kathy hugged him next

"I love you sweet brother. Take care of yourself."

"I love you too sis," said Mike. Mike's dad walked with him to his car.

"Son," he said. "Make your dreams come true. Work hard and don't let anyone, especially beautiful girls distract you. Take good care of yourself. I will see you hopefully at Thanksgiving. Good luck Mike."

"Thanks dad," said Mike, "I will work hard and spend most of my time studying." Mike then pulled out of the driveway and down the street. Mike was on his way to his first year of college and a new and exciting experience.

CHAPTER TWO

Good Times and Bad times

Mike arrived at Toledo Wednesday afternoon for his first year at the Medical University. He took out his map and found his way to the University. He parked his car and went to the main building. He was not sure that it would be opened. He was more than a week early. The door was opened so he went inside. On the left was an office door with a sign that said Registration Office. Mike knocked on the door.

"Come in," said a voice from inside. Mike opened the door and entered the office. "Come in and have a seat in front of my desk," said a middle aged woman. "My name is Lisa Brown. I am the University registration Officer. I guess you are here to register for classes in the university. So, give me your name."

"My name is Mike Costello," said Mike. "I am registering for the doctor's degree in Medical Surgery."

"Let me look up my records," said the woman. "Yes, I see from my record book that your first year attendance has been paid. I need you to sign this entrance agreement. Here is the pamphlet that has all the school rules." She then went over all the rules verbally. "If you break one of these rules you will be expelled from the university."

"I promise that I will follow all the University rules," said Mike. I suspect the rules are similar to the ones I had at Ohio state university"

"I'm sure they are," said Lisa. "Here are the floor plans for the two buildings that you will be in. The first is the classroom building. It is the one where you are right now. The building on the right is the dormitory building. All the dormitories are on the second floor. There is a short covered bridge between the two buildings. You will not have to wear a jacket when you go from one building to another. Your dorm room is 215. The dorms have a bathroom, a family room where your desk will be, and a bed room. On the far side of the bathroom wall is a counter with storage cabinets under it. The counter is about three and a half feet high and is used for pictures or other things you want to store on top of the counter. One of the things some students rent is a Cooler unit. It is like a refrigerator without a freezer in it. It is only about two feet high and is used only to store liquids like milk. It has a drawer where you can store lunch meat and other meat products. If you like I can give you the phone number of the renter."

"What will be the rental cost for the cooler?" asked Mike. Lisa looked at the folder she had and then, to see what the total would be she hesitated.

"Just a minute," said Lisa. "I see that your paid bill has that cost included. You knew about this when you called to pay your bill for the first year as a student."

"No," said Mike. "I didn't know anything about it. It was my father who called to pay for the bill after I got the letter of acceptance."

"Well there is nothing left to take care of," said Lisa. "Go and move into your dorm."

"Thank you for your time and information," said Mike as he left the office. He then went directly to his dorm bringing all his possessions he brought with him from California. In the room it was just as Lisa had described. Mike sat for a while trying to get used to the place. He then started to read all the information Lisa gave him. After a while he decided to call Carol. He had not heard from her in months. He had called several times but got no answers. He understood her problem. She had said something about not liking long distance relationships. Mike called her number. Again, he got no answer. However, he decided to leave a message. The other times he called, he never left a message. This time he did.

"Carol sweetheart," said Mike. "I know that you don't like long distance relationships, but I am now in Ohio. I think we are close enough to see each other." After he hung up he decided to go to the nearest bank and set up an account with it. Before he left he plugged in the power cord of the cooler. He then drove to town and stopped at a sign that Read PNC bank. Mike set up an account with the cash he had and the checks he got from his bank account he had in California. Mike ended up with an account of a little over one thousand dollars. He also got a check book and a credit card. He then went out to look for a grocery store to buy some lunch meat and milk and perhaps some ginger ale. As he drove around town looking for a grocery store he spotted a small restaurant. He decided that before he did the shopping, he should get something to eat. He had not had any food since breakfast the day before. He ate a hearty dinner and then went to the grocery and bought enough lunch and breakfast food for the rest of the week. He then drove around the town to get acquainted with the city. Before it got dark he went back to his dorm. He was tired and went to sleep early. The next day he got up early. He was very excited. He had cereal for breakfast and then decided to check out the dorm building. He found that on the first floor there was a cafeteria. It was closed. He could look at the inside through the large front window. It looked like the food would be behind the counter. At the far end he could see a large amount of trays. At the end near the door was a register. Mike realized that the student who wanted to eat there would grab a tray and walk down the counter, get the food that he wanted and pay for it at the other end. There were several tables that I could eat at. Mike then went to the main building to see the classrooms. Most of the class rooms were on the second floor. Much of the first floor had offices.Mike then went up to his dorm and reviewed the pamphlets that he got yesterday. At noon he had lunch from his cooler and went back to driving through the city. One of the places he was looking for was a bookstore. He found one that was not too far from the University. He realized that he would have to buy books required from each class. The next days were all very similar. Mike had all that he needed at the present time. He ate breakfast and lunch in his room and ate dinner at different restaurants. Finally, it was Monday, the first day of classes. He got up early, ate breakfast and was at his first class five minutes before eight. Some of the students were already there. The rest of the students came around the same time as Mike arrived. When everyone had taken a seat the professor closed the classroom door.

"I am Professor Nicolas Remer. The subject in this class will be a study of all the body internal organs. To get acquainted, please stand up when I call your name." He then started to call all the names one at a time. When the student who heard his name stood up the professor took a good look at him and then called the next student. It took about ten minutes to call all the students. When he was done he gave a quick dissertation of all they would cover that semester. He also gave the name of the book and the author who wrote it so that the student would get the right book. After that they were dismissed Mike then went to his next class. The actions there were very much the same as it was in the first class. The professor was Professor Clarence Witicar. The subject of that class was the cause of organ's break down, and the possible cures. After a brief discussion of the subject the class was dismissed. Mike then went to his room and had a sandwich and a fruit for lunch. Mike at the right time went into his afternoon Classes. His two classes that afternoon were very similar to his morning classes. The subjects of the two classes were the possible diseases that a person could catch and the cure for all diseases. Mike had four books to buy. That evening after the last class he went to the bookstore he had seen the day before and was able to get all the books he needed. He then went into the cafeteria and got in line to get his dinner. After paying for the meal he sat at a small table and ate his dinner. He learned that if he got his food with the copper tray he had in his room and the paper dishes that were provided at the counter, that he could take the dinner to his room and eat in privacy. From that day on, that was what Mike did. Before he went to bed he called Carol one more time. There was no answer. Next, he called his family phone number. His mother answered the phone.

"Hi Mon," said Mike. "Is everyone OK?"

"We are all fine," said his mother, "except we miss you. How are you doing?"

"I'm fine," said Mike. "I just came out of my last class. You would never believe how great the University is. It has a cafeteria and a refrigerator in our dorm room. I think that I am going to enjoy my time here. However, I do miss you all."

"Well you enjoy and take good care of yourself. Thanks for calling Keep in touch." They then said good bye and hung up. Mike had a good night's sleep.

The next couple of days were a shock to Mike. He never dreamt that the study of the organs in the body could be so complex. He was also overwhelmed with the number of organs that were in the human body. In one of the classes they studied the problems each organ can have from just normal existence. In another class they studied what could cause the organ to fail and how to repair it. Another class covered the outside diseases that can attack the organs. Another class studied the different curses and drugs that could be used in each case. After the first week each class and from there on only covered a half of the organs. The more tender and complex organs would be covered next year. That week caused Mike to realize that the study was going to require a lot of hard work. There was so much to learn. From that day on, Mike concentrated on homework and independent study. Because of this determination, Mike forgot about Carl and never found time to call his parents. Mike spent most of his time studying. He only went out on the weekend to buy food for breakfast and Lunch. Soon it was Thanksgiving week. The Monday after Thanksgiving An import test was scheduled. Mike wondered why the University would do that. It was heartless, he thought. He called his parents' phone number. His mother answered as usual.

"Hi Mom," said Mike. "I have bad news. I don't think I could make it home for Thanksgiving. The rotten people have scheduled an important midterm test. I have a lot of studying to do. I think it will be a very difficult test."

"That is alright," said Mike's mom. "I am not cooking a turkey this year. Your father is out of town to finish a very important job. He will not be home for about two weeks. So, I pray that you pass that test with flying colors."

"I will call you on Thanksgiving Day," promised Mike. They then said goodbye and hung up. Mike was not wrong. It turned out to be a very difficult test. Mike got a B minus on the test. Mike did call his mother on Thanksgiving Day. Mike liked the fact that he also got to talk with his sister Kathy. After that, the time went by very quickly. Soon it was December. Mike made plans to drive to Chicago and take a plane to San Francisco. He called his mother and told her the time the plane would land. She assured him that she would be there to pick him up. Christmas that year fell on Wednesday. The school closed from Tuesday to the day after New Year. That gave Mike seven days to be with his family. On the weekend he went to the mall and bought his family some Christmas gifts. He bought his mom a nice necklace. He bought his sister a wrist watch. He had noticed that she didn't have one. He bought his father a blue shirt and matching tie. He knew that his father loved blue. He wrapped them up in nice separate packages and placed them in his suitcase. On Tuesday the 24th of December Mike drove to Chicago. He had to leave early to get the flight to San Francisco. Since there is a two hour difference between Ohio and California Mike got there around ten o'clock. His mother was there waiting for him. When Mike stepped into the Airline waiting room, his mother threw her arms around him.

"Mike honey," said his mother. "It is so good to see you. I

have missed you so much. Kathy will be home this afternoon. And your father will be home for dinner. It will be so good to have all of us together."

"It is so good to see you, mom," said Mike with a shaky voice like he was ready to cry. However, he soon got his control back and continued. "I will be home for five days. We will have a fantastic celebration." Mike's mom then drove them home. When they got there, Mike went directly to his room and settled all the clothes he brought with him. He then went downstairs carrying the gift packages. He placed them under the Christmas tree that was set up in the living room. He noticed that it was not finished.

"Mom," said Mike. "What is the story about your Christmas tree? It only has the light and a few bulbs hanging on it."

We just didn't have the time to finish setting it up," said his mother. "If you would like to help, the rest of the ornaments are in the closet. I am busy making a nice Christmas Eve dinner." Mike went into the closet and got the ornaments and before Kathy and His father got home Mike had finished setting up the tree.

"Hi Mike" said Kathy as she got home. She then gave Mike a great hug. "It is so good to see you, Merry Christmas."

"It is so nice to see you too," said Mike, "and Merry Christmas to you too."

"How are you doing in school?" asked Kathy. "Have you gained any good doctor type knowledge?"

"You would never believe what I am going through. If we have time later I will give you a more detailed answer. However, I would like to hear about your schooling. I understand that you are in law school. How are you doing?" Before she could answer, their father came in.

"Hello everyone," said Mike's father as he came in. "Mike, it is so great to see you. I was hoping that you could come home for at least Christmas. How long can you be here?"

"I have to be back the day after New Year," said Mike.

"Great, that gives you about seven days to be with us," said

Mike's father. "Let's enjoy every minute of it." They did enjoy being together those seven days. They exchanged gifts like they did the year before. At New Year's Eve dinner Mike gave them an hour by hour description of the subjects that he was taught so far this year. They enjoyed the dinner and a couple of jokes that Mike had memorized for the patient at the hospital. Soon it was January one. Mike and his mother left after lunch. It was about one O'clock. They were all so sad to see him go. Mike's plane left at one-thirty. The flight time was four hours but there was a two hour difference so the plane landed in Toledo at eight. After setting his suitcase in his dorm, Mike drove to the nearest restaurant and had dinner. After dinner he went to his room and went to bed early resting for the hard work at the university.

Soon it was April. Mike took his last exam and when he got back to his room he packed and was ready to leave for California. The next morning after breakfast, Mike got into his car. He had decided to drive instead of taking a plane. He would need the car in California. Mike left for the three day drive at eight in the morning. He arrived in San Leandro on Wednesday at about five. His mother, his father and his sister were all home waiting for him.

"Hi son," said his father. After he hugged him his mother and sister did the same.

"I have cooked your favorite dinner," said his mother. They all sat and had dinner. The rest of the evening Mike explained to them all that he was studying. The next day only Mike and his mother spent the day together. That evening they were altogether for dinner and this time Mike asked all the questions. That Friday Mike went to the Fairmount Hospital. He went straight up to Mr. Cromer's office. He knocked on the door.

"Come in," said Mr. Cromer. Mike opened the door and walked in. "Hello there Mike. It's so good to see you. Come in and sit down. How have you been?"

"I have been fine," said Mike. "It was a hard first year. I had a lot to learn."

"Well it is good to see you," said Mr. Cromer. "Are you ready to come to work through your summer?"

"If the job is available," said Mike. "I would love to come to work here. I hated to leave last fall. I love working here."

"Well this is the time of year when people get out and get hurt."

"When can I start," asked Mike, thrilled that a job was available for him.

"Can you start Monday?" asked Mr. Cromer.

"That would be perfect," said Mike.

"Wait here while I get the paperwork," said Mr. Cromer as he left for the hiring office. After all the paperwork was done Mike went down the hall to see if Tammy was still there. She was still there.

"Hi Tammy," said Mike. "How are you doing?"

"Hi Mike," said Tammy. "It is so good to see you. Will you be available this summer? We need you badly."

"I start on Monday," said Mike

On Monday Mike went back to work in the hospital as he had done the year before. Everything was the same. It was like he never left. However, because they were all different patients it was always an exciting job. Mike did spend a little more time on the third floor then he did the last time he worked there. It was because now he recognized some of the diseases and problems. However, he used his normal conversation trying to encourage patients that they were lucky because it could have been worse. He told them about a patient that had it worse. It turned out that he brought much delight to most of the patients. However, time went by too quickly. It was time for Mike to return for his second year of college.

The next months were as Mike expected. Things got harder, not easier. There was so much to learn. Mike went back to his normal routine. He went out only once a week to buy the food that he needed. He always ate lunch in his room and always brought his dinner up to eat in his room. The days rolled by slowly. It seemed to Mike like several years went by since he was home. He did call his mother at least once a week. He gave up on calling Carol.

Soon it was November. He found that there was no special class for the holiday weekend. He decided to go home for Thanksgiving. He made all the arrangements as he did for Christmas the year before and as before Mike's mother picked him up at the airport. It was three years ago since he spent Thanksgiving with his parents and sister. Mike's mother made a nice turkey dinner. They all enjoyed the time together. Soon however the time went by too fast. Sooner than Mike wanted he found himself back in Toledo. Life somehow has a way of repeating itself. A month later, Mike found himself at home for Christmas. After a joyful Christmas and New Year, Mike went back to the University to finish his second year. In early April Mike took his exam and soon was home. This time he also drove. He got home in the early afternoon on Wednesday. His mother and Kathy were home. His dad would not come home until dinner time. At dinner Mike's dad asked Mike about his year in college.

"Dad," said Mike. "The year was very much like the year before. We just studied a different set of organs. It was a little harder in one way but easier because now I knew what to expect and was ready for it."

"How did you make out," asked Mike's father, "on this year's final exam?"

"It was better," said Mike. "If you remember last year I got a B minus. This year I got a B plus."

After the next four days together Mike went to the hospital. He went right up to see Mr. Comer. He was surprised that he got the job back. The summer went by just like it was still the summer before. Mike had the same results as he had before. He brought much joy to the hospital patients and hospital staff. Soon the summer was over and Mike left for his third year at the university. This time his study was about the third and last set of the human organs. Everything was like it was the semester before. Mike was now well prepared for the work. He followed the same routine as the year before. In November he flew home for Thanksgiving dinner and again in December he flew home for Christmas. Both holidays were experienced with great joy. Soon it was April and Mike drove home. He again got the job at the hospital. They were all very happy to have him back. At the hospital Mike spent more time on the third floor since he had much knowledge of the problems the patients had. All of the hospital staff was happy to have him here to help them. That summer went by too fast. However, Mike was thankful for the experience. Mike then went back to the University for his fourth and last year. When he got to the first class he was surprised. It was not a study from the textbooks as it had been the three years before. It was studied using some real and some plastic organs. Only a few actual organs could be used. The real organs were the ones that could be cut open and the student could see the important parts to investigate. Some of the organs showed what they would be like when they failed and what caused the failure. The plastic ones were built so that they could represent the real ones. They too were cut open to show what the student was to suspect when they opened the real organs. Most of the body organs were not opened but the study was to see what they looked like and to recognize them as failed organs and what made them fail. This type of study went on until November. They were then given the Thanksgiving week off. Mike then flew to California. His mother picked him up at the airport as usual. His family was happy to see him. At the dinner table Mike was loaded with many questions.

"Well this is your final year," said Mike's father. "Does this year differ from the other years?"

"Oh dad," said Mike, "the answer to that question could take all week."

"Just give me a brief description of what the difference is." Mike then started to briefly explain what he had experienced the last few months. Mike's father later explained that he was kind of lost in Mike's explanation. Then he changed the subject.

"Well tell us, what are your plans after you graduate this spring?" asked Mike's mother. "Are you planning on opening a private doctor's office?"

"Only if I have to," said Mike. "My main study, if you understood my answer to dad's question, was to be a medical surgeon. I don't think I would like to take care of simple problems for the general public. I am going to check with the Fairmount Hospital first to see if I can get a job right here near home. If I can't get one there I will try other hospitals around the area. Let's not try to guess what will happen months from now."

"Well," said Mike's mother. "I hope you get one here. I would love to have you live here." She then went into the kitchen to wash the dishes and put away all the leftovers. Mike's father excused himself. He said that he had something to take care of. That left Mike alone with his sister Kathy, who had been silent up to present time.

"Mike," said Kathy. "I think I understood a little more of what you said about your work at school then dad did. It sounded like they were preparing you for the surgeon's job you long for."

"Thank you," said Mike. "I was wondering if it was me that couldn't tell it right."

"You would have to be a doctor to understand all that you were describing," said Kathy.

A couple of days later Mike flew back to school. The study was as it was before, with plastic organs. It seemed like only a couple of days went by when Mike flew back home for Christmas. Mike's father was very happy to see him, however he did not ask Mike any more questions about his school experience. The Christmas joy was overwhelming. The thought that this would be the last Christmas that Mike would have to fly home from the University excited them. No one considered that if Mike didn't get a job nearby he might have to fly or drive home from a distant hospital. After they had a fantastic Christmas and New

Year, Mike had to go back to school for his last few months. He was excited to go back. He was tired of going back and forth. When he went into his first class he was shocked at what they were going to do the rest of the semester. He never dreamt that they would surprise him again. However, when he entered his first class, the professor made an unexpected statement.

"Students," he said, "we have a change to make this morning. Most of you will continue as we have done the previous years. However, there are four students who have signed up for Surgery class. John Brown and Troy Windon please go to room 3112 on the third floor. You are dismissed." After they left the professor continued. "Mike Costello and Ralph Nicolson please go to room 315. You are dismissed." Mike and Ralph left together and went to room 315. There they found Professor Whitmyer and Professor Garner. Please come in," said Professor Garner. "Ralph, you are assigned to me. However, our session will not start until this afternoon. So please go into the study hall or your dorm room and study this document." He then handed him the document. I will meet you here at one after lunch." That said they both left. The other professor then turned to Mike who was so confused that he kept silent.

"I'm sure you remember me from your past classes but to be sure, I am Professor Ken Whitmyer. I will be your instructor from now on till Graduation. We are going to study heart surgery first. It is the most important." All of the rest of the morning he was explaining every detail of the heart surgery. After lunch they met again in room 315.

"Are you ready for the heart surgery?" asked the professor.

"Are we going to watch a real surgery?" asked Mike.

"Come with me and you will get the answer to your question," said the professor. Mike was then taken into a room that looked like an operation room. In the middle of the room there was what looked like a casket. The professor opened the casket and pulled out a human body and placed it on the operation table. That was when Mike noticed that the body was a dummy body made of plastic. That afternoon they performed heart surgery on the dummy. When they had finished they put it back together and placed it back in the box that looked like a casket. It was then that Mike saw his name on the name tag attached to the dummy. He then realized that he would be doing many more surgeries on the dummy. He also noticed that there was another casket-like box. Mike assumed that it was Ralph's dummy

"Well," said the professor. "You have done a great job. You will make a great surgeon. We will see you tomorrow morning. We will study the surgery on the human lungs." Mike left being so excited with what he had done that afternoon. He could hardly wait till the next day. The following days were all the same. In the morning he studied what surgery he was going to do in the afternoon and in the afternoon he performed the surgery. He noticed that Ralph always entered the class room when he left for the surgery. He then realized that Ralph studied the surgery he was going to do while Mike was doing his surgery and he would do his surgery the next morning when Mike was preparing for his next surgery that afternoon. The days went by very slowly. Mike felt that it would last forever. Every day he would study what he would do in the afternoon and then in the afternoon he would do it. Although it seemed like it would never end, the end finally came. On the last day of school, he had his final exam. Mike passed it with flying colors. The day of the graduation was set. Mike called his parents. They flew to Toledo a few days before graduation was to take place. Mike went to the airport to pick them up.

"Hi dad, mom, Kathy," said Mike. "It was so nice that all three of you could make this a fantastic occasion." Mike hugged all three one at a time. "How come you all flew instead of driving up here?"

"We thought that after you graduate, we would drive back with you," said Mike's father, "that way we could celebrate at every place we stop for the night.

"Dad," said Mike with a smile on his face. "You didn't have to do that. We could all have celebrated when we got home."

"We could do that two," said Mike's mother. "This is a very special occasion. I don't see that we will have another one like this."

"So be it," said Mike. "It's too late to do anything else. Kathy, honey, don't you have anything to say?"

"All I can think of is congratulations my dear brother."

"How are you going to get to the graduation," asked Mike. "I may not be available."

"We will get a cab if we must," said Mike's father. "Don't worry about us. Just take us to the nearest hotel." Mike took them to the hotel which was just one block from the university. He left them there and went back to his room. It was soon graduation day. Mike drove over to the hotel and picked up his family. At the auditorium Mike's family was directed to the balcony. Mike then went back to his room, got dressed in the graduation costume and went into the auditorium. There he was seated in the third row from the front. When he looked back he could see all the people in the balcony that came to see the graduation. It was too dark there to see his family there. It was about an hour later that the university's chief manager came up to the microphone that was on a stand in the middle of the stage. He gave a wonderful speech about the success of the students. Mike was too excited and nervous to comprehend what the manager was saying. The proceedings only got his attention when one of the other professors called the first line of graduates. They all walked to the right end of the stage. One by one, when their name was called, they walked across the stage and were given their diploma and they walked back to their seats. Finally, the third row was called. They all got at the end of the stage as the two rows before them had done. As their name was called, they walked across the stage and received their diploma. Finally, Mike was called and he walked across the stage and received his diploma. He walked back down to his seat in a daze. It was finally over. After all the diplomas were given out one of the professors gave a final speech congratulating all the students. Finally, he released them. All the people on the balcony clapped their hands. As Mike walked out into the lobby he saw his parents. His father took a picture of Mike as he walked toward them. When he got to them they hugged each other. All three of his family congratulated him.

"Let me go to my room and change clothes," said Mike. "We can then go and have lunch somewhere. They are having a graduation party in the cafeteria tonight. They will serve dinner and have a band playing dance music. Some people I'm sure will dance. Do you guys want to go?"

"I think it is too late to head home today," said Mike's father. "I think it will be a good start to our celebration. What do you guys think?" he said as he turned to his wife and daughter.

"Let's go," said Kathy. They went to lunch and after lunch they sat and talked about the future. They then spent the rest of the afternoon at the hotel where Mike's parents were staying. At about five thirty they went to the university cafeteria. The band was already playing dance music. Some students were dancing. They had a fine dinner and Mike got to dance with his mother and sister. Mike's father also got to dance with both ladies. They had a great time. Soon it was eleven O'clock.

"We had better go if we want to leave early tomorrow," said Mike's father. They all agreed. Mike took his family back to the hotel and went back to his university dorm room. Before Mike left they agreed that they would have breakfast at seven in the morning and leave at about eight."

In the morning Mike goes up at six. He packed up all his belongings. He searched the room from corner to corner and floor to ceiling. He knew that he would not ever come back to the room. He wanted to be sure that he got all his stuff. He checked his cooling box. He had about a pound of assorted lunch meat and a complete loaf of 100 percent wheat bread. He placed them all in a plastic bag. He thought that maybe they could have a sandwich for lunch on the way home. He also checked the cabinet under the cooler. There he found a package of eight Coca Cola cans he had forgotten about. He took them, the food bag and his suitcase and put them all in the trunk of the car. He then made a last final check of the room. Then he got into his car and drove to the hotel. As he entered the lobby he saw his family waiting there with all their suitcases.

"Good morning," said Mike's father who saw him first. The women then said good morning and hugged Mike.

"I see that you are all eager to go home," said Mike.

"Let's put our suitcases in your trunk," said Mike's father. "Then let's have a quick breakfast and be on our way." Mike helped his father put their belongings in the trunk and then they all went into the hotel's cafe. They had a quick breakfast and finally they were on the way home. When they were on the road for about two hours Mike remembered the food he had stored in the trunk.

"By the way dad," said Mike. "I forgot to tell you. I had a lot of food in a cooler that I had in my room. Being that it is cold outside, being April, I think it will be good for us to eat for lunch."

"What do you have and how much of each," asked his father.

"I have about a pound of lunch meat," started Mike. "You see I always ate lunch in my room while I did some homework and studying. I also have a loaf of sliced bread, and eight cans of soda.

"Great," said Mike's father. "That will give us more time at the hotel where we will be staying and celebrating tonight." At about twelve-thirty Mike's father spoke out. "Mike, pull over here. Do you see that there is a pull off place to give drivers some place to rest?" Mike did as his father requested. When he had parked Mike turned to his father.

"Do you want to have lunch?" asked Mike.

"Go and get the food," said Mike's father." Mike opened the truck and got the lunch meat, the breads and four cans of Coca Cola. He made four sandwiches and brought four cans of Coca

Cola. Each had a sandwich and a can of Coca Cola. When they finished eating, Mike requested they give him the cans so that he could put them in the trunk.

We are not finished with the soda yet," said Mike's mother. "I would like to keep mine. I will drink it while you are driving."

"Me too," said Kathy.

"I would like to keep mine too," said Mike's father.

"All right," said Mike, "as you wish. I drank all of mine. I was very thirsty." Mike then went back on the road and drove until they got to Omaha. They went to the hotel where Mike had been when he had driven home during the summer. He was pretty familiar with the area. After they got settled in, Mike and his father went down to the entrance counter.

"Can you recommend a good restaurant," asked Mike's father, the clerk at the counter.

"We have a very good café here," said the clerk. "Our cook is a fantastic chef."

"We would like somewhere that has music where we can dance. Our son has just graduated and we would like to celebrate."

"There is a fantastic restaurant two blocks left down the road across the street," said the clerk. "It is called Drano's Place. It does have an orchestra." Mike went up and got the girls and walked down the street to the restaurant the hotel clerk recommended. They had a great dinner and Mike got to dance with his mother and sister and Mike's father did also. It was a great evening. But like all good things it ended and they went back to the hotel.

The next day went much like the day at Omaha. They stopped at noon and had the sandwiches and the Coca Cola as they did the day before. Soon they were in Salt Lake City. There they could not find a restaurant with a band. They ate at the hotel and went to bed early. The next day they stopped and had the last of the lunch meat and Coca Cola. They decided to go straight to California without stopping that night. They got home at about midnight. They all went straight to bed. The next day they celebrated all day. That evening Mike's mom made

Cavatelli and had a large cake after dinner. It had written on it the words, Happy Graduation Mike.

The next few days went by with a happy celebration feeling in their hearts. Finally, it was Friday. Mike decided to go and see Mr. Cromer to see if he would hire him as a surgeon. When he got there the door was open and Mr. Cromer was sitting at his desk.

"Hi Mr. Cromer," said Mike. May I come in? I would like to talk to you about a job."

"Hello Mike," said Mr. Cromer. Come on in. It's so nice to see you. I guess your school year is over."

"All my school years are over," said Mike. "I graduated last week."

"Boy," said Mr. Comer. "How time flies by. Come in and sit down and let's talk." Mike sat down across from Mr. Comer. "What is your final degree on? "

"I graduated and have a doctor's degree as a surgeon," said Mike.

"I'm sorry," said Mr. Cromer. "We have two surgeons at this time and they handle all that is needed. However, I would like to make a recommendation. We do have an opening at our Medical Center for a Personal Physician. All members of the Medical center are members of Fairmount Hospital. They are not independent centers that just rent space like some hospitals do. You will have the right to serve anywhere in the hospital."

"What are the chances for me to get a surgeon's position with the hospital some day?" asked Mike.

"I think it is very good. I have confidence in your ability, said Mr. Cromer. "Also, we have two surgeons. One takes care of all the bone surgeries, the other one takes care of all the other problems who is about sixty years old. He may retire any time. I am offering the physician's job because I want you available for the job in the future."

"I will then take the job," said Mike. "I can try it and see if I would like it. When can I start?"

"You can start Monday," said Mr. Cromer. They then signed all the papers and Mr. Cromer took Mike to the Medical center and one at a time introduced Mike to the doctors who would be working with him. He introduced two doctors, Doctor Art Hawlins and Doctor Richard Dwyer since they were free. They had to wait until the other two were finished with their patients. The first that was free was Doctor John Panzen. Ten minutes later Mike met Doctor Carl Netley. After some get to know each other, Mike left. Mr. Cromer went back to his office. Mike went down the hall to the nurse's desk.

'HI Tammy," said Mike when he walked up to the counter. "How are you?"

"Hello Mike," said Tammy with a large smile on her face. "It is so good to see you. Are you coming back?" Mike then explained to her what his next job would be." After a few cheerful talks Mike left for the second floor. There he met Debbie. Debbie was so happy to see him she threw her arms around and hugged him. After some cheerful comments and Mike telling her of his new job Mike left for home. When Mike got home his mother met him at the door.

"Well honey, how did it go?" she asked.

"Well, we will have to see," said Mike. "I didn't get all that I wanted but I have a promise that I may get it in the future."

"So what did you get?" asked Mike's mother.

"I got a job as a general Physician," said Mike. That evening both Mike's father and sister wished him good luck. The days went by slowly. Mike realized that the job wasn't as bad as he had imagined. He found that with most of the patients he was very familiar with their problem. In most cases he knows exactly what drugs to give them to cure their problem. Some, recognizing the problem, he sent them to the lab so that he could get all the information that he needed to provide a cure. A few he sent to the third floor for surgery. After a few weeks, since his hours were from nine in the morning to about four in the evening, he decided to come to work at eight and go to the third floor and meet the patients that needed some cheering up. After his last patient at the Medical center in the evening, Mike went to the third floor to cheer all the patients there. All went fine. All the nurses loved Mike. He brought cheerful life to the hospital. Soon it was spring. Mike was enjoying the patients that got cheered up when they saw him. One day Mike was called up to Mr. Cromer's office. Mike entered his office and sat at his desk.

"Mike," started Mr. Cromer, "I promised that you will someday get the surgeon's position. Well the time has come up. You know that the two surgeons. We have Curtis Becker, the one that takes care of all the bone surgeries and Eric Davison who does the rest of the surgeries. Well Eric is retiring this month. So, if you want his job you can have it."

"I have enjoyed the job I have now. It was more satisfying than I expected," said Mike. "However, I'm sure that the job as surgeon will be much more satisfying. Of course, I accept the position."

Mike did a fantastic job as a surgeon. All the people praised him. He had saved many lives. Some had died on the way to the hospital but Mike revived them and gave them their lives back. It was about the end of his second year when a strange thing happened. Mike was walking down the hall on the third floor towards Tammy's counter when he was shocked with what he saw talking to Tammy. It was the most beautiful girl he had ever seen. Her face thrilled him. As he got closer she turned towards him. She suddenly stopped talking and looked shocked. Mike didn't notice it because he was also shocked.

"Hi," she said with a shaking voice. Tammy noticed the strange action of the two so she spoke up.

"Hi Mike," said Tammy." "I would like you to meet Tina Bano. Tina," she continued, "I would like you to meet Mike Costello."

Hi," said Mike, feeling something strange in his stomach he had never felt before. He realized it was what some people called butterflies. He also thought that she was the most beautiful girl he had ever seen.

"Hi" said Tina, "nice to meet you."

"Nice to meet you too," said Mike thinking that it was a stupid answer. He also realized that he was not himself at the moment. Before he could recover she turned to Tammy.

"I have to go now," said Tina. "I have too much to do. She then turned to Mike, smiled and left. It took a few minutes for Mike to recover.

"Who was that?" asked Mike of Tammy.

"She is the financial director," said Tammy. "She has the job of reviewing all of the hospital's operations. I think it is her job to make financial changes so that the hospital could increase its income."

"Sounds like a major undertaking," said Mike and then left for his office. He had a surgery to do in a few minutes. Because of the surgery Mike had a late lunch. He ate lunch normally at around one in the hospital cafeteria. The rest of the day went by as usual. The next day Mike had a small surgery and spent the rest of the morning reviewing the third floor patients. At one he went down to the hospital cafeteria. As he walked in he saw Tina sitting by herself at a small table. He then got in the cafeteria line to get his lunch from the food counter and after paying at the end of the counter he then walked to the table where Tina was sitting.

"Hi Tina," said Mike, better able to control his actions than he did when he first met her. However, he still felt the fireflies in his stomach. Her face showed a bit of shyness. Mike didn't notice it. "Do you mind if I join you?" asked Mike.

"No," said Tina. "I would love the company. They talked for a while. She told him all that she was doing and he told her of his accomplishments. This happened several days during the next months. They got to know each other better. Both had butterflies in their stomachs when they were together. Several times he asked her what she was doing in the evenings after work. He was trying to find a way to ask out with him. She always told him that during the day she would analyze each section of the hospital's organization and that in the evening she would work trying to find a way to improve it. Each time he would ask, she would tell him what she was working on that day. She just didn't understand what he was trying to do. Several times she would ask him what he did at night. She was trying to get him to ask her out. He misunderstood her motive. So she assumed, since he didn't ask her for a date, that he had a girlfriend. Mike one day told himself that he was going to ask her out. The reason he had not asked her was that he felt unworthy of her. However now he was going to ask her and if she turned him down he would have to accept it. The next morning since he didn't have any surgery he was going to ask her for sure. He was too nervous to ask her. They ate lunch together for the next two weeks. They looked like a very loving couple. He told himself that the next time he saw her he would ask her out for dinner. On Monday at about ten Mike got a call from Debbie on the second floor. She asked him to come down immediately. It was an emergence. When he got down there he found out it was a woman that had an auto accident and was not breathing. They had her in the surgery room with a doctor who was trying to save her life. He then was told that it was Kathy Costello. Mike almost fell over. Debbie took him to the room where Kathy would be brought after the surgery. When Mike got his senses back he asked the nurse how bad she was injured. He was told that the worst was that she had a bad injury to the head. He was told that she also had a broken arm and a broken leg. But what worried the doctor was the head wound. A piece of medal had protruded the side of her head. Just then Kathy was brought into the bedroom.

"How did she do?" asked Mike nervously.

"I have placed a device on her to take the pressure off her heart. Her brain is not working to control the body's actions. We will keep her under sedation to prevent any load on her brain.

I think that her survival is less than fifty percent. She was dead when she was brought in to me. I think I got her living, giving her a small chance of survival. Mike was shocked. He went to the chair that was next to the bed. He tried to sit on it and hold Kathy's hand. He slipped off the chair and fell on his knees. He stayed on his knees and leaned against the bed and held Kathy's hand. Just as Tina walked in, Mike started to cry out loud.

"Kathy honey, " said Mike, out loud. "Please don't leave us. What would we do without you? I love you Kathy. Please Kathy, don't leave me. I can't live without you." Mike kept repeating this over and over. Tina hearing this became very sad. Not only because she felt very sad hearing how much Mike was suffering, but because it told her that Mike had a girlfriend. Then as she walked further in the room she noticed that her last name was the same as Mikes. Suddenly it entered her mind that Kathy was Mike's wife. She assumed that was the reason Mike never asked her out for a date. Feeling broken hearted she left feeling more depressed then she had ever been before in all of her life. She thought that she was madly in love with a married man.

After a while Mike stopped his yelling and still on his knees started to pray. Later that evening Mike's Father and mother came to the hospital. They comforted each other.

It took two days for Kathy's body to be back to normal. On the third day she woke up. However, she was in a daze. The next day Mike decided to take her home where he could take better care of her. Before he left he went to Mr. Comer's office and asked for time off from his job. He got the time off and headed for home. They were home for about one hour when they got a phone call. It was from Kathy's boss.

"Hi," said the caller. "I am Cutis Becker. I am Kathy's manager. About a week ago she was promoted to the Corporate Attorney for our New York main office. She was supposed to pack and be there by now. Is she home so I can talk to her?"

"I'm sorry that you have not been informed," said Mike.

"Kathy was in an auto accident and has been in the hospital. I understand now why she was on the road at ten in the morning."

"How bad," asked Mr. Becker, "was she hurt?"

"She has a bruised shoulder, a broken arm and a broken leg," said Mike. "She is now at home recovering." Mike didn't want to tell him of her head injury. He wasn't sure she would ever be the same.

"Well I'll hold off on the transfer until she is able to travel," said Mr. Becker. "Tell her to call me when she is ready to leave." Seeing that Kathy was so much better Mike considered going back to work. Mike's father had already returned to work knowing that Kathy was in good hands.

It was three days later when Kathy came out of her daze. Her family was so happy and couldn't stop thanking God. It seemed like a miracle but Kathy was back to normal. She explained that she was on the way home to tell them about the promotion and she had to start packing her clothes. It was too good a deal to turn down. Here she was just an assistant. There she was the top attorney, besides her salary was almost double.

The next day Mike took off the casts on Kathy's arm and leg. Three days later Kathy was on her way to New York. Mike decided to stay home until Monday. After he had lunch with his mother he noted something different in his mother's behavior.

"Are you OK mom," asked Mike. "Are you sad that Kathy has gone to New York to work?"

"I am fine. I am very proud of Kathy. Why do you ask?"

"You do not seem like the upbeat person you normally are," said Mike.

"I guess we should let you know what we are thinking about," said Mike's mother. "We held off because we feel that you have enough to think about."

"What are you talking about?" asked Mike, puzzled by her statement.

"Your dad is thinking of retiring," said Mike's mother.

"That is great," said Mike. "So why does that make you sad?"

"We want to move back to Ohio," said Mike's mother quickly to get it over with. Mike stood in shock for a while.

"Wow," he finally said. "I have a lot to think about."

"We are going to sell this house and move everything back to Ohio. I know that you have a fantastic job. You can buy a small apartment. This house is too large for a single person."

A week later, Mike's father put their house up for sale. Mike helped his father put all the furniture they wanted to keep in the large truck they still owned. Mike asked his father to take all of Mike's furniture to Ohio if there was room in the truck. The next Monday Mike's father and mother left for Ohio. Mike went back to work. He asked all the nurses and other hospital employees if they knew where Tina Banio was. No one knew. Finally, he went to see Mr. Comer.

"Mr. Comer," started Mike. "I would like to contact Tina Bano but no one seems to know what happened to her. Can you tell me where she is? Doesn't she still do work for you?"

"I will look up my record," said Mr. Comer. "By the way do you know what happened to her?"

"I don't know of anything that happened to her," said Mike. "Why do you ask?"

"Well when she came in to tell me that she was leaving the job, her eyes were red like she had been crying." Mike shrugged his shoulders. Mr. Comer checked his booklet of employee information and told Mike the address that was written in his book. "I think that is an apartment building. Other than that I have no idea where she is." Mike accepted that answer and went back to his job. The next day he checked the apartment building and found that she had moved out. He checked every place he could think of. He used the computer to see if he could get some information. All his efforts failed. From that day on he was not the same jolly doctor he was before. Not only did he miss Tina, but everywhere he went reminded him of his father, mother and sister. One day he found that his parent's house had been sold. Finally, it seemed like it was not getting better so he made up his mind that as great his job was he could no longer take the loneliness. A Couple of days later he told Mr. Comer of his decision to move back to Ohio. Mr. Comer told him how much he will be missed but in respect he had for Mike he gave him a letter of recommendation. The next Monday he called his mother and told her of his decision. Then he packed up all his belongings and left for Ohio. While driving on his way to Ohio he wondered what his life would be like from then on.

CHAPTER THREE

A New Beginning

Mike arrived at the Fairlawn Ohio house at about six thirty on Thursday evening. His mother met him at the front door. She grabbed him and hugged him before either could say a word.

"How are you mom?" said Mike when she released him from her grip.

"I am so excited to have you home," said Mike's mother after she got her breath back. "I never thought you would leave the fantastic job you had. I am worried about what you will do."

"Don't worry mom," said Mike. "My boss at the Fairmont Hospital gave me a fantastic letter of recommendation. That will go a long way getting me a new job.

"I hope you are right," said Mike's mother. "Anyway, you can live here as long as you want."

"Where is dad?" asked Mike.

"He is at the airport getting tickets for us to go to San Francisco California."

"You are kidding," said Mike with a large smile on his face. Why in the world would you want to go back there?"

"I am not kidding you," said Mike's mother with a very serious look on her face. We are flying there this coming Monday."

"You have got to be kidding me," said Mike. "Why in the world would you want to go there?" Seeing that Mike was getting distressed she answered him.

"We are going there because that is the best place for us to get a flight to Hawaii. We are going to Hawaii for a month. I think we told you that we are going to spend the rest of our life, or as long as our money holds out, to travel all over the world."

"That is wonderful," said Mike. "For now what I want to know is what is there for dinner. I didn't stop for lunch and I am very hungry."

"As soon as your father gets home we will eat," said Mike's mother. "The food is ready." She just finished that statement when his father walked in. After a few hugs and hellos they sat down to eat.

The time for Mike's parents to leave went too fast. They had to leave on Wednesday to be in time to get the flight to Hawaii. Before they left Mike's father pulled Mike aside.

"Listen Mike," said his father. "You are to feel like this is your home. You are free to make any changes you like. It is your home. We will only be like guests since we will only just spend a few days here between trips."

After they left Mike felt lonely like he felt in California. He decided that he needed a job. He checked with Akron General Hospital but they did not have an opening. He wanted to check around the Akron area before he went to Cleveland. He thought of Universal hospital but when he left they did not have a surgery facility or any patient rooms that he could remember. However, what would he lose? He remembered that on the east side of the building was the Medical center where as a kid he had his family doctor. Maybe he could be a family doctor. He remembered that at the Fairmount hospital where he spent his first year, he learned that it could be a very satisfying job. The next day, which was Friday, he went to the University Hospital. It was only a ten minute drive from his house. He arrived there at nine O'clock. The first nurse he met he asked to be directed to the Head Manager.

"That will be Mrs. Sophia Keen," said the nurse. "Her office is the last office on the right at the end of the hall. Mike walked down the hall to the last office on the right. He knocked on the door.

"Come in," said a woman. Mike walked in and sat across from

her at her desk. "I am Sophia Keen," said the lady at the desk. "I'm the Chief Administrator of the hospital. How can I help you?"

"My name is Mike Costello, I am a Medical Surgeon. I have worked for two years at the Fairmount Hospital in San Leandro California. The first year I was only a family doctor. At the end of the first year they promoted me to the hospital surgery post. I recently resigned from there and am looking for a job here in Ohio." Mike then handed him a folder with his qualification, his degrees and the reference letter from Mr. Comer.

"Why did you leave your job at the Fairmont Hospital?" asked Sophia.

"I was born here in Ohio," started Mike. "I got my first Degree from Ohio State University in Columbus Ohio. My father is a carpenter. At the time I graduated my father got a Construction Managers job in California. We all move there. We kept the house my father designed and built here in Ohio. It was for rent since we moved to California. My father always considered moving back to Ohio after he retired. I went to the Toledo Medical University while my home was in California. About a month ago my father retired and moved back to Ohio. I didn't like being alone in California. After a few months I decided to come to Ohio to practice."

"Well I will need a little time to consider your request for employment. I don't know if you are familiar with this hospital. We have been expanding the hospital's capabilities."

"Yes, I did notice some differences," said Mike. "You see, until I went to college I came here to be examined by my family doctor. So, I was very familiar with it at that time. That was over seven years ago. However, the first thing I saw was that there is now a wall across from the elevators and that the area on the other side is now a café."

We have expanded the hospital in many other ways," said Sophia. "We are now under construction to make this a complete hospital. If you remember just a few years ago it was only a medical center for family doctors, a lab and an emergency room. Now we are expanding it to be a full hospital."

"I know that you must be very busy," said Mike, "but would you have time to tell me what the expansions are?"

"I will be glad to," said Sophia. "Maybe you can make some recommendations. You see we have heard so much of the success of the Fairmount Hospital in our hospital Journal. Let me call Ralph. He is in charge of the expansion." It took Ralph about fifteen minutes before he came to the office. While they waited Mike told Sophia great things about the Fairmount hospital.

"One of the intelligent things they did was to hire a Financial Adviser to review and reorganize those that could be improved. Because of her work, the Hospital's income increased by over thirty percent. They used the increase in income to purchase better and more modern equipment."

"Do you know who this Adviser was?" asked Sophia.

"Yes," said Mike. "Her name is Tina Banio." Sophia wrote the name down on her pad.

"We can't use her now, but after we do most of the construction I may contact her. Thank you for the information." Just then Ralph walked in.

"Sorry it took me so long to get here," said Ralph. "I was in the middle of giving a man the building instructions."

"That is alright," said Sophia. "I want you to meet Doctor Mike Costello. He is here requesting a job. He comes from Fairmount Hospital."

"Please tell me what they did to become one of the highest rated hospitals," asked Ralph.

"Before you answer," said Sophia, "I would like to know that you are hired. We will talk about the different jobs that are available after Ralph is finished."

"It will take all day to tell you all I know about the hospital," said Mike.

"Just give us a brief description," asked Ralph.

"First," started Mike, "the basic setup is the same as this

hospital, the lab is on one end, and the Medical center on the other end. The emergency entrance is next to the lab. The main floor has all the equipment like the things that are necessary to clean the rooms after a patient has been released. The second floor has all the patients that had a bone braking accident. The third floor had all the patients that had body organ functions problems and all patients that had some kind of disease. On the third floor there are two surgery rooms. One had a surgeon whose patience requires bone related surgery. The other has all the other types of necessary surgery. Basically that is the Fairmount Hospital set up."

"That is very helpful information," said Ralph. "There is one thing I would like to mention. We have one surgical room and it is on the second floor. The doctor is presently doing surgery for accident victims."

"That is better," said Mike, because the surgeon will be on the same floor as the patient he will take care of."

"I think you are right," said Ralph. "I hope you will be available during the rest of the construction effort. We can use the input from a knowledgeable doctor."

"I will be glad to help," said Mike.

"Well I have to go now," said Ralph. "Call me if you need any information." Ralph then left.

"Well Mike," said Sophia." We don't have too many jobs at this time. The only thing I can offer you is an office in the Medical center. You will spend most of your time as a family doctor. However, in your spare time you can visit and help any patients you feel you could help. When the third floor is complete we will add a surgical room that you can use as the hospital surgical doctor."

"Sounds great to me," said Mike. "What I did at the Fairmount Hospital in California is that I went to work at seven and that gave me an hour to visit the patients before I saw my first patient at the Medical center. I also spent an hour on the third floor before I went home in the evening"

"That is great," said Sophia. "You are free to do the same thing here." She then took out the paperwork needed to hire Mike. Mike finally had a job about ten minutes from his home.

Mike soon became well known in the hospital. He got to know Joana Kozar, the second floor nurse. He spent a lot of time on the third floor helping Ralph with the construction. When he got a patient that needed surgery he used the second floor surgery room when it was available. He also spent a lot of time with the patients that were placed in the second floor hospital rooms that slowly became available. Slowly all the rooms on the second floor were finished. As the news about the hospital's new additions got around, more patients became available. Soon the third floor was completed. Sally Ross was hired to be the top nurse on the third floor. Mike got to know her well. They became good friends. Lastly the third floor surgical room was completed. Mike was soon back operating like he did In California. About a month later, Mike's parents came home from Hawaii. They spent time telling each other what they did in the last month. One day during breakfast Mike's father turned to Mike.

"It has been so nice for us to spend time with you," However I would like to tell you that we are going to leave on our next trip next Monday."

"Where are you going this time?" asked Mike.

"Since it is summer it is a good time to go to Alaska," said Mike's father. "We hear so much about all that can be seen there."

"Well I hope you have a fantastic trip," said Mike. "I will have to get used to being alone again."

The next Monday as planned Mike's parents left for their trip. Mike decided that while they were away that he would start the upgrading of the house as his father said he could do. After all, his father was a carpenter and some of that might have been passed on to Mike. Mike got a piece of paper and walked through the house and wrote down all the things that he thought should be upgraded. First he decided to paint the rooms that needed repainting badly. Mike decided to go to the mall to one of the department stores to see what they had. As he was walking through the mall he saw a person that looked like Carol. He approached her and as she turned away from looking at a store window she spotted Mike walking towards her.

"Carol is that you?" asked Mike.

"Mike," said Carol, looking very surprised. "What are you doing here? You live and work in California."

"Not anymore," said Mike. "We all moved up here over two months ago. What are you doing here? Did you get a job here in Fairlawn?"

"No," said Carol, "I am going to school at Akron University. I am studying towards my Master's Degree. I am going to the summer class to get enough point to graduate this fall"

"I have missed you so much," said Mike. "You stopped answering my calls and never called back."

"I'm sorry Mike," said Carol, "you know how I feel about long distance affairs. They never work."

"Well I now live just around the corner," said Mike, "do you want to start over?"

"I am not seeing anyone else if that is what you are asking," said Carol. "I would love to be your girlfriend again. I never stopped thinking of you. I take it that you have not had a girlfriend since it was me."

"No," said Mike. "I was too busy. I also did not get over you."

"Sounds great," said Carol. "Where do we go from here?"

"Well it is near five. Why don't we go to dinner where we can tell each of us all that has happened to each of us over the last seven years or so?"

"Great," said Carol. "I have a great desire for some fish. I was thinking after I got what I wanted I would go to Red Lobster."

"Sounds like a good place to have dinner," said Mike. "Let me drive and after we leave Red lobster I can drop you off at your car. However," said Mike, "did you get what you wanted to buy here?"

"I can come back another day," said Carol. "How about you, didn't you come here for something too?"

"After meeting you I forgot what I came for." They both had a hardy laugh. A few minutes later they arrived at the Red Lobster restaurant. They were seated near a window. The waitress gave them a menu. They each ordered their dinner and then they started to talk.

"Tell me," said Carol, "what have you been doing since we last communicated?"

"After I left you, I got a job at the Fairmont University. I was the nurse's assistant for most of the year." Mike then told her about all the patients he helped. He then told her about his going back and forth from college to home. He told her that every summer when he got home that Fairmount Hospital gave him a job. Then told her how each year he was elevated to a better job.``

"When did you become a Primary Surgeon?" asked Carol.

"After I graduated," said Mike, "I got the job as a family doctor in the Hospital's medical Center. It was after the first year that I was elevated to hospital's primary Surgeon."

"You had a very interesting life," said Carol.

"How about you," said Mike, "what was your life like?"

"My life was very boring," said Carol. "After I graduated from college in Columbus, I got a job as a store sales lady in Hartville where my parents live. I sold women's clothes. After a few months of working as a clerk I tried to find a better job. I found that there was no one that would hire me. I was told that the Company management job required at least a Master's Degree in Management. So I went back to college. However, I found that Akron University had better courses in Corporate Management. Besides, it is closer to home. I'm in my second year. I will graduate this fall after my summer classes."

"So when will I see you?" asked Mike. "I would like to start taking you out on a date as we did before I went to California."

"Well we can do exactly as we did when we were in college

together. What I'm saying is that I cannot go out during the week. We can be together on Friday nights and Saturdays. The other evenings I will have too much homework. If I would go out with you when I get home my mind would be too excited to do homework."

"Sounds like a plan," said Mike. "I was afraid that you would not want to take up where we left off."

"You must understand that I broke up with you because of the great distance between us. I never stopped caring for you," said Carol.

"I never stopped caring for you," said Mike. "The proof is that I have not dated anyone since we parted."

"I can say the same," said Carol. The waitress then brought them their dinner. They ate with only small talk about the dinner and other restaurants they would like to try. After dinner Carol requested that they leave.

"I still have some things to purchase. So, take me back to my car." Carol then took out a piece of paper from her purse and wrote down her address and phone number. Call me when you are free to go out." They then left and Mike dropped her off at her car and went home feeling more joyful than he had felt for a while.

The next Thursday Mike called Carol.

"Hi honey," said Mike, trying to be romantic. "Can I pick you up at about five tomorrow? We can have dinner and then we can go to see a movie. There is a very romantic picture I would like to see. I think you would too."

"Hi sweetheart," responded Carol. "It sounds great to me. I will be ready." On the next day Mike picked up Carol. They went to dinner at Olive garden. After dinner they went to the movies. They both loved it very much. Then Mike took Carol to her dorm. At the doorway he kissed Carol good night. Carol did not resist. Things were getting back to normal. This went on for the next few weeks.

Soon it was Carol's graduation. Mike went to it and they

both enjoyed it very much. After the graduation party Mike took Carol to her dorm where she was going to pack and get ready to go home.

"Do you want me to help you find an apartment here?" asked Mike. "I can also help you find a job. I can give the University Hospital where I work a good report for you. I have a great reputation there."

"Not yet," said Carol. I am going home for a while. My mother isn't well. I would like to spend a little time with my parents. I'm not in a hurry. I would like to spend the holidays with them. I will call you when I plan on coming to Fairlawn for a job. I will keep in touch." Mike then left feeling a little sad at her decision. He had no idea as to what would occur in the future.

Mike then went back to his normal work at the hospital. He brought some joyful atmosphere to some of the patients. He did some surgeries, but he became known for his ability in saving some patients from having surgery. At home he was lonely. His parents were in Alaska. Carol had stopped calling him and would not answer the phone when he called her. One day when things were slow he took off. It was on a Monday. He decided to drive down to Hartville to see if Carol was well. Perhaps her mother died and Carol was just suffering the loss. He left early in the morning and got home at about ten. He knocked on the door. An older woman answered the door.

"Can I help you," she said.

"I'm Mike Costello. I am a friend of Carol. We went to college together." Mike assumed that Carol had not told his mother about their relationship.

"I'm so sorry Mike," said Carol's mother. "Carol is on the way for her honeymoon. She was married on Saturday. She met an old boyfriend that she had in high school. I know that this must be very sad news to you. I told her that she should have notified you."

"You have this all wrong," said Mike trying to defend his

sadness. "I love Carol like a sister. We were just great college friends. She told me that she had a possible job here in Hartville and would stay here with her family. Did she get the job?"

"I guess Carol meant that she loved you like an older brother," said Carol's mother. Are you much older than her?"

"I'm not sure," said Mike. "It is about ten years. We were just lonely in college and found our relationship satisfying that problem. Look I was in the neighborhood so I thought I would stop and see Carol. I have an appointment here so I have to go. I wish Carol a long and happy life." Mike then said goodbye and left. He went back to the hospital

It was early in November when Mike had just finished dinner and was sitting in the family room looking to see what movie he wanted to watch when he heard his front door bell. He wondered who it would be. He answered the door. It was a young lady with a handsome man standing next to her. For a while Mike just stood there. He thought that he recognized the girl. Suddenly he remembered who she was.

"Hi Sylvia," said Mike suddenly. "I remember you. You were Kathy's best friend in high school. Come on in. How are you?"

"I'm fine, Doctor Costello," said Sylvia. "I don't think you have met my husband Larry. This is Kathy's father." She told her husband.

"Please call me Mike," said Mike. "I'm not your doctor."

"I don't feel right just calling you by your first name," said Sylvia.

"Then just call me Mr. Mike or Doc or something like that," said Mike. "If you call me Doctor Costello I feel like we are complete strangers."

"Ok doc. How have you been?" said Sylvia. "I understand that your parents are out of town. That must make you pretty lonely."

"How do you know all that?" asked Mike.

"Oh," said Sylvia. "We are constantly in touch with Kathy. She is my best friend."

"Why are you here?" asked Mike. "Is there something wrong? Is Kathy alright?"

"Kathy is fine," said Sylvia. "We were asked by Kathy to visit you. You know that Larry is a police officer with the Fairlawn police force.

"I thought I recognized you," said Mike. "What job do you have with the police department?"

"My job is to investigate any crime, especially murder," said Larry.

"So, you are a Detective," said Mike.

"Something like that," said Larry. "I am known in the department as Lieutenant Benten, but you can call me Larry."

"You know," said Mike. "Some of the work that I do at the hospital is to investigate the cause of a patient's death if it is not from an accident or a known disease. I have a young lady doctor check the blood and all the possible causes of the death."

"Maybe someday we will work together," said Larry. Mike then offered them a soda drink but they both preferred coffee. After some small talk Larry got a phone call.

"Yes, this is Officer Benten," said Larry. After listening for a minute he answered, "I will be right there," and hung up. "Listen you guys, I have to go to a possible crime scene. Would you consider coming with me Doc? We may need a doctor's opinion."

"I will be glad to," said Mike. "I will drive so that Sylvia could go home in your car. After we finish at the crime scene I can take you home."

"Great," said Larry. "Let's go now." Mike under the direction of Larry got to the house where there could have been a Crime. A police car was already there. As they walked in, a police officer came up to them.

"I think it is an open and closed case," said the officer. "I think it was a suicide. We found him lying on the floor with the gun in his hand. We spoke to the woman next door who was a close friend and she said that he was very unhappy because his wife had left him." Larry and Mike walked over to the body.

"It does look like he shot himself," said Larry. "What do you think Doc?"

"Don't believe that he shot himself," said Mike. "First look at his wrist watch. It is on his right hand. That indicates to me that he is left handed. He would not shoot himself with the right hand."

"That is a good point but he could be double handed," said Larry.

"There is another point that makes me think that this was a murder," said Mike. "Look at that stand there in the corner of the room. It has a book there half open. I think it is a bible. If he is a strong Christian he would never commit suicide."

"I'm so glad you came with me. You have given us a strong point that would direct us to look at who would benefit from his death. We should also look for someone that could hate him enough to kill him."

"Besides looking at what his wife will receive I suggest that you check his place of employment," said Mike. "I have seen a lot of cases where a promotion could cause some problems." Mike then drove Larry home and went to his own home. It was a few days later that Larry called Mike.

"Hi doc," said Larry. "I thought you would like to know the results of the crime that we went to."

"Yes," said Mike. "What did you find out?"

"First of all, we check with his wife," started Larry. "She said that she left him only to punish him for his treatment of her about having children. She said that she was a Born-Again-Christian, and that she would never divorce him. Then we checked at his place of employment. We found that there was going to be a promotion and that the guy that was shot was next in line. We finally got the guy to confess to the murder."

"Thanks for letting me know the conclusion to that case," said Mike. "I will be available any time you may want my opinion in one of your cases."

"Thank you," said Larry. I will take you up on that."

Back at work the next day Mike had a surgery that he had to do. When he did surgery he always had to use the second floor surgical assistant which was really the surgical assistant to Doctor Broderick who was the accident patient's doctor. When she assisted Mike she was not as helpful as Mike wanted her to be. But he had no choice. About a week later Mike decided that he would only use his surgical room on the third floor. However, Mike still had to use Doctor Broderick's assistant. He then asked Sophia for an assistant who had experience with patients who had disease or body organ failure. Sophia then put out a sheet requesting the hiring of a surgical assistant. It was about two weeks later that a young woman was hired for the job. When the hired person came into the hospital she was directed directly to Sophia's office. Sofia then called Mike to her office. When Mike got there he was stunned at what he saw. She was a very beautiful young lady. He just stood there looking at her. He wondered why he was called. It couldn't be that this was his assistant.

"Mike," said Sophia, "I want you to meet Melanie Lane. She will be your surgical assistant. She has two years' experience as a surgical assistant for a hospital in Utah. "Melanie, I would like you to meet Doctor Mike Costello. You will be working for him.

"Hi doctor," said Melanie, "It is so good to meet you. I promise that I will do my best in assisting you.

"I'm sure you will," said Mike, getting his control back. "I will not have surgery until tomorrow morning. But come with me and I will show you around. I will show you the surgical room and all the equipment we have and if time allows I will introduce you to some of the patients that are waiting for possible surgery."

"That sounds great," said Melanie. Mike then took her to the surgical room. After all, he thought that was the most important place. He was surprised that she knew all about the new equipment that he had in the room.

May I ask you a question?" asked Mike.

"Yes of course," said Melanie. "What do you want to know?"

"You seem to be well experienced in this field," said Mike. "Why did you leave the job you had? By the way please just call me Mike except in the presence of a patient"

"Ok Mike," said Melanie with a big smile on her face. I left because I had a problem with one of the people down there. We just didn't get along. After much effort to settle our problem I decided to leave."

"Well I'm glad that you are here," said Mike. Then he went on his normal routine taking Melanie with him. Melanie was very well accepted by the patients they visited. Mike was encouraged that she was a good choice. The next day they went into the surgery room to perform surgery on a middle aged man who had a heart attack two days ago. They got him settled and began performing the surgery. He needed three Coronary vessels replaced. After the surgery the patient was moved to a recovery room. Mike and Melanie cleaned up and decided to go to lunch together in the hospital cafeteria.

"Well," said Melanie. "How did I do?"

"You are hired," said Mike with a smile on his face. "I will keep you."

"Thank you," said Melanie. "I think I will stay. I was very impressed with your procedure in the surgery. It looks like you know what you are doing. "The truth is that I was very impressed by your assistance. I felt like I had four hands. You are the best I have had so far.

"Thank you doc, or can I say, thank you Mike?"

"Mike is fine except in the presence of a patient," said Mike. After they had lunch Melanie went to check on the patient. Mike was called to Sophia's office.

"Well," said Sophia, "How did she do?"

"She was fantastic," said Mike. With her there I felt like I had four hands. She is the best I've ever had."

"That is great," said Sophia. "We will keep her then. That's all I wanted to know. You may leave now." Mike left and went on to see some of the patients. Mike and Melanie work fine together.

Two months went by with great success. Mike and Melanie became great friends. They dated at least twice a week. It was now the middle of august. Mike missed his parents very much. He wondered when they would come home from their trip. It was one beautiful day that Mike saw a black car drive next to him as he was leaving his house. Suddenly he heard a gunshot and felt pain in his chest. The next moment he passed out. He woke up in a hospital bed. He had no idea how much time passed. He thought it was a minute ago. He looked up and saw three people there waiting for him to wake up. He looked around a notice that he was in the recovery room.

"Did I have some kind of surgery," Mike asked.

"Hi Mike," said Doctor Broderick. "I did a quick surgery. I removed the bullet from your chest. Fortunately, you must have turned just as you were shot. The bullet entered your chest at an angle and set in your shoulder. I removed the bullet and had to replace the vein that was perched. I think you will be well. I think I repaired the vein so that you will not have any internal bleeding."

"Thank you doctor," said Mike, coming back to his normal thinking. "I would like to ask you to keep all that is going on a secret. I have an idea how we could find the one who shot me."

"Did you see who shot you?" asked Larry.

"Hi Larry," said Mike. "No, he had a big black mask on. He was a very tall male."

What is your idea as to how to catch the shooter?" asked Larry. "Before he could answer Melanie walked up to Mike.

"Oh Mike," she said with tears in her eyes. "I'm so sorry."

"Why should you be sorry?" asked Mike.

"Oh Mike," said Melanie. "I care very much about you."

"Come on Melanie," said Mike. "Come out with the truth. I don't know of any one that would want to hurt me. So, come on Melanie. It's a matter of life or death."

"All right Mike," said Melanie. "I graduated from Westminster College in Utah. After I graduated I got a very great job at the

City hospital in Salt Lake City. It was there that I met George. He said that he also was a student at Westminster College. I think he was not telling the truth. We dated once. I found that he was an over self-rated arrogant. He was the most selfish person I had ever met. When he asked me out a second time I refused. He then told me that I belonged to him and that I was his girlfriend. He said that after he got the job he was after that they would get married. I told him that I did not love him. He said that I will get to love him after a few more dates. He said that in only one date I could not have known the future we would have together. It was then that he got aggressive and hit me, repeating that I belonged to him and that if I gave him trouble that he would beat me up. I told him that I would never go with him. He then beat me up. My neighbor heard the yelling and being a good friend called the police. The police arrested him and called an ambulance. He got six months in jail. When He got out he came after me. He told me that I was his and that nothing was going to change the fact that I belonged to him. Apparently, he did something illegal because as he left my house the police stopped his car and arrested him. That's when I decided to leave Utah. I found that the job was open here in Ohio so I applied and got the job. I have not heard from him since but I wonder if he has found me. From the description that you gave Mike it sounds like him."

"I'm sure that he was the one," said Mike.

"Mike," said Larry, "what was your Idea on how to catch the shooter?"

"I think the best way is to let him believe that he was successful," said Mike. "I think that after a couple of days he will go to Melanie's house to get her back."

"Then what do we do?" asked Larry, "How do we prove that he shot you?"

"Well we set up a recorder and any other equipment you can think of and we placed a police officer hidden in her house. "Melanie will make him confess to the crime and the police officer is there to protect Melanie. We have no idea what he has in mind." Larry went out into the hall and got on the phone. After a little while he came back.

"I have a young woman police who can help you set things up," said Larry to Melanie, "and can stay with you until he shows up. Being a woman she can sleep in one of your spare rooms until it is all over."

"Sounds like a good plan," said Mike. "You have to make sure that he gets the message that I died."

"I will have that all handled," said Larry. Larry then turned to Doctor Broderick. "Doctor Can you have a roiling bed with two covered pillows that look like a body? I noticed that a couple of reporters are downstairs trying to get information. I will not tell them anything but the covered pillow. I'll give them information. We will use an ambulance and take it to a mortuary. I will inform them that they should burn the pillow and place the ashes in a bottle with Mike's name on it."

"I'll get right on it," said doctor Broderick.

"Go Melanie," said Larry, "the woman police officer is on the way to your apartment." Melanie left with the okay from Sophia. When she got home the police officer was there waiting for Melanie.

"Hi," said Melanie. "You are quick. I am Melanie Lane.

Hi," said the police officer, "I am Officer Martha Winder.

"Glad to meet you," said Melanie.

"Now if you will help me bring in the equipment we need," said Martha, "we can get all set up. You never know when the criminal will show up." They went inside bringing in all that Martha had in her police car. They then started to put everything up. The first thing they set up was the recorder. It was important to get a confession from him. They set the recorder behind the couch. The next thing they started to set up was a camera. They were discussing where they could set it up so it was easily seen. While they were discussing the different possibilities, the doorbell rang.

"I wonder who that could be?" asked Martha.

"I don't know many people around here," said Melanie, "I have not lived here very long."

"It is probably Larry," said Martha, "but just in case it is someone else we should keep what we are doing a secret. I will hide in the hallway to the bedroom. I want to check to see which bedroom I will stay in anyway." Melanie went to the door and opened it, and then with a great surprising voice she yelled out.

"George, what are you doing here?"

"I come to get you back," said George. "Did you really think you could run away from me?"

"I didn't run away from you," said Melanie. "I am not your girlfriend."

"You belong to me," said George. "You are mine and you always will be."

"I was never yours and I will never be yours," said Melanie.

"Why can't you understand that you no longer have a choice," said George. We are spiritually married. We just have to make it work."

"Listen carefully," said Melanie. "I am engaged to a fellow who is a famous Doctor. Why would I go with you? Consider us divorced."

"You do not have a boyfriend anymore," said George. "He is no longer available."

"Why would you say that?" asked Melanie. "I was with him just yesterday. I belong to him."

"He is no longer alive," said George. "I saw to that."

"How did you see that?" asked Melanie trying to get him to admit that he had shot Mike. "Did you kill him by a strong wish," said Melanie. "I don't see how you could get rid of him. You could never talk him out of it. He loves me too much. It is only your stupid dream. I am going to marry him this coming spring. And you and your silly lies will not stop it." Melanie tried to get him aggravated so that he would confess his shooting. Apparently it worked.

"I shot him this morning and I watched the hospital and saw them take him out covered with a sheet. I followed them to the undertaker. So you see you can never be his."

"That does not make a difference. I would never go with you. I hate you more than I thought I could hate anyone. You shot the love of my life. How could I ever forgive you?"

"I guess you would rather die than to come with me," said George

"You got that right," said Melanie, understanding what he was really saying.

"Well I guess there is only one thing left to do," said George as he pulled out his gun from the rear of his belt. "If I can't have you, no one else will." As he pointed the gun at her, Martha came out of the hallway where she was hiding and pointed her gun at George.

"Drop your gun and put your hands up," said Martha expecting him to do just that. She never expected him to do what he did. Before she could say another word George shot at her hitting her in her left shoulder. As she went down she fired at George. As fortune would have it the bullet went directly into his heart. He was dead before he hit the ground. Melanie ran to George, kicked the gun away from him and then went to Martha.

"How badly are you hurt?" asked Melanie as she reached for her phone and dialed 911. When the phone was answered she told the one that answered the phone about the shooting and gave them the address. She then looked back at Martha.

"I am only shot in the shoulder," said Martha. "It hurts so badly."

"Just hold on for a minute and let me get some medical equipment," said Melanie." She then ran to her bathroom and got the medical box. "I have to stop the bleeding." She then removed the clothes from the shoulder and proceeded to take care of the wound. It was around five minutes later, though to the girls it seemed like hours, the ambulance got there. Two young ambulance men got George and Martha and brought them to the ambulance and left for the hospital. Melanie was about to follow the ambulance when Larry walked it.

"Hi Melanie," said Larry. "Where are you going?"

"I thought I would follow the ambulance," said Melanie. "I wanted to be sure Martha was alright. I tried to stop the bleeding."

"It won't be necessary for you to go," said Larry. "She will be well taken care of. I need you here to retrieve all the equipment."

"The recorder is behind the couch," said Melanie. "George came so soon that we didn't have a chance to set up any other equipment. Everything else is still in the boxes."

"Help me put them all in the police trunk," said Larry.

"What about Martha's car?" asked Melanie, "how will you get it back to the police office?"

"I came with another officer," said Larry. "He is driving it to the police office."

"By the way," said Melanie, "here is the DV disk with George's confession. Although you have George's body, you still have to prove that he did the shooting to close the case."

"Thank you," said Larry. "You have a good point." Melanie then helped Larry get all the equipment into his trunk. Then Larry said good night and left. Melanie then went inside and turned on the TV to listen to the news.

The next morning Melanie went to work. The first place she went was to see Mike in his hospital room. Mike greeted her as she entered his room.

"Hi Melanie," he said before she could speak. "I see you found and got rid of the one who shot me and harassed you. How do you feel?"

"How I feel is not important," said Melanie with a smile on her face. "It is how you feel that is important."

"I am going to survive," said Mike, "that is what is important."

"Come on, Mike," said Melanie. "Please answer my question.

Do I have to go and see the doctor to find out how you are doing?"

"Well if you find out come and tell me," said Mike trying to be funny.

"Very funny," said Melanie, "I guess I have to ask a doctor. So, doctor Costello, please tell me how my good friend Mike is doing?"

"You got me there," said Mike. "Ok then, I had a surgery that removed a bullet from my chest. The surgeon also replaced a blood vessel that had been damaged by the bullet. This morning He sent me down to the lab for an x-ray. Just before you walked in he was here and told me that everything looked good. I will be out of here in about two weeks."

"There now," said Melanie, "was that too hard?"

"No," said Mike. "I am just working to keep you here longer."

"Well it worked," said Melanie, "I have to go to see all of our patients."

"Will I get to see you later," asked Mike," before you go home?"

"I will," said Melanie. "I promise." She then left and went into the third floor where their patients were. This went on for the next two weeks. During that time they received eighteen patients with body organs that were not working properly or diseases that needed attention. Fortunately, none needed immediate surgery. Mike had Melanie send them to the lab for a test. Mike then reviewed the test results and gave prescriptions as he felt would relieve the problem. What surprised both Mike and Melanie was that the prescriptions that Mike prescribed completely cured six of the patients. The other twelve showed that the drugs relieved their problem and postponed the requirement for surgery. Everything seemed to go in Mike's favor. It was on Thursday, about two weeks after Mike got shot, that Mike was told that he was ready to be released. After he was informed Melanie walked into Mike's hospital room.

"I understand that tomorrow will be your last day in the patient hospital ward," said Melanie.

"Yes," said Mike, "however Doctor Broderick said that I should rest at home for at least another week."

"Well tomorrow will be a special day for both of us," said Melanie. "It will be a date that both of us will remember."

"I don't think I will like what you are about to tell me," said Mike with a very sad look on his face.

"You know that I left Utah to get away from George," said Melanie, "I had a very fantastic job there. My parents and all my friends are there. I hope you can understand. I have a great respect for you. I love you but as an older brother. There is no romance between us. I hope that we can keep in touch with each other."

"Oh Melanie," said Mike with a very sad voice. "I will miss you so much not only because I love you as my little sister, but I will miss the work you help me with in the surgery job."

"Please keep in touch," said Melanie and left. As soon as Melanie left, Sophia walked into the room.

"Hi Mike," she said. "I see Melanie told you that she has resigned. She wanted to tell you privately first. However, the reason I'm here is to inform you of what I have accomplished since she informed me of her resignation. When I first sent out a request to hire a surgical assistant I got three answers. I picked Melanie because she seemed to want it the most. I can understand it now. However, I did call the other two. One was not interested at all. The other with the increase in pay I offered decided to accept the position. She will be here on November 28th. Her name is Vera Raven. She has three years' experience as a surgical assistant. I hope she will fill in all that you will need as an assistant."

"Thank you," said Mike. "I'm sure that she will do it." The next morning Mike started to get all his things together. He put on his regular street clothes and was about to leave when Melanie walked in.

"I see you are ready to leave," said Melanie. "I have all my stuff in the car and I am about to leave also. I just want to say goodbye one last time." She then hugged Mike kissing him on his cheek very close to his mouth. Mike hugged her back. Then with sadness Melanie left. Mike had to withhold his tears. He then got his stuff ready and walked down to the parking lot. There Sally Ross, the third floor nurse, who had offered to take him home.

We are going to miss you at the hospital," said Sally. "We enjoy your upbeat personality."

"I will be back after the holiday," said Mike. "It will go by very quickly. However, I will miss all of you also." They then got into Sally's car and soon arrived at Mike's house. Mike grabbed all his stuff and left the car.

"Have a wonderful holiday," said Sally as she started to drive away.

"You have a wonderful holiday too," yelled back Mike. Mike then entered his house and put all the stuff he brought home away. Then he looked into his refrigerator. He was wondering what he had that was still good that he could have for dinner. The only place he figured he could find something good to eat was in the freezer. All the things in the refrigerator he had to throw away as he was searching through the freezer compartment he heard a noise that seemed to come from the garage. He wondered if a rabbit or deer had entered the garage somehow. As he walked to the door from the family room that led to the garage the door opened. Mike jumped back. He was surprised. Then he noticed that it was his mother.

"Mother," said Mike. "You scared the heck out of me. I didn't expect you back so soon."

Hi Mike," said his mother. "How are you? It is so good to see you. Sorry if I scared you. We came home earlier than expected because first we had seen all that we wanted to see. There isn't that much to see. And also, because it was snowing so badly and it was predicted that it would get worse, so we decided we had enough." Then Mike's father walked in.

"Hi Mike," said Mike's father. "It is so good to see you. Let us get settled in and then we will have dinner and talk about all that has happened to both of us."

"Of course, dad," said Mike. "It is just that you surprised me." Mike's dad and mom then brought in their suitcases and other packages and got settled in. After they did that Mike's mother went into the freezer and brought out enough lamb chops for all three of them. They were all very hungry. After they ate, Mike turned to his father.

"So, dad," said Mike, "tell me about all that you saw in Alaska." Mike's father then gave a very detailed account of all that they did in Alaska. After he finished he turned to Mike.

"Now it's your turn," said Mike's father, "what have you been up to?"

"First let me say this," started Mike. "I have a job almost identical as the one I had in California. I have been doing surgery just like I did before. I had a surgical assistant named Melanie that was out of this world. I had so much respect for her. We dated several months. We cared for each other with lots of friendly feelings. However, there was no romantic action taking place. We were just good friends before I told you about the terrible thing that happened. Let me tell you about Melanie. She had a very good job as a surgical assistant and she never wanted to leave. However, she made a big mistake. She dated a fellow that she knew nothing about. It turned out he was an arrogant person who thought that he was a gift from heaven. The next time he asked her to go out on a date she turned him down. To make the story short he told her that she was his girlfriend and that he owned her. He hounded her and one day he caught her alone and after she refused he hit her several times telling her that she belonged to him. A person saw what was going on and on her cell phone called the police. The police got there just as he knocked her out. He was arrested and was given six months in jail. That was when she decided she had to leave the area. She found a job here in Fairlawn and went to work with me. About eight months later as I was getting in my car a tall fellow with a mask shot me. Fortunately, I was just about to turn away from him so that the bullet entered my chest but went sideways through my shoulder. I was all right. The surgeon took out the bullet and I was recovering in the hospital recovery room"

"Dear Lord," said Mike's mother who was listening to Mike's whole story. "Did they catch him?"

"Please let me finish my story," said Mike. "After some investigation and Melanie telling us of her crazy boyfriend named George, we decided that he was the one to watch out for. So, we set up a trap. First, they set it up with the media that I had died. That way George would feel free to visit Melanie. We sent a police woman with Melanie to set up the trap. They were going to set up a recorder and a TV system and the police lady was going to sleep in one of the guest rooms until George showed up. They only finished setting up the recorder behind the couch when the evil George showed up. He told her that she belonged to him and that she had no choice. She had to come with him. When she declined and said that if he didn't leave she would call the police. She asked him why he shot her boyfriend. That is when he confessed. He told her that he had to get rid of him. He said the reason why he shot him was that he couldn't compete with a famous Doctor. Melanie told him that she will never go with him. Then he pulled out a gun and told her that if he couldn't have her that no one would have her. He then pointed his gun at her. The police woman that was hidden behind the hallway to the bedroom came out and told him to drop the gun. Instead he shot at her. She shot back and hit him in the heart. He was dead before he hit the ground. So that is the story. I recovered and came home just before you got home."

"Wow," said Mike's father. "You should write a novel with all the experiences you have gone through."

"I will do that probably after I retire," said Mike. "Right now I want to help people who are very ill. That is why I became a doctor." Before Mike's father could answer, Mike's mother called them to dinner. She had made something special. It was Lamb Chops that she got out of the freezer and defrosted in the microwave. They all ate. Nothing more was said about the past days. They did discuss a little about the future.

The days went by very slowly. Soon it was Thanksgiving. Mike's mother made a very special turkey for lunch. They were sitting around discussing how badly the government was controlling the country when they heard a knock on the door. Mike was the closest so he went and opened the door.

"Cathy," he said and grabbed and hugged her. "Mom said that you probably were not coming home for this holiday. Glad you could make it."

"I had a very important court session but it was canceled so I was free to come home," said Cathy. "How have you been?"

"It's a long story," said Mike. "After our dinner we will talk. Right now mom has dinner ready and I am very hungry."

"Looks like I came home just in time," said Cathy. Suddenly both her parents came and hugged her for ten minutes.

"I thought that you were too busy with a court session to come home," said Mike's mother.

"It got canceled," responded Cathy. They then all sat at the kitchen table and had the turkey. Mike's father said grace thanking God for all the blessings they received and the great holiday dinner. It was obvious that they all were very hungry, especially since it was a very delicious dinner. After they all ate they sat down in the family room. They were so stuffed that they did not talk too much. Mike did tell Cathy all that had happened to him the week before. Cathy was very shocked at the information. Soon it was dinner time. They were all so stuffed that they could not eat anything. Mike's mother brought out the leftovers from their holiday meal but no one had anything except a cup of coffee. After watching a very romantic movie they all went to bed.

On Friday and Saturday they had sandwiches for lunch and leftovers for dinner. Sunday they all went to church and after they returned from church they had Sirloin steak for lunch. It was a wonderful four days for Cathy. However she got ready to leave Sunday afternoon for New York. She had to be at work Monday morning. Mike also had to be at work Monday morning. At the hospital Mike went back to his normal job. He had several surgeries and helped several from not needing surgery. Vera was just as good a surgical assistant as Melanie was. Everything at the hospital went by very successfully.

The days went very slowly. Mike was very happy at his job. Vera became a good friend as well as a great assistant. Mike was very careful not to get a romantic relationship with any of the hospital staff. He had enough problems with that type of relationship. It was in the beginning of December that Mike was called on an emergence. A woman was hit on her car side by a drunken driver. She was rushed to the hospital. She had a metal piece of the door window and some glass entered the side of her head. It looked terminal.

"Take her quickly into the surgical room," said Mike, "I need to stop the bleeding right away." They brought her into the room and Mike cut open the side of her head. After removing the metal and glass he fixed the blood vein that had a hole in it. He then closed the wound and stitched it together. Vera who assisted him didn't say a word during the surgery. After the surgery she turned to Mike.

"Do you really believe that she will survive," said Vera, "without some change in her mental capacity? If she survives at all"

"We did our best," said Mike. "I believe that if her mind is affected we can reteach her to continue a happy life."

"I hope you are right," said Vera. "She is a very pretty woman,"

"Well let's see what she is like tomorrow," said Mike and left the room to visit some of his other patients. That evening when he got home he told his parents what had happened that day. He told them that her brain may have been damaged. At dinner he prayed that she would survive with all her mind back to normal.

The next day Mike went first to check on his patient with the head injury. Sally the third floor head nurse was there,

"Hi doc," said Sally when he walked in. I was checking on your patient. She is doing well."

"Good morning Sally," said Mike. "Yes I see that her heart beat is normal and her body temperature has risen to normal. I think she will survive. However we have to see how her brain has survived. Keep giving her the medication. We don't want her to wake up until the hole in her head heals a little more. Keep watch on her. By the way, have we recovered her purse from the car? I would like to know who our patient is."

"I'm sorry," said Sally, "the police have recovered the purse and given us her credit cards, her insurance card and her driver's license. Her name is Rosemary Mason."

"Thank you Sally," said Mike and then left to visit his other patients. The next day everything was the same. It was on the third day that they stopped giving her the medication. Mike wanted to see if she would wake up with normal actions. However, when she did wake up it was with painful sounds that made Mike decide to give her the medication back.

"Wow," said Sally who was helping Mike. "What was that about?"

"I think we should try again tomorrow," said Mike, "but let's first give her some pain relief medication that will relieve the pain that she must feel in her head." When Mike got home his mother asked him about the woman that he was taking care of.

"How is that woman that got hit in the head doing?" asked Mike's mother.

She almost woke up this morning but it seemed like she was in great pain so we put her back to sleep again." Nothing was said after that.

The next day Sally did as Mike told her. It was in the late morning when Sally was checking on her that she heard a little moaning. Mike had visited her earlier that morning and was now visiting other patients. Sally then called Mike. Mike came running in.

"Mike," said Sally, "I think our patient is waking up."

"Yes," said Mike, "I can hear the moaning. Let's get ready to put her back to sleep if the sound is one of pain." Finally, Rosemary woke up. She opened her eyes and looked around.

"Hi," she said when she saw Mike who was near to her. She then looked around again and spoke.

"Where am I?"

"You are the University Hospital in Fairlawn Ohio," said Mike, giving as much information to see what her reaction would be.

"What am I doing here?" she asked, "and why do I have a headache?"

"You had a very bad auto accident," said Mike. "A car driven by a drunk hit your car right on your side of the car. The reason your head hurts is that you had a head injury that needed some surgery."

"Am I going to be alright?" she asked.

"That is what we are trying to find out right now talking with you," said Mike. "How do you feel? More importantly, what do you remember of your life before the accident?"

"I remember that my name is Rosemary Bruster," said the patient. "I think I remember everything."

"But your credit cards and your driver's license," interrupter Sally, "says that you are Rosemary Mason."

"That is my maiden name," said Rosemary. "That is funny. I had all my papers updated. I must have forgotten. Did my husband call me? I would think that he would have heard of the accident and be here. Perhaps he has nowhere to leave our little daughter Mia. He should have called anyway. Will you please try to reach him or my parents? We all live in Phoenix Arizona."

"We have tried to reach your parents for the last three days but we have not been able to reach them," said Sally. "We left a message. We will try again later."

"Maybe they are out of town. My father is a lawyer and is sent away to other cities often. Sometimes my mother goes with him but most of the time, when she can't get out of work she goes to grandma who often takes care of Mia."

"What," asked Sally, "is your grandmother's name?" Perhaps we could contact them."

"That is a good Idea," said Rosemary. "I think I had a personal phone book in my purse. If you check it out it will give you all the names addresses and phone numbers of all out relatives and friends"

"I didn't get to see all that was in your purse," said Sally. "I will check that out. I think your purse is still in the police station. It was the police that gave me your credit cards, insurance card, and your driver's license."

"Please go and get my phone book," said Rosemary. "I miss not having someone from my family here."

"I will go tomorrow early in the morning," said Mike. "Now that you seem to be back to normal, can you tell us what you are doing so far from your home?"

"I don't remember," said Rosemary. "I think I had a job somewhere near here. I think maybe that information is in my phone book."

"I will go home now," said Mike "I will see you in the morning. I will get your phone book before I come here." Mike then left for the police station. When he got there the first person he saw was Officer Larry Benten.

"Hi Larry," said Mike. How are you doing?"

"I'm fine," said Larry. "Why are you here? Do you have a problem?"

"I'm here to recover the purse of the woman that was hit by a drunken driver."

"Yes, I remember that," said Larry. "We have all of her possessions that we recovered from her car. We have also arrested the driver and he was willing, without any problem, to have his insurance pay for repair of her car and agreed to give her fifty thousand for her medical bills. We will need her to approve and sign a document where she agrees with the court results and will not file a suit against him. We are having her car fixed and it will be available when she is ready to leave and go home." Larry then went into the storage room and brought out the phone book. "We didn't know what to do with all her stuff and so we stored it here. It will all be available when she comes for her car. The car and all her stuff will be here when the car is completely repaired." He then handed the phone book to Mike.

"Thank Larry," said Mike. "She is still in a dazed state but I think she will be well soon. Take care and I will see you soon." Mike then went home and after he said hello to his parents he went and sat at the table where his father was sitting waiting for dinner.

"How was your day?" asked his father. "How is that girl that was in the auto accident?"

"She woke up," said Mike, "and after a while she was back to what seemed pretty healthy. Her heartbeat was normal and all the other signs were good. However she did have a strange problem. She claimed that she was married with a little daughter, but the information we have tells us that she is not married. The nurse who took care of her said that she is still a virgin."

"That is not unusual," said Mike's father. "When people are in a coma their thoughts are deeper in the mind so that a dream seems more like a memory of the past. After they wake up the dream seems more like remembering something that happened in the past."

"Thanks dad," said Mike. "That makes sense. She must have dreamt that she and her boyfriend got married and had a child. Now that she came too she thinks that it all really happened."

"I think that you should gently inform her of this information so that she doesn't end up with a broken heart."

"I will do my best," said Mike. Mike's mother then brought them dinner and they all ate and enjoyed the food.

The next morning Mike then went back to the hospital. When he entered the room he went right to Rosemary. He explained the result of the court action first.

"I will think about it," said Rosemary. "I am too confused at this time to make a decision."

"Anyway," said Mike. "I have your phone book and I will call Mr. Bruster in a little while. I think there is a two or three hour difference between Arizona and Ohio."

"Please call as soon as you can," said Rosemary. "I want my husband and daughter here with me"

"But before I call," said Mike, "I have something I have to discuss with you."

"Is it that important?" asked Rosemary.

"Yes,' said Mike. "It will answer a few questions. Let me explain what I have come across a few times. I want you to consider this as a possibility in your condition. When a person gets hit hard in the head and goes into coma he can have dreams when in that condition. However, in the coma condition the brain places the dream deeper than a regular dream is normally in the brain. So that when that person comes out of the coma the dream being deeper in the memory becomes a memory of something that seems to the person to really have taken place."

"So why are you telling me this?" asked Rosemary.

"I want you to consider the possibility that this maybe is the same with you," said Mike. "I don't want you to get a broken heart if it turns out that Jay is not really your husband and that you don't really have a daughter."

"Why do you think that this is a possibility with me?" asked Rosemary.

"I feel it is a possibility for two reasons," said Mike. "First you were in a coma for three days and I'm sure you had a dream or two. Secondly it would explain why all the information we get about you and all the information in your purse has your maiden name." Rosemary looked very shocked at that information.

"Do you really believe that is a possibility?" asked Rosemary.

"With all my medical experience as a doctor, I believe that is a very good possibility." With that said Mike grabbed his phone and called Jay Bruster

"Hello," said a young voice. "What can I do for you?"

"Hi," said Mike. "I am Doctor Mike Costello. Do you know a woman named Rosemary Mason?"

"Oh, dear Lord," said Jay, sounding like he was near to having tears. "How is she? Is she OK?"

"She is fine," said Mike, hoping that would settle him down. "We have been trying to call her parents. We have not been able to reach them."

"I know," said Jay. "I have been trying to reach them too. I think they are out of town. I have also been trying to call Rosemary for the last three days. I have not been able to reach her. What is her problem that a doctor has to call me?"

She has been in a car accident," said Mike. "But she only has a few bruises," added Mike to keep him from having another alarming situation. "A drunken driver hit her car on the driver's side. Do you know where she was headed too?"

"She is a Financial Adviser," said Jay. "The company she works for sends her out to different companies that have financial problems. Rosemary is great. She reorganizes their financial department so that the company ends up with a great profit. I have been trying to get her to leave that company and take a job where she is an assistant manager that also controls the company finances."

"Here is the hospital address where Rosemary is located. She is very lonely without you and her family here," said Mike. "I also want to inform you so you will handle it with care. While she was unconscious she dreamed that she was married to you and that you both had a little girl named Mia. Now that she is awake she thinks that that dream was real. Treat her so that she doesn't have a broken heart."

"Thank you," said Jay. "I will be there as soon as I can get transportation." Mike then hung up and went back to Rosemary.

"I just talked with your boyfriend Jay," said Mike. "He said that he will be here as soon as he can."

"How about my family," said Rosemary, have you contacted them?"

"It looks like they are on some sort of a trip," said Mike. "Jay has been trying to contact them and you for the past three days. He couldn't get anyone. I will try to reach them every day. However, I don't think you will need them. You are healing very well. You will be able to go home soon. I'm sure Jay will be on your side until you are home. Why don't you now get your afternoon nap? I have to go now and visit some of my other patients." Mike then left to visit a young man who had just recovered from a surgery that Mike had performed yesterday afternoon. That evening he visited Rosemary before he went home. She was soundly asleep. That evening Mike explained all that happened that day on the insistence of his parents. After dinner they sat and discussed all the possibilities that could occur.

The next morning Mike went into Rosemary's room just to say hello. He had surgery to perform. He found that she was fast asleep. He then went into the surgery room and performed the surgery. After the patient was placed in the recovery room he went back to Rosemary's room. She was just waking up.

"Wow," said Mike. "It is almost ten o'clock. You have had a nice night of sleep."

"Hi Doc," said Rosemary. "Somehow I feel that I am going to have a nice day." She barely finished talking when a young man walked into the room. He ran up to Rosemary.

"Rosie sweetheart," he said, grabbing her and hugging her. "I thought I had lost you."

"Jay honey," said Rosemary with a great smile on her face. "I have missed you so much."

"I have been calling you for the last three days," said Jay. I couldn't get a hold of you or your family."

"Are you going to get in trouble leaving your job?" asked Rosemary.

"No, I have some vacation coming."

"I am Doctor Mike Costello," said Mike introducing himself. "And of course you are Jay."

"I'm sorry doc," said Jay. "I was so happy to see Rosie that I didn't even see you."

"I understand that," said Mike. "What kind of work do you do?" asked Mike, "can you take a vacation any time you please?"

"I am an engineer," said Jay," I help design electronic control devices."

"Are you and Rosie married and have you been married before?" asked Mike.

"No, we are not married and we are both virgins," responded Jay with a look that told him that he asked that question so that Rosemary would hear it.

"And what was the reason that brought your sweetheart Rosie," asked Mike, "all the way out here."

"Hasn't she told you?" asked Jay with a very surprised look on his face. I see that she had her head wrapped up. Does she have a memory problem?"

"I didn't have a chance to tell him," said Rosemary. "You see I was hit in the head in a car accident. I had a medal piece enter my head. I had surgery to remove it and heal the area that was opened. I was kind of in a fog when I first came to. Also, I may as well bring you up to date on everything. You see, when I was in a coma from the head injury I had a dream. I dreamt that you and I were married and had a daughter named Mia. When I came too, I thought that it was a true memory and not a dream."

"Well if I have my way it will not be long before it becomes true," said Jay. "I also would like you to know that our first daughter will be called Mia. It is my grandmother's name. It is a custom in our family to name our first daughter after the woman's grandmother and the first boy after the man's grandfather.

"Well that is all cleared up," said Mike, except my question did not get answered."

"I was headed for Pittsburg to a company that has financial problems," said Rosemary to show all that her mind was back to normal. Their financial problem is so bad that they are losing money. I was supposed to reorganize their finances so that they would get a profit. Unfortunately, I will not be going there because I am going home with Jay."

"That brings up an important piece of information that I have," said Jay. "Rosie, do you remember a week or so before you left for Pittsburg, you went to the Phoenix General Hospital for a job. If you remember they needed someone to analyze the six departments for the financial status. I couldn't get transportation here yesterday so I called the Hospital. They have checked your background and are very impressed. They would like you to see them. They want to make you an offer. The main job is as an assistant hospital manager with the secondary job as a financial manager with the responsibility to investigate the finances of each department, reorganize if necessary, and keep them profitable. It is a permanent job."

"I accept," said Rosemary. "I don't care if the offer is peanuts."

"Great," said Jay. "I also have a ring that I had before you left. I was waiting for the time you and your parents were together to give it to you. If they are not home when we get there I will not wait.

"Whatever you have in mind I accept," said Rosemary.

"Good then as soon as we get home we will start making arrangements," said Jay.

"I have started already in my mind," said Rosemary.

"I see that you two have a lot to talk about so let me ask one question and then I can leave," said Mike.

"What do you want to know?" asked Jay.

"I was wondering if you have a place to stay?" said Mike.

"You know that there is a nice hotel across the street just down the street about a block away."

"Thank doc," said Jay. "I will look into it later today." With that said Mike left the lovers alone.

The next two weeks went by smoothly. Jay got a room in the hotel and spent every day holding Rosemary's hand. Mike during the week went to the police office and got Rosemary's suitcase. He knew that the clothes she came in were bloody and she would need clean clothes. He brought it into the hospital room and set it into the closet. He didn't have to explain much to Rosemary and Jay. Soon it was time for Mike to redress Rosemary's wound. After removing the bandage he had on the wound he checked it to see how well it had healed. It looked good enough for Mike to remove the stiches. Feeling that everything was OK he sent her down to get the lab test which will tell him how the healing had taken place inside the brain. The test came back and everything was positive. After examining the lab reports he walked into Rosemary's hospital room.

"Well you two," said Mike, "the tests are all positive. You are released to go home."

"Finally," said Jay. Mike called the nurse to help Rosemary get dressed. Jay and Mike waited outside in the hallway. When she got dressed they placed everything in the suitcase and they went down to the first floor for Rosemary to check out. Mike then drove them to the police station where Rosemary's car was and all her other possessions.

"Wow," said Rosemary when she saw her car. "It looks like it is new. I don't even see a dent where I was hit." They loaded everything in the car and were ready to leave.

"Please honey," said Jay. "Let me drive. We have to stop at the hotel so that I can get my suitcase and check out." She gave him the keys and then turned to Mike.

"Doc," she said with tears in her eyes. "How can I ever thank you for all that you have done for me? I can't but I pray that God blesses you with much love and happiness." She then hugged him and said goodbye and got into the passenger's front seat. Jay then hugged Mike.

"Rosie is right," said Jay. "Only God can give you enough thanks. Have a beautiful life." He then got into the car and soon drove away.

CHAPTER FOUR

Life Goes On

Mike suddenly felt lonelier than he had ever felt before. To get over it he went back to the hospital and visited his other patients. He felt better when he placed his mind on other patients. At the end of his shift he went home thinking it would help him to spend time with his parents. When he got home the first thing that his father asked him was about Rosemary.

"What did you find out today?" asked Mike's father. "Is she well enough to go home?"

"They not only are ready but they left early this afternoon," responded Mike. He then gave him details of the last hours with them.

"Well that was a happy ending," said his father. "That at least was very good news. I now have news that is not good for you."

"What have you guys been up to?" asked Mike. "What are you planning now?"

"We are planning to go to Sicily," started Mike's father. "Your mother has several cousins in Barrafranca Sicily. Your mom's cousin Stellina invited us to stay with her family. It happened to be the house your grandmother was born in."

"Well how long," asked Mike, "do you think you will be away?"

"I don't know," said Mike's father. "It all depends on what they have planned for us. Over the phone they talked about taking us on a tour. We will see when we are there."

The next week went by quickly. It was time for Mike's parents to go on their trip. Mike hugged them and after they left He went to work. At the hospital he got a patient that needed an emergency surgery. Mike and Vera didn't waste time. The fellow, named Brandon, had a heart attack and was barely breathing. Mike then opened his chest and found a blocked artery and quickly replaced it. Mike then stitched the opening he had made and seeing an improvement in the patient Mike felt better. The fellow was then brought to the recovery room. Mike then went to visit his other patients. He brought some happy times for the patient by convincing them that they are lucky because it could have been worse. He convinced them to thank God that they were still alive and will soon be back to normal.

The next two weeks were very slow. The number of patients was less than normal. One day Mike decided to take a few days off. In the morning of the first day, he went to the mall to buy himself some shirts and underwear. The ones he had were getting old and some had holes in them. He remembered that the men's apparels were located close to the side entrance which was on the south side of the building. It was a little smaller than the main entrance which was on the west side of the building. He parked his car next to the side entrance and walked to the doorway. As he entered he saw a young lady open the adjacent door and then fall to her knees yelling.

"Oh no, oh no, oh lord help me." She then started to cry. Mike walked up to her.

"Miss, can I help you?" said Mike. He then walked up to her and helped her get up. "What is your problem?"

"Someone stole my car," said the young lady. "I parked it right there at the end of the row. Now it is gone."

"What is your name?" asked Mike. "I can take you home where you can call the police to report the car stolen."

"I don't know how to get there," said the woman. "I left my cell phone in my car which I used to find my way around here."

"You are not from around here are you?" said Mike. "What is your name? I promise I will not leave you alone. I will help you until we solve your problem."

"My name is Lina Borio," said Lina. "I'm from Charleston, South Carolina."

"What are you doing here in Ohio?" asked Mike.

"I came here because my mother is very ill," said Lina. "I came to take care of her."

"Look, I know that it is hard to talk here in the doorway. Let's go inside where I know that near men's shirts there is a small bench," said Mike. "We can talk there to see how I can help you."

"Why," asked Lina, "do you want to help me? You don't know me."

"That is what I do for a living," said Mike. "I help people in trouble. Most of my work however is medical. I work at the Universality Hospital. I am a doctor. My name is Mike Costello."

"God is looking out for me," said Lina. Mike then grabbed her by the hand and led her inside. As he had said, right there by the doorway was a small bench. They sat down there and began to talk.

"Now," said Mike. "Let's start from the beginning. I know that you are from North Carolina. I know that your mother is ill. What I don't know is where your father is. And what are he and your mother doing here in Ohio?"

"My father, who was here on business, got the opportunity to buy a Hardware Store," started Lina. "Unfortunately my father passed away two years ago and my mother has tried to run the store."

"All right," said Mike. "What is your mother's home address?"

"That is the problem," said Lina. "I don't know. All the information I have is in my car. I need the direction finder on my cell phone to find my mother's house."

"What is the full name of your mother's hardware store?"

"It is Northside hardware," said Lina. "It is located across from the freeway exit."

Let me see if I can find information on your mother," said Mike. Mike then using his cell phone tried to get any information on her mother. He could not get anything.

"Let's see if I can get the phone number of the hardware store," said Mike. "Perhaps I can get your mother's address and phone number there." Mike went back to his cell phone. After a little while he smiled. "I got the number of the hardware store. I'm sure they will be able to give me the information we need. But before I call, there is a thing that has puzzled me."

"I can't believe that there is anything that will puzzle you," said Lina with a smile on her face. "You have succeeded with all that we need. What would puzzle you?"

I just wondered," said Mike. "Why in the world would you enter the mall through the side entrance instead of the main entrance?"

"I did enter through the main entrance," said Lina with a frown on her face. "Isn't this the main entrance?"

"Oh Lina," said Mike with a large laugh. "You are so sweet. You will never guess what the answer to your problem is. It is something you are going to laugh about. See Lina, your car was not stolen. Come with me."

"I don't understand anything you are saying," said Lina. Mike then grabbed her by her arm lifting her from the bench and led her through the men's clothing section, around and past the jewelry counter to the front entrance. He took her to the door. Lina was silent from the shock she felt.

"Look out there," said Mike. Do you see your car?"

"Oh Mike," said Lina with a big smile on her face. "Thank you so much. You are such an angel I am such an idiot. There is my car right where I left it." She then gave Mike a big hug.

"Let's go see where you live but first you probably should call your mother," suggested Mike. They then went to the car and Lina opened the door. She then leaned in and grabbed her cell phone. Lina then called her mother

Hi Mon," said Lina. "This is Lina."

"Lina sweet heart," said her mother. "I have been trying to call you all day. Where have you been?"

"Why have you been trying to call me?" asked Lina. "Are you OK?"

"I'm fine," said Lina's mother. "It's just that I wanted to tell you that I have gone to the hardware store. We are having financial problems. I have to stay here until I can clear some of this out. What I want to tell you is that I will not be home for dinner. Go home and make yourself dinner. You can have anything that is in the refrigerator."

"Thanks Mom," said Lina. "I will take care of myself."

"You didn't answer my question, said Lina's mother. "Where have you been?"

"I have no problem," said Lina. "I just left my cell phone in the car. I spent most of my time in the mall." Lina's mother then hung up. Lina turned to Mike. "My mother had to go to work due to some kind of financial problems. She will be there till probably after nine tonight. So, I will go home and make myself a sandwich for dinner. But before I go I want to thank you from the bottom of my heart. How can I ever repay you?"

"Well to start,' said Mike, "I am a very lonely guy. You see, my sister moved to New York and both of my parents are in Sicily. They will be gone most of the summer. I can use a friend to keep me company. I would especially like company when I go out to dinner. Will you join me?"

"I assumed that you had a girlfriend and was only being a nice gentleman. I would love to be your company. I can't believe a handsome and intelligent guy like you doesn't have a girlfriend."

"I have a few girls that are friends but it is against the company for a University Hospital Employee to have a relationship with any other hospital employee. So, you see, at work I have many friends, male and female. But after work I have no one."

"That is a very sweet story," said Lina. "I don't believe a word of it. However, I too can use a friend. So, I'm your friend. What do you want to do at this time?"

"Well," said Mike, "It is too early to eat dinner so let's go in the large cafeteria and get a cup of coffee and a cup cake or something like that and get to know each other." When they stopped at the mall cafeteria it was about four O'clock. Mike told Lina all that he went through to become a doctor. He even told her about the girlfriends that dropped him because he was too far away or that they had a boyfriend that was more available then a surgery doctor who was on call twenty four hours a day. When Mike was finished and Lina got answers to her questions it was Lina's turn.

"It's your turn now," said Mike.

"As you know my name is Lina Borio. I am a high school Mathematics teacher. I am on vacation. I had a summer job but resigned to come and take care of my mother who had a heart attack. I have been dating a fellow named Jeffery Palmer. I have not seen him for a while because he is in college. He is studying to be a mechanical engineer. He wants to teach at South Carolina University. There he will need a doctor's degree. I guess that covers it all."

"So you plan on going back after you are sure that your mother has recovered from her heart attack," said Mike.

"That was what I originally planned but now I wonder if she will be alright. You see the hardware store is in financial trouble. I'm hoping that if I can help bring the store back to providing some profit I can leave her. But if I can't then how can my mother survive without an income?"

"Why don't we go to the Hardware store and see what the problem really is? Perhaps I could help."

"Would you do that?" said Lina. "It would probably take more than a few hours. How about your job, can you take some time off?"

"I have some vacation coming," said Mike. "I would like to help. Let's see what we can do." After they finished their coffee they left in Mike's car and drove to the store. When they got there Lina took Mike directly to the office. There they met Lina's mother Stella.

"Mom," said Lina. "I want you to meet Mike. He has offered to help if he could. He is a very good friend of mine and he wants to help."

"Hi Mike," said Lina's mother. "I'm not sure anyone can help."

"Let me try," said Mike. "What can it hurt? Let me have the use of your computer." Lina's mother then pulled a chair up to the desk with the computer.

"It's all yours," said Lina's mother. Mike sat and turned the computer on. He was surprised at what he saw.

"What in the world," said Mike? "You are not hooked up to the internet. What use is a computer without the internet?" Mike then got on his cell phone and called the company that provides Mike his internet. They promised to come and install the internet the next day. Mike then searched through all the financial files and found many that the purchase price, that the hardware stored paid, was more than the competition was selling the product for. There were four that were the worst. Mike got on his cell phone and looked for a manufacturer that would produce it for less. The next day Mike used the internet to continue his search. He was having a little success but not enough to save the store. It was on the third day that a woman came into the store. Lina was with a customer and Lina's mother was with Mike in the office. The woman walked up to the office door and knocked on the open door.

"May I help you?" said Mike.

"I would like to talk to the owner," said the woman.

"The owner is here and I represent her," said Mike. "What can I do for you?"

"My name is Dona Right," said the woman. "I am a Financial Adviser. I would like to be hired to help you get this store back on the profit side of the business."

"Why do you think you could help?" asked Mike.

"I have been doing this for about three years. I have helped a dozen or more businesses get back on their feet. Three of them were hardware stores. So, I have experience in your type of store. I have succeeded in all of them."

"You are exactly what we need," said Mike. "However, we are deeply in debt and don't have the funds to hire you. We are losing money every day. I am trying to find suppliers that can reduce the cost of the products that we handle."

"I will make a deal with you," said Dona. "I will work for your company without a salary until I can get my salary from the profit that I will get for you. That is after the profit I will get for you will have paid off all your debts."

"You are that confident?" asked Mike. "You write that all on paper and then I believe that we have no choice. What do you think of Mrs. Borio."

"Like you said, we have no choice. I am for it."

"I have one condition," said Dona. "I have to have complete control of the business until I'm finished.

"You can take over right now," said Stella.

"I will be back tomorrow morning with all the paperwork," said Dona and then left. After she left Lina walked into the office

"What did the woman want?" asked Lina. They explained the complete picture of what was to take place for at least the next few weeks Lina was excited at the news.

"Look," said Mike. "You two can discuss the new arrangement; I am not needed here anymore. I have to get back to the hospital. I probably have a line of patients that need my help, so goodbye Lina. I will call you an evening when we are both free." Mike left.

"Great," said Lina, "I will see you later in the week." Then Lina turned to her mother. "I like this new arrangement. Even if it fails it would have failed anyway. We have nothing to lose. However, it also means that you do not have to be here, mother. You need some time to rest. Don't forget you have a heart problem."

"I'm fine," said Lina's mother. "I only have a little pain in my left shoulder. I have had that for a long time. I would like to be here to see what this lady is doing."

"I disagree, mom," said Lina. "Knowing you, you might interfere with the reorganization the lady is doing. Please go home and relax. I will keep you informed of all that is going on." Lina's mother did go home, but two days later she showed up at the store. In the meantime Dona was reorganizing the complete store. She has ordered some new products, especially the ones that were not able to be sold at a profit. She arranged the counters so that they all had an upper shelf. In the area that was freed when the products there were moved to the added shelve, she added some new products. She added things like toasters and waffle irons. She did the same thing on the other side. There she added Paint and all the painting equipment one would need to paint their house or individual rooms. To Lina's surprise, Dona changed the cash register. She moved it to the entrance lobby and added another. They were both lined up like they were in a grocery store. The grand opening advertising started to bring people in. The next thing Lina found was that she was tied up in one of the cash registers. Lina's mother came in every day but only talked with the customers. Lina was so tied up with the customer line that she never got to help the customers as she had done before. This went on for days. Soon Lina learned that all the debts and mortgage were paid up. Dona soon started to get her salary. Things look pretty good. One day after the day was over Lina went to the office to talk to Dona.

"How can I help you," said Dona, "do you have a problem?"

"I think we have two problems," said Lina. "First I think we have to hire someone to take over the cash register job."

"You are not happy with that Job?" asked Dona.

"No," said Lina, "I love the job. I am a high school teacher in South Carolina. I came here to take care of my mother after she had a heart attack. I will have to go at the end of the summer."

"We can do that," said Dona. "What is your other problem?"

"When you are finished and leave I don't want my mother to take over the job of store manager. I recommend that we hire a manager."

"After I leave you will increase you store income by not having to pay me the large salary that I am getting now"

"I think paying someone like you would be a great and worthy decision," said Lina.

"Well since you think that way I would like to make a

suggestion," said Dona. "You see I have been running around the country doing the job of Financial Advisor. I'm very tired of traveling. I would like to stay in one position and perhaps build a home here. So, I suggest that you hire me as the Store manager.

"That would be fantastic," said Lina. "God has answered my prayers."

"Are you and your mother a strong Christian?" asked Dona. "I am a Born- Again-Christian."

"We are also Born-Again-Christians," said Lina. "That will make any agreements we may have an honest one."

The day that Dona took over the hardware store Mike went back to work. He had a line of patients to take care of. Several need surgery. Lina wanted her mother to go home but she refused. She wanted to hang around and confer with the customers. Lina was so tied up at the cash register that she didn't have time to argue with her. As long as she felt well she let her alone. Mike got to see Lina at least once a week and everything was going well. Mike seldom went to the hardware store. It was about three weeks later that Mike just got out of performing a surgery on an old man when he got a call from Nurse Sally.

"Mike, " said Sally, "You are needed in the emergency room. I think a friend of yours is there." Mike rushed to the emergence room. There he met the ambulance men who had brought the patient into the emergency room. It was Lina's mother Stella that was brought in.

"Tell me all that you know about this woman," asked Mike, the ambulance medical attendant.

"His daughters call us about her mother passing out," said the young ambulance attendant. When we got there she was already dead. We brought her here but though we did everything we could to bring her back to life we did not have any success. She has been dead for around fifteen minutes or more. I don't think she can be saved.

"Let me determine that," said Mike. "Bring her up to the third floor surgery room." They did what he asked, thinking that it was a waste of time. Mike got Vera and they proceeded as usual to operate on the patient.

Her body is cold," said Vera. "Are you ready to save her? She has been dead too long.

"I am going to do my best, "said Mike. "She is a personal friend. At least we can say we tried." They hooked up the heart bypass equipment that pumped blood through her body and gave the oxygen mask. They found that she had four blocked arteries. One was completely blocked. Mike did a quadruple bypass surgery. When finished they took her to an empty room. Mike didn't want her in the recovery room. He wanted more control of her. He kept the heart bypass equipment on her and the oxygen mask as it was in the surgery room. He then went into the waiting room. He found Lina there.

"Mike," said Lina with tears in her eyes. "How is she?"

"I did the best I could," said Mike. "Time will tell how well I did. Come and sit with her. I have her in one of the hospital rooms." Mike took her into the room where her mother was. Lina ran to her side and hugged her.

"I will sit here until she wakes up," said Lina.

"That could be days and even weeks," said Mike. "She had a quadruple bypass heart surgery. That will take some time to heal."

"It could take all year," said Lina. "I will not leave here until she does." Before Mike could answer her Vera walked into the room.

"Mike," she said, "Sophia wants to see you."

"I wonder what she wants?" said Mike. Mike then left the room and walked up to Sophia's office.

"Hi Sophia," said Mike as he got into her office. "What is the problem?"

"I am wondering what you are doing," said Sophia.

"I am doing what I usually do," said Mike. "Do you have a problem with what I am doing?"

"Yes," said Sophia. "I see that you are doing surgery on a

woman that has been dead for more than a day. Why are you tying up our equipment on a person who has been pronounced dead?"

"I know this woman," said Mike. "Outside of her heart problem, she is a very healthy woman. I believe that I can save her."

"I will give you one day," said Sophia. "Then I am going to ship her to the undertaker."

"Are you a doctor?" asked Mike.

"Of course not," said Sophia, "but I have been in the business long enough to know when a person is dead. Anyway, I got the information from the ambulance people. They said that the woman was dead when they picked her up. They had no idea as to how long she had been dead. They also said they used everything they could to try to revive her in the ambulance on the way to the hospital. They said they had no success. Do I need more than that?"

"Yes," said Mike. "You need my OK as her doctor. I will pronounce her dead if I find that she will not recover from my medical procedure."

"All right," said Sophia. "I will give you two days. Then I will call the undertaker and have her delivered to the Morgue."

"We will see," said Mike. "You will be sorry if you do it without my permission." Mike then left and went into the room where Stella and her daughter were.

"How is she doing," Mike asked Lina as if she knew. Mike said it just to make conversation.

"She has not moved at all," said Lina. "I have just been sitting here praying that she will survive."

"Prayer is the best medicine," said Mike. Mike then checked all of Stella's Vidal signs. Her heart was not beating. Her body temperature was way lower than normal. We will have to wait a day or two."

"I am holding her hand," said Lina. "Her hand is so cold. Is that normal?"

"It is for the first day," said Mike, not really knowing. He had never had a person that had been dead that long before surgery. Mike just hoped that he got to her soon enough.

"Do you really believe that my mom will survive?" asked Lina.

"You know that I am doing my best," said Mike. "However, from my experience she has an eighty percent chance of surviving." Mike just made that up to give Lina some encouragement.

"I know that you are doing more than expected," said Lina. "I heard the nurses in the hallway talking about you doing more than they expected and would normally do."

"Don't listen to them," said Mike. "They are not doctors. I had a couple of experiences with patients that had the same problem as your mother has. I had success. However, it has not happened in this hospital."

"I trust you," said Lina.

"Thank you," said Mike. "Listen, it is close to noon. Do you want to go down stairs for some lunch?"

"No," said Lina, "I want to stay here with my mother."

"You don't need to stay here," said Mike. "She isn't going anywhere. Anyway, I will get the nurse to look into her every once in a while."

"I'm sorry," said Lina. "I want to stay here with my mother. I want to spend as much time with her in case she doesn't survive."

"As you wish," said Mike as he left. At the cafeteria Mike had a bowl of soup sent to Lina. After lunch Mike visited his other patients. Before going home to have his dinner, he visited Lina in Stella's room.

"Have you noticed any difference," asked Mike of Lina.

"Not anything important," said Lina. It seems like her hand is a little warmer. But it may be that I am warming it up with my hand." Mike checked the thermometer on Stella's body. It did show the temperature to be a little higher, but not enough to consider it an improvement.

The next day as Mike walked into Stella's hospital room Sophia caught him by her bedside.

"Well there doesn't seem to be any improvement," said

Sophia. Before he could answer Mike noticed that the body temperature had improved quite a bit.

"I think things are going as expected," said Mike. "I see a great improvement in the patient's body temperature." Mike then pointed to the thermometer for Sophia to see it.

"That may be because you have been pumping hot blood into her," said Sophia. "I will give you until tomorrow. If you cannot show me a great improvement then I'm getting this body out of here." Sophia then left. Mike then turned to Lina.

"How are you doing, Lina," asked Mike.

"I am doing a lot better," said Lina. "Her hand is now pretty warm. I think she is getting better. What do you think of Mike?"

I think you are right," said Mike. "The only thing that I am worried about is her brain. The brain is very delicate. I am just worried that some loss of brain activity may occur. Let's pray that there will be no problems with the brain" Mike then led Lina into a prayer session.

The next day Mike walked right into Stella's hospital room.

"How is she doing today?" asked Mike of Lina who had just woken up from sleeping on the soft chair that Mike provided for her.

"I just woke up," said Lina. "The only thing I notice is that her hand is warmer. Is that good news?" Before Mike could answer, Sophia walked in.

How is she doing today?" asked Sophia.

"Her temperature is way up," said Mike. "Look at the body temperature. It is almost back to normal."

"Well," said Sophia. "I will give you one more day. I think you are just delaying" She then walked out.

"How are you doing?" asked Mike of Lina. "Have you gotten enough to eat?"

"I'm fine," said Lina. "Please just concentrate on my mother."

"As you wish," said Mike. Mike then did a thorough check on Stella.

"Everything is as expected," said Mike. "I now have to go

and see some of my other patients." Mike then left and went into the next room. The rest of the day went by as usual. Lina was fed breakfast, lunch and dinner.

"The next day Mike went in earlier than usual. He wanted to build up a story before Sophia came in. Lina was asleep. He looked at the heart monitor and was so glad at what he saw. He saw a very light heartbeat. Thank God Mike yelled with joy. The noise woke up Lina.

"What was that noise?" asked Lina.

"It must have been someone in another room," said Mike, not wanting her to know the truth. He wanted her to believe that the heartbeat was what he expected.

"Have you checked on my mother?" asked Lina.

"Yes," said Mike with a smile he could not withhold. "Her heart has started to beat as I expected."

"That is good news is it?" asked Lina.

"Well that was what I expected. The only thing that we are not sure of is the effect this all has on the brain."

"Well," said Lina. "Thank God things are going as expected. God is good. He will not let us down." A little while later Sophia walked in.

"Well I think I will call the undertaker," said Sophia before even saying hello. Mike became upset.

"The woman is still alive. Look at the heart monitor," said Mike. "Her heart is starting to beat. However, why are you harassing me? I am the doctor here. You are meddling in my attempt to save this lady's life."

"We will see," said Sophia. "We will see how long that heartbeat lasts. Tomorrow will be your last day." She then left. Mike decided to check with Akron General Hospital for a job. He had a good background history that would help him get hired. Mike decided that the next time he saw Sophia he would tell her of his getting another job. The day went by as the day before. Stella's heart beat increased dramatically. Mike decided that if the heart was beating well the next day that he would lower the instrument that pumps the blood, relieving the heart's job. The next morning came quicker than Mike expected. Stella's heartbeat was even better. Before Lina woke up Mike lowered the heart bypass instrument by fifteen percent. The heart still worked well. That day he didn't hear from Sophia. He was glad. He had enough of her. The next morning Mike lowered the bypass equipment by fifteen percent. The heart seemed to take over quite well.

"What are you doing?" asked Lina as she woke up.

"Good morning sweet lady," said Mike. "I am fixing it so your mother's heart starts to take over the job of keeping her alive. Mike did not wait until the next day. Before he left he removed all the equipment that was keeping Stella alive. He was sure that her heart would do the job. The next morning he woke up Lina.

"Lina honey," said Mike. "Today will be an important day. We have been feeding your mother and keeping her asleep with intravenous shots. I am going to give her a shot that will wake her up. We have to check if her mental capability is OK." Mike called in Nurse Sally. He instructed her and soon she gave Stella the shot Mike requested. It was about fifteen minutes later that Stella started to moan. Mike leaned over her and called her name. Stella opened her eyes but it seemed that she wasn't seeing anything. She then closed her eyes.

"Stella," said Mike. "How do you feel?" Stella just moaned for a minute. Then she opened her eyes. But this time she looked around.

"Mom," said Lina, "I'm here mom. How are you?" Stella turned her head and looked at her daughter.

"Lina," said Stella with a very weak voice, "where are we?"

"We are in the hospital," said Lina. "You had a heart attack and I called 911 and they brought you here. How do you feel?"

"I feel like I have no strength at all. I can hardly lift my hand."

"That is normal," said Mike "You just came out of surgery. You had a triple bypass surgery. You will be better soon."

"Mike," said Stella. "I didn't recognize you when I first woke up. How are you?"

"I'm fine," said Mike. "It is you I am worried about. What do you remember?"

"I remember being in the hardware store and getting a terrible pain in my chest and left arm. I remember feeling dizzy. The next thing I remember is waking up here."

"That is fine," said Mike. "I was worried that the heart attack would affect your memory. You are going to be fine. You had surgery to fix the reason for your heart attack. I performed a bypass surgery. You now only need time to heal."

"Thank you so much Mike," said Stella. "Is it alright to call you Mike or should I call you Doctor Costello?"

"Mike is fine," said Mike. "Don't call me Mike in front of the nurse or another doctor. Just call me sir." Stella then turned to her daughter Lina.

"Honey, how long have I been here and how long have you been here?"

"Mom," said Lina, "you have been here for about four days. I have been here next to you all day and night. They let me stay all night. I slept on this comfortable soft chair."

"Oh honey," said Stella. "You didn't have to do that."

"Yes, I did," said Lina. "I was worried that you would not recover. I wanted to spend as much time with you as I could. I held your hand all the time."

"How about our store," said Stella? "Who has taken care of the store?"

"I guess I should tell you," said Lina. "Dona has asked to be the permanent store manager. She is tired of all the traveling her company had her doing. She wants a permanent location to work. I hope you don't mind my agreeing to that. She has improved the store's income so much that she not only has the salary we promised but we also have an income that we have never had before."

"That is fine sweetheart. You made a good decision. I approve."

"Thanks mom," said Lina. "When you get better we have to talk about the future. I have something I want to suggest."

"We will talk later," agreed Stella, "However I am wondering about something, if you have been here all the time how did you get food?"

"The good nurse brought me breakfast, lunch and dinner, by sweet Mike's request."

"Let's see if we can lift up the rear of the bed so that you could sit up for a while," said Mike. He raised the rear section of the bed."

"Stop," said Stella. "My head is spinning like crazy." Mike then lowered it a little until she seemed OK.

"How is that?" asked Mike. "It is now only half way up. It will take a little while for you to get used to sitting up. We will lift you up later slowly."

"Thanks sir," said Stella, trying to be funny.

"I think you will be fine," said Mike. "A good sense of humor shows that you are improving. I have got to leave now to check on some of my other patients. I will see you later." Mike then left. After lunch Mike went in to check on Stella. She was sitting up in her bed.

"Hi doc,' said Stella when she saw Mike. "You see that I am sitting up now. You were right. So now when can I go home?"

"You can go home when I have removed the stitches from your chest and the cut is healed."'

"That will be tomorrow I hope," said Stella with a smile on her face that told everyone that she really didn't believe it herself.

"Very funny," said Mike. "I think it will be at least another week." Before he could say more, Nurse Sally came in.

"Mike," she said, "Sophia wants to see you."

"What is she unhappy about now?" said Mike as he got up to go to Sophia's office.

"I don't even want to guess," said Sally. When Mike got to Sophia's office he knocked on the open door.

"What is your problem now?" asked Mike.

"Come on in and have a seat," said Sophia. "I have three things I want to discuss with you."

"I'm all ears," said Mike, having no idea of what Sophia was talking about.

"The first thing I want to tell you is that I am extremely sorry for how I acted. I had no right to question what you were doing. You are the doctor. I should not have interfered with your job. And from this day on I promise that I will never question you. I hope that you can forgive me."

"You are forgiven," said Mike, feeling a little better. "I understand what you were feeling. I have brought back to life a couple of dead patients before but not at this hospital. I hope that from this day on you will trust me completely. Although I must admit that I am human and can make mistakes."

"Good then we will be friends as well as co-workers," said Sophia. "My next thing I want to discuss with you is your work with the city police force. They have asked for your help when they have a crime that you could help. They offered to pay your salary during the time you spend with them. So, if you are willing to help them you have my approval as long as you will still perform your duties here in the hospital."

"I will make my work here at the hospital my first priority," said Mike. However, I would like to help the police whenever I can."

"Great," said Sophia, "I will call and let them know that you will be on call."

"Thank you," said Mike, "so what is the third thing you want to discuss?"

"The third thing I want," said Sophia, "is to inform you that because of the excellent work you have performed as a surgeon, and your medical capabilities that are above what we thought you had, we think you deserve an increase in your salary. Therefore, I am informing you that you will be given an increase of twenty percent on your salary."

"That is so kind of you," said Mike. "I don't know what to say. It is a surprise I didn't expect."

"Well you deserve it," said Sophia. "Now go and take care of your friend Stella." Mike left in a state of shock. That was nothing he expected. He immediately went into Stella's room. Lina and Sally were laughing at something Stella had said.

"Well I see you are both doing well," said Mike. "Looks like I am not needed here."

"What did Sophia want?" asked Lina.

"She just wanted to tell me," said Mike, "that it was OK to help the police department. Listen since you are both doing fine I will go to visit my other patient." Mike then left. It was only about a minute after Mike left that the phone in the room rang. Lina picked up the phone.

"Hello," said Lina. "Who am I talking to?"

"Hi Lina," said Dona, "How are you doing, and how is your mother doing?"

"Hi Dona" said Lina recognizing her voice, "How are you doing?"

"I'm doing great," said Dona, "and the store is doing fantastically."

"So, what's up?" asked Lina wondering why she called.

"I have been checking the value of the store," started Dona. "I talked with your Real Estate Agency and they told me that when I first came to help that they had evaluated the store to be worth about a half a million. Today, they evaluated it, at my request, saying that it is worth one and a quarter million. I have worked very hard on improving your store"

"That is very interesting," said Lina, "but why are you doing that? Do you want a pat on the back or an increase in your salary?"

"No," said Dona. "Let me finish and it will answer your question. The reason I did all this is that I was thinking that you wanted to go back to South Carolina and that you didn't want to leave your mother here alone. She would be better living close to you and after you get married, she will enjoy taking care of her grandchildren. Not only that, I thought that if you sell the store she would have one and a quarter million to live on. My parents are living on forty thousand dollars a year. If your mother lived on a thousand a month for a total of fifty thousand a year she would have enough income for twenty three years. I understand from the information I obtained that your mother is 75 years young. That means that she will have enough money until she is 98 years old, not considering the interest on the money or the difference it will make by the effect of inflation."

"What you are saying," interrupted Lina, "is that you are suggesting that she sells the store. I appreciate all the valuable information that you are giving us. We have been thinking about it but your information is great in helping us make a decision. Do you have a buyer in mind?"

"Yes, I do," said Dona. "I have made the store worth more than three times since I started to work there. I think I should have some of the benefits of that achievement."

"So, do you want a percentage of the sale?" asked Lina.

"You don't understand," said Dona. "What I am saying is that I want to buy the store. I am willing to pay the total value that the Real Estate Company said it is worth. I love this area. I would like to spend the rest of my life here."

"That is a fantastic offer," said Lina, "Let me tell my mother all that you have said. I will discuss it with her and call you back." Lina then repeated all that Dona had said. Lina's mother was shocked at the offer. After a little discussion they both agreed.

"That is an offer," said Stella, "that we cannot turn down." Lina then called Dona.

"Dona," said Lina. "My mother and I discussed it and decided to accept your offer."

"That is great," said Dona with a joy in her voice. "I will start the procedure and get back to you when I have all the paperwork." Lina then turned to her mother.

"You know mom," said Lina. "We should start thinking about selling your house. I want you to move down to South Carolina with me. Dona was right. You should be near your family."

"Well first," said Stella, "We have to move all the furniture and belongings to Charleston. But where would I store all that I have and want to keep?"

"We will store it in my garage until we can find a place for you to live. In the meantime you will stay with me. I am not married yet. I will have a lot of room." That evening Lina told Mike all that had taken place. Mike offered to help wherever he could.

A week later all the paperwork was gone and after Stella signed the sales document the store belonged to Dona. Lina then took pictures of all the rooms in her mother's house. She then took them to the hospital to show them to her mother.

"Mom," said Lina. "I have taken pictures of all the rooms in your house. You look at the picture and tell me what furniture you want to keep."

"That was a fantastic Idea, " said Lina's mother. "You are such an intelligent daughter." Just then Mike walked into the room.

"What are you gals up to?" said Mike.

"Hi Mike," said Lina and her mother at the same time, "we are checking to see what furniture my mother wants to keep," said Lina. "We have to start moving her things to my house. When can my mother leave for the hospital?"

"We will see," said Mike. "I will have to remove the stiches and see how well she is healing.

"Can you give a rough estimate," said Lina. "You see we have to move my mother's furniture and I would like to know if I can leave her while I move the furniture."

"It will be at least a week," said Mike, "and probably be more like two weeks."

"I have ordered a truck that will be delivered this afternoon," said Lina. "I would like to move the furniture tomorrow. But some furniture that my mother wants to save is too heavy for me to move it alone. I wonder if you could help me move the heavy things tomorrow morning."

"I will be there about seven in the morning before I have to go to work," said Mike. "I'll be happy to help you."

"Thank you so much," said Lina. "Mom, I will have to leave you for a couple of days. Will you be OK?"

"Go and get that done," said Lina's mom. "Just drive very carefully."

The next morning, after Lina got up and dressed, she went down to the driveway where the truck was parked. She opened the back door of the truck to get ready to start loading her mother's furniture. Suddenly two cars pulled up her driveway. One she noticed was a police car. Mike got out of the first car and Larry with two police officers got out of the second car.

"Hi there Lieutenant Benson," said Lina trying to be formal in front of the other policeman. "What are they doing here?"

"We came here to help you pack the heavy furniture. These are Benny and Ryan. They are here to help you."

"Hi fellow's," said Lina. "It is so nice of you to come and help me." Lina then took out the photos that her mother had marked that showed what she wanted to keep. Lina explained the markings on the photos and they began to load the furniture in the truck. When they got into the main bedroom Mike noticed a large pile of clothes on the bed.

"Are you going to ship all these clothes?" asked Mike. "Where are you going to put them?"

"I have no Idea," said Lina. "I guess I will have to throw them on top of the furniture."

"Look," said Mike. "I have two very large suitcases that you can borrow. You can use them and return them when you come back. You keep on loading the truck and I will be right back." It only took about twenty minutes for Mike to come back with the suitcases. With those suitcases and one that Lina's mother had they were able to store all the clothes. The clothes that Stella wanted to keep to use in Ohio were stored in Stella's small suitcase. The clothes that Lina wanted to keep in Ohio she stored in her own small suitcase. Both suitcases were then placed in

Lina's car trunk. It was about eight thirty when they finished packing. Lina then locked the house and got into the truck.

"Thank you so much fellas," said Lina as she got into the truck. "See you in a couple of days."

"Drive carefully," said Mike as Lina pulled away. That evening when Lina got home in Charleston she was met by her boyfriend Jeffery. Lina pulled the truck backwards up to the garage door. When she got out of the truck Jeff grabbed her and kissed her with a big hug.

"It's so good to see you," said Lina. "It's been too long."

"I know honey," said Jeff. "I have missed you terribly."

"How long," asked Lina, "have you been waiting here for me?" asked Lina.

"Well, you called when you left Ohio," said Jeff, "I figured how long it would take you so I came here and sat in my car. I wasn't too far off. I have been here for about an hour." Lina went into the house and from inside she opened the garage door. She then opened the truck door and saw a car pull up behind the truck. It was Jeff's brother and father. They came to help her unpack the truck. When all the furniture was removed from the truck and placed in the house where Lina directed, although a lot of it remained in the garage, they all went to dinner. Lina insisted on paying for the dinner in payment for their help. Lina spent the next day with Jeff.

"When do you think you will be back permanently?" asked Jeff.

"I will come home as soon as my mother is able to travel," said Lina. "We also have to sell her house and take care of all the paperwork that will be required to leave Ohio. I hope it will be less than a couple of weeks." The next morning Lina left for the drive to Ohio.

It was three days later when Lina got back to Ohio. As soon as she got the truck back she drove to the nearest motel and after getting a room she had a good night's rest. The next morning she went to the hospital to see her mother.

"Hi Mom" she said, "How are you today?"

"I'm fine," said her mother. "Did you get everything over? But before you answer I want to inform you that the house was sold. They offered about twenty thousand less than we asked but that is OK. We don't need the money. I have accepted the offer.

"That is great," said Lina," but we have another problem. "We have two cars here and I think you will want a car in South Carolina. I don't think you will be able to drive. So, if the doctor is not going to release you within the next week I think I should go back and drive your car there so you will have one to drive there. I can fly back. Then I will drive you home in my car when the doctor releases you."

"Whatever you say," said her mother. "I will leave everything in your hands."

When Mike walked in he was happy to see that Lina was back safely.

"Hi Lina," said Mike. "Nice to see you got back safely."

"Hi Mike," said Lina. "However, I may have to go back soon. How long before mom can be released?"

"I am going to redress her bandage to see if I can remove the stiches yet.

"When," asked Lina, "are you going to that?"

"Well I can do it right now," said Mike. Mike then asked Lina to leave the room and after Lina left he removed the dressing. After checking he replaced the dressing covered Stella and then called Lina back to the room.

"Well what did you find?" asked Lina."

She is doing fine," said Mike. "But I will not remove the stiches for at least four more days."

"Thank you Mike," said Lina. Then turning to her mother she informed her mother. "Mom, tomorrow I will drive your car to your new home."

"Well," said Stella with a smile on her face. "It really is my old home. I think I still own it."

"Of course," said Lina. "I just live there until I and Jeff get married"

"Don't stay too long," said Stella. They spent most of the day together. They were separated only when Lina went to lunch and dinner. Lina left about eight and went straight to bed. The next morning she got into her mother's car and drove straight to South Carolina. As she did the last time she called Jeff and told you she was on her way. Jeff was there waiting for her.

"Hi Lina," said Jeff as soon as she got out of the car. He then hugged her and kissed her. "We don't have anything to unpack so my mother has invited us to dinner. Lina parked her mother's car in the garage and went with Jeff. When they went there Jeff's mother met them at the door.

"Hi Lina," said Mrs. Palmer, Jeff's mother. "It is so good to see you. Come on in. Dinner is almost ready."

"Hi Mrs. Palmer," said Lina. "It is so good to see you too." Jeff's mother led them into the dining room where Mr. Palmer was already seated at the table.

"Hi Mr. Palmer," said Lina as she sat across from him at the table. I see that you are getting ready to eat."

"Hello Lina," said Mr. Palmer. "I admit that I am very hungry." Just as Jeff sat down next to Lina, Mrs. Palmer brought in the food and set a plate in front of each person at the table and one next to her husband where she then sat.

"Before you say grace dad," said Jeff "I have something that may make the dinner taste better." Jeff then got up and knelt beside Lina.

"Lina," he started, "I have missed you so much. I want to make an action that may make you want to come home as soon as you can. Lina, I love you with all my heart. I want to spend the rest of my life with you." Then Jeff took out a little box. He opened it and took out an engagement ring. "Lina, will you marry me?" "Lina looked at him with tears in her eyes.

"Yes," said Lina. "I will marry you. I would like to spend the rest of my life with you." Jeff then put the ring on her finger. Jeff's parents then both hugged Lina and told her that they loved her. Lina was so surprised at all this. It was not expected at all. Lina hardly remembered the rest of the evening. She remembered Jeff driving her to the airport. The next thing she remembered was the plane landing in Cleveland Ohio. She then took a taxi to the hotel where she had a room. It was now around noon. Flying was so much better than driving, she thought. After a short lunch at the hotel she drove to the hospital.

Hi mom," said Lina. "I have a surprise for you."

"Hi Lina," said Stella, her mother. "I have a surprise for you too. But give me yours first." Lina didn't say a word. She just lifted her hand and showed her the engagement ring. "Wow, he finally proposed. That is so great. I am so happy for you. Have you decided when the wedding will take place?"

"We just got engaged," said Lina. "We didn't have time to talk about it. Well now, I told you my surprise, what is yours?"

"The doctor examined me this morning," said Stella, "and he removed the stiches. He said that I could leave tomorrow."

"That is great, said Lina, "We can leave for South Carolina the next morning. I'm very eager to go to our real home." That day the two of them spent the time enjoying the company together. The next morning Mike went in and gave Stella a last examination.

"Well ladies," said Mike. "You are well and I will release you. I will miss you both so much. I suspect that you will leave for South Carolina soon."

"We are going to leave early tomorrow morning," said Lina. "We have nowhere to stay here in Ohio. We sold the house and I have a room at the hotel. We will miss you too. I hope we can stay in touch." Lina then helped her mother take off the hospital clothes and get dressed with the clothes she had when she was brought into the hospital After getting everything together they went down to the hospital financial office. After signing a document and paying the co-pay they left in Lina's car.

"Boy," said Stella, "I am so happy to get out of there. Where are we going now? It is too late to travel."

"We are going to the hotel where we are going to stay

tonight," said Lina. "I brought your suitcase and mine to the hotel room. You can pick your traveling clothes. But first let's stop at the small restaurant and have some lunch." After lunch they went into the room that Lina had in the hotel.

"I think you can be comfortable here," said Lina. "I was lucky to get a room with two single beds. You can have the one next to the window. I have already slept in the other one." That afternoon they discussed how they would live until Lina got married. Lina decided that after she and Jeff got married that she would move out and leave the whole house to her mother. At about seven they went down to the hotel restaurant and had a light dinner. They went to bed early. The next morning at about seven they got up dressed in their travel clothes and got all their other clothes in the suitcases and took them down to Lina's car. They then had a quick breakfast checked out of the hotel and were on their way. At about twelve o'clock they stopped at a small cafe where Lina had stopped the other times she traveled to South Carolina and had a sandwich and a cup of coffee for lunch. They got to Charleston South Carolina at about six pm. When they got out of the car they were met by a large group of people. It was Lina's aunt, her uncle, and her cousin Bryan. There was also Jeff, his parents, and his brother Carl. Lina also recognized some old friends that she went to school with. They were throwing a homecoming party and an engagement party. You can imagine the surprise this was to Lina and her mother. That evening they all had a fantastic time.

Back in Ohio Mike went back to visiting all his patients. There were about a dozen patients that were under Mike's care, but even though he was among them he still felt lonely. He missed Lina and her mother. The days went by as usual. Mike only had two that needed surgery. It was about two weeks after Lina and her mother left that Mike got a call from Larry.

'Mike," said Larry, "please come to the emergency entrance area. I have an emergency that requires your help." Mike immediately went to the emergency area.

"Hi Larry," said Mike, "what is the problem?"

"I just brought in a woman who was shot in the chest," said Larry. "She died just as we brought her here. See if you can save her." Mike didn't ask anything more. He instructed the nurse that was there.

"Take her immediately to the third floor surgical room." Mike then called Vera his surgical assistant and they met in the surgical room. Mike proceeded to hook the woman to the heart bypass equipment and the oxygen equipment and open her chest. He found that the bullet just missed the heart and that it punctured the main artery to the heart. After he repaired the artery he was happy to see that the heart started to beat. After he finished all the repairs that were needed he stitched the surgical opening and brought her to the recovery room. Just outside the room he found Larry waiting for the results.

"Well Mike," said Larry, "were you able to save her?"

"I think she will recover," said Mike, "We got to her just in time. Now tell me what this is all about."

"Well her name is Vanessa Brenner," started Larry. "Her neighbor was out walking her dog when she heard a gunshot and saw a person wearing a black hood run from her house and left in a small foreign white car. She didn't know what it was. She then called us and we found her by her front door. It looked like she was about to leave. We then bought her here as quickly as we could. It was important to help her since we got to her so quickly. Also, perhaps she could tell us who shot her."

"I doubt that," said Mike. "If her neighbor said the killer was in a black hood, she probably didn't recognize the shooter. Perhaps she could tell us if it was a male or a female."

"I guess you are right," said Larry. "I think if you can leave Vanessa, you should be the one to check her place of employment. I will check on her family and friends. As a police officer, I will be a better person to get their cooperation."

"I will give her a quick check up and then go to where she works," said Mike. Do you have a place of her employment?"

"Yes, I have her purse," said Larry. "We will both go through it together when you get back. For now, here is her card that gives you the address and name of the company she works for."

"Can I make a suggestion?" asked Mike.

Of course, you can," responded Larry, "that is why I have you working here with me."

"I would like to suggest that we let every one thing that she died," said Mike. "Do you remember when I got shot how we drew out the shooter by thinking that he had succeeded?"

"Great Idea," said Larry. "I agree. Go and get it done." Mike got Sophia's approval and then got the nurses together and told them the plan. They all agreed to keep it a secret that Vanessa was still alive. Then they covered several pillows with a white bed sheet and brought it up front where the news people were yelling for information. They put the fake body in the ambulance and sent it to the undertaker. Some news men followed the ambulance to the funeral parlor but were not allowed to enter. They were told that the body will be cremated. The news men then left with the story they were led to believe.

"That went well," said Larry. "Meet me at the police station when you are finished with what you need to do." Mike then went to a women's clothing store. As he went in he was met by a sales lady.

"Hi," said the sales lady, "how can I help you?"

"I would like to talk with the owner if I may," said Mike.

"That is Olivia Wilson," said the sales lady. "You will find her in her office at the back of the store." Mike walked to the back of the store and found the office. The door was open and he could see inside that the woman was facing the other way because she was facing her cabinet. Mike knocked on her door to get her attention.

"How may I help you?" said the woman as she turned around and sat at her desk now facing him.

"My name is Mike Costello. I am a doctor with University

Hospital. I am assisting the police department. I am here to ask you about Vanessa Brenner."

"She did not show up today," said Olivia." She is seldom late. I hope she is alright."

"She has been shot in the chest," said Mike. "Do you know anyone that would hate her enough to want to kill her?"

"Oh my lord," said Olivia with a shocked look on her face. "She is the nicest person I have ever met. I can't imagine anyone wanting to kill her. We are going to miss her very much. She had such a cheerful personality that some people ask for her when they come here to purchase something "

What about the other sales ladies," asked Mike? "Is it possible that one of them is jealous of her?"

"We only have one other sales girl," said Olivia "That is Kelly Perton. They are like sisters." She then got on her phone and called Kelly to her office. "Kelly, this is Dr. Mike Costello. I hate to tell you, but Vanessa has been killed." It looked like Kelly was about to pass out. Fortunately, there was a chair near her and she sat down. Mike and Olivia waited until Kelly got control of herself. After a few minutes Mike spoke.

"I'm sorry to bring that kind of news," said Mike, "but we need your help. Do you know anyone who hated Vanessa enough to shoot her?"

"No," said Kelly with a very sorrowfully sounding voice. She was an angel. We all loved her. I think whoever shot her made a mistake. He probably thought that she was someone else. Vanessa was too kind to hurt anyone."

"That is a good point," said Mike. "Were you and Vanessa good friends?"

"We were more than good friends," said Kelly. "She was such a good help to me. If I had trouble with a customer she would come and help me. I don't know what I will do without her."

"Well thank you very much for your information," said Mike. "Girls have a great day" Mike then left and drove to the police station where Larry asked him to meet him after his talk with the people at Vanessa's workplace. Larry was there talking on the phone. When Larry hung up he turned to Mike.

"Well Mike," said Larry. "Did you find out anything?"

"I found out only that they were devastated to hear of Vanessa's death," said Mike. "There were only two people there, the manager and a sales lady. They are going to miss her very much. She was a very important part of their operation. There was no indication of any bad relationship. How about you, what did you find out?"

"I didn't find out anything either," said Larry. "With the help of the local police I found all the relatives of Vanessa. There were only two, the father, the mother and a sister. I checked where they worked and found that they all were there during the shooting. I didn't want to contact them until it was a last resort."

"I guess the only thing to do now is to look for her fiancé'," said Mike.

"That is right," said Larry. "I forgot that she had an engagement ring on her finger." Larry then took out Vanessa's purse. They went through everything in there but only found a card with the name David Brian.

"Can you find out where he lives and where he works?" asked Mike. Larry then got on the phone and called the police secretary who had the city's public directory. After a few minutes Larry hung up.

"He is an auto mechanic for the Cadillac dealership on Main Street," said Larry. "It's still early, so let's go to the place he works and talk to him. We can both go."

"Ok," said Mike. "Let's get it over with. I have to go back to the hospital soon. I have a patient that may need surgery." They immediately left and were at the Cadillac auto repair area of the dealership twenty minutes later. When they got there, they walked into the main office.

"I am officer Benten," started Larry to the man sitting at the desk in the office. "And this is my assistant Dr. Costello. "We are here to talk to David Brian. Does he work here and is he here today?"

"Yes," said the man behind the desk. He then picked up the phone and called for Dave to come to his office. A few minutes later a good looking young man showed up.

"What can I do for you Frank?" asked Dave.

"These gentlemen would like to talk with you," said Frank the manager.

"I am Larry Benton and this is Dr. Mike Costello," said Larry. We want to know if you know a girl named Vanessa Brenner."

"Yes," said Dave. "She is my fiancée. Is she in trouble?"

"She was shot in the chest," said Larry. "Would like," but Larry was interrupted by Dave. "Is she alive?"

"I'm very sorry," answered Larry. "He didn't want to tell him the truth until he got some answers. David almost passed out. He started to cry out loud. He finally fell into a chair. He kept on crying so that he couldn't answer any questions.

"Try and control yourself," said Larry as he put his hand on his shoulder. "I'm so sorry to give you bad news. We had no idea that you even knew her." Dave shook his head and kept on crying.

"It's pretty obvious that he didn't have any idea of her being in trouble," said Larry.

"What," asked Mike, being disturbed with what was going on, "do you want to do it now?"

"I think we should wait until he gains control of himself," said Larry.

"That may take hours," said Mike.

"You may leave if you need to go back to the hospital," said Larry. "I will stay and take care of him."

"I will stay," said Mike.

"I will give him a couple of days off," said Frank, finally coming out of his state of shock. "I think he needs some time off."

"I hope you don't mind," said Larry. "I would like to stay here until David accepts what has happened." It was about twenty minutes later that Dave turned and spoke.

"Who would want to hurt Vanessa," said Dave. "She was such a sweet and loving person."

"Can you think of anyone who would want to harm her?" asked Larry.

"No," answered Dave still with tears in his eyes. "They all loved her. Even when her lips were not smiling her eyes always smiled."

Listen," said Larry, "Let me take you home. I think you need some time to get control of yourself. You have to rest for a while. Mike will follow us to your house in your car. I do not want you to drive yourself home." Dave got up and gave Mike his car keys. He then followed Larry to his car. Dave gave Larry instructions on how to get to his house. When they got there Larry let Mike in the driveway first. Mike got out of the car and after locking it he walked over to Larry's car.

"Do you have your house keys," said Larry as they got out of the car and walked up to the front door.

"Yes," said Dave as he pulled the key from his pocket. "Look fellows, I am very sorry for how I have acted. I loved her so much. I expected to spend the rest of my life with her. Now I don't know what to do. Also, I want to thank you for your kindness to me. Thank you so much. When you find out the person who did this terrible thing please let me know. Knowing that the evil person who did this is punished will give me a little relief from my broken heart."

"Take care," said Larry. "We will keep in touch." After Dave went into his house Mike turned to Larry.

"Listen Larry," said Mike. "I have to go to the hospital. Let's get together tomorrow morning. I should be finished with my surgery and the other patient tonight. We have some thinking to do and determine our next move."

"Yes," said Larry, "Get into my car and I will take you to

your car" Twenty minutes later, Mike was in his surgery room performing his first surgery.

The next morning Mike went into Larry's office.

"Good morning Larry, said Mike as he walked into his office.

"Good morning Mike," said Larry. "How are you doing this morning? Have you given this crime any thought?"

"I'm doing fine," said Mike. "I have given this much thought. I think that we should look to see if Dave's fiancée was shot to hurt Dave."

"I'm not sure of what you are suggesting," said Larry.

"Well when I was in California, I heard of a fellow's wife getting shot to punish the husband. When they finally caught up to the shooter he confessed that he shot the wife because he wanted to have the husband suffer like he made him suffer. Apparently, the husband did something that made the shooter suffer very much. He said that if he shot the husband he would only suffer for ten seconds, but by shooting his wife the husband would suffer for a long time like he made him suffer."

"I guess what you are saying is that we need to go and speak with David," said Larry.

"We do have to talk with him," said Mike. They both got into Larry's police car and drove to David's house. When they got there they knocked on the door. A few minutes later Dave opened the door.

"Hi fellows," said Dave, being very happy to see them. "Come on in. I'm so happy to see you. I am so lonely here by myself. I hope you have found the one who shot Vanessa."

"Hi Dave," said Larry,"

"Hi David," said Mike, being more formal.

"I'm sorry," said Larry. "We have not found the shooter yet. That is why we are here. Mike here has an Idea of who this could be. Go ahead Mike explain it to Dave."

"When I was working in California," started Mike. "I came across a similar situation. A man's wife was shot to death. The police found no evidence that any one hated the wife. Later they found that the one who shot the wife did it to punish her husband. The killer said that if he shot the man he hated he would only suffer for a few minutes. If he killed his wife he would suffer for a couple of years."

"That is why we are here," said Larry. "We want to check if anyone hates you enough to want you to suffer. Have you done anything that hurt a customer badly?"

"I can't think of anyone," said Dave. "I am friends with all the guys I work with. And most of the customers don't know who fixed their car. Anyway I never worked on a car that I couldn't fix."

"How about some personal friends?" said Mike "Is there anyone that you have had problems with, even some personal friends of your wife?"

"I can't think of anyone who is not friendly with us," said Dave. "We loved all of our neighbors"

"How long," asked Mike, "have you known Vanessa?"

"I have known Vanessa for almost two years. We have been engaged for about a month now. We were planning to have a spring wedding."

"Did you have a girlfriend," asked Mike, "before you met Vanessa?"

"Yes, I did," said Dave. "Her name is Martha Bradly. It is strange because she called me yesterday. She read in the paper that my fiancée had passed away and she called to tell me how sorry she was. She wanted to get together with me as a friend to try and console me. I told her that I was too sorrowful to be with anyone. I told her to call later when I felt better."

"Why did you break up with her," asked Mike.

"We only dated about three times," said Dave. "She was too arrogant and wanted her way all the time. She also was not a Christian. I am a Born-Again Christian. She said that religion was a scam created by the governing body to control the people. I could never have had a relationship with her back then."

"Does that mean that you could have a relationship with her now," asked Mike?

"She is a very beautiful girl," said Dave, "she said that she had changed and now has accepted Jesus as her savior."

"Well Larry," said Mike. "I think we have all the information that we need. Let's go because I am needed in the hospital."

"Well Dave," said Larry, "I'm glad you are feeling better. We will keep in touch and let you know what we find out."

"Goodbye Dave," said Mike. "Take care of yourself. God will take care of you. Have fate."

"Goodbye Larry, Mike. Thank you guys for coming to see me, Keep in touch." Mike then got into Larry's car and they left for the hospital where Mike's car was and where he was badly needed.

"I believe we have the possible shooter," said Larry.

"I think she loved Dave so much that she shot his fiancée to get him free and was even willing to lie and say that she became a religious woman."

"That is the way I see it," said Mike. "You will have to get a warrant to search her car and home. She is too confident to have disposed of the weapon." Twenty minutes later Larry dropped Mike off at the hospital and proceeded to get the warrant. Mike went up to the hospital on the third floor. He had to perform two surgeries before the day was over.

It was three days later that Mike heard from Larry. He was just coming out of a surgery.

"Hi Mike," said Larry. "Well we solved the case. It is closed.

"Was it the ex-girlfriend," asked Mike, "as we suspected?"

"Ye," said Larry. "Using my skills to upset, I got her really raving mad. It made her confess. Fortunately, I had my phone on so I recorded all that she said. She said that she thought that Dave would eventually come back to her, but when she found that they were engaged she went into a furry. She yelled that the witch stole Dave from her. She felt that if she was out of the way that she would woo him back. With the information I had and the confession she was sent directly to jail."

"Well that leaves me one thing to do," said Mike.

Have fun," said Larry. "I wish I could come with you, but I have some work to do by tomorrow." After they hung up the phone Mike left for Dave's house. He hoped that Dave had not gone back to work. Since he had not returned to work he answered the door when Mike knocked.

"Hi Mike," said Dave. "Have you found the murder?"

"We have solved the case," said Mike, "but you have to come with me to identify a witness."

"Who is that?" asked Dave.

"I can't tell you anything," said Mike. "If I do it will nullify the identification."

"Give me a minute to get ready," said Dave. About five minutes later Dave came out. He had changed his clothes. "Where are we going?"

"Just come and follow me with your car," said Mike, "You will need it to come back home. I have some surgery to do so I can't bring you back home." Mike had no idea how long Dave would stay in the hospital after seeing that Vanessa was still alive. Dave did as Mike suggested. They were soon in the hospital parking lot. Dave followed Mike to the hospital's third floor. Dave had no idea where they were going and why. Mike then entered the room where Vanessa was recovering from her surgery. Dave walked up to the bed and a soon as he recognized Vanessa he yelled out

"Vana darling, is that you?" he then threw his arms around her and kissed every part of her face.

"I'm sorry to have kept her condition from you," said Mike. "But we had to pretend that she had died to let the shooter think that she had succeeded. As you can see it worked."

"We understand completely," said Dave. He then turned and hugged Mike to Mike's surprise. "We will never forget what you have done for us."

"Thank you Mike," said Vanessa. "I know from talking to the nurses that I died and you brought me back to life by your fantastic surgical abilities. Like Dave said, we will never forget you." Mike then went to see his other patients. Before he went home that evening he checked Vanessa's room. Dave was still there and Mike guessed that he was going to stay there all night. Mike said good night to them and left for home. On his way home he noticed that the happiness that was in Vanessa's room was catchy. He had never felt so good for a long time.

CHAPTER FIVE

The long and lonely days

The following days were back to normal. Mike went to the hospital and visited the third floor patients when he was not performing surgery or taking personal care of patients recovering from surgery he had performed earlier. When he had time, he brought them some relief from their problems. It was his joyful and upbeat personality that brought some pleasant and happy atmosphere to the patients. This went on for more than a week. It was on a Sunday after Mike got back from church that Mike began to feel the loneliness again. Mike was a good Christian. He never missed church on Sunday. Mike would not do any work on Sunday as the Bible directed. He was sitting at the table ready to make himself a sandwich when he heard a noise in the garage. Before he could check to see who it was the door opened and his parents came in.

"Hi mom, hi dad," said Mike. "I'm surprised to see you home this early in the year. It is only the middle of August."

"Well we decided that we were not going to miss your thirtieth birthday," said his father. "We had more than enough of Sicily."

"I would like to know all that you did in Sicily," said Mike.

"After we have lunch," said his father, "I will give you a brief description of all that we saw. And if you are really interested I can show you the videos we took on all the trips we took." After they had their lunch Mike turned to his father and mother.

"Well it's time to tell me about your trip to Sicily," said Mike. "I don't understand why you stayed so long. I think after a while you would get Bored."

"Just the opposite is true," said Mike's father. "We have been on the move every day that we were there. If you will remember, we have a cousin named Rosina living in Barrafranca. Well she has a son named Salvatore. He drove us all over Sicily. The first place he took us was to Agrigento. I'm not sure I remember all the names. If you are really interested I am going to have the videos I took transferred to DVDs and then you can see them on the TV and get all the proper names. Anyway, there we walked through a piece of land that took us forty five mines to walk through. As we walked through we saw the amazing Greek ruins. There were three remains of a large building. Next Sal brought us to Messina to mount Peloritani. Near there was the Etna Volcano. We were brought up there using those hanging cars. When we got there they brought us to a little cabin and gave us jackets. It was freezing up there. Up there we got to look down the mouth of the volcano. It was fantastic. One day Sale brought us to Gel which was just south of Agrigento. There we went swimming in the Mediterranean Sea. The whole time we were there, we were always taken somewhere. The places we went to are too many to remember them all. However, I do remember another place we went. They took us to Palermo. One of the fantastic places they took us was the famous Catholic Church. Inside it was fantastic. All the inside walls were covered with gold sheets."

"It is very different from what I thought your trip was like," said Mike. "It sounds like you two had a fantastic time. I'm almost sorry I didn't go with you."

"If you are really interested in seeing what we saw, just wait a couple of days. I am going to take my videos to the Dodd Camera Shop to have them converted to DVDs. It will be like you were there with us. While I am taking the videos I described everything we saw."

"I can hardly wait," said Mike. "It sounds like watching it will be a wonderful and exciting time."

It took three days before the videos were transferred to DVDs. The evening when they were available, Mike's father set one up after dinner so that it would be shown on the TV.

"There are eight DVDs. It will take at least two weeks to see them all. This first DVD is different from the rest. Seven of the DVDs are set in Sicily. This one was taken in Italy. You see, the plane landed in Rome. We thought since we were in Rome we could get a look at some famous places like the famous Roman Coliseum. You see, we thought that this was our only chance to see places in Italy. We never imagined that they would drive us around Sicily and show us more fantastic places." Mike's father then started the video. It lasted about one hour.

"That was fantastic," said Mike. "I can't wait to see the others. Are they all for about one hour?"

"No," said Mike's father. "Most will be close to two hours. This one is shorter because we only stayed there two days."

"Well, I can't wait to see the other," said Mike. "Especially since you suggest that they are more fantastic than the one we just saw."

"We will see one tomorrow," said Mike's father. "We cannot see one the day after tomorrow. It is August 23, which is your thirtieth birthday. We have to celebrate that special day." It turned out like Mike's father said. They watched one DVD the next evening and then they celebrated Mike's thirtieth birthday. They did surprise Mike. Some of his co-workers he was very friendly with were invited. They had a very happy celebration.

It was two days later that Mike's father decided to play DVD number three. They enjoyed it very much. Nicola and Joseph, Mike's mother and father, felt like they were reliving their trip. Mike felt like he was traveling in Sicily. They viewed the other DVDs about two times a week. There were days when Mike's parents wanted to view other programs that were available in the evening. They could watch the DVDs any time. Mike however was impatient. He enjoyed them so much. It was like he was taking a vacation. They finally viewed the last of the DVDs. It took over a month to see them all. Mike was very pleased to see them all. He then went back on thinking about his patients. Mike's father and mother, when there was nothing on TV that they wanted to see, would replay some of the DVDs of their Sicilian trip. Mike however did not stay with them when they replayed any of the DVDs. He went upstairs to watch movies that he liked. Life after that went back to normal. Mike dedicated himself to his job at the hospital. Mike's parents spent a lot of time traveling around town and sometimes went to other nearby cities. Mike was so pleased to have his parents around. His life was no longer a lonely life. Sometimes he went with his family on their city trips. When he was with them, his parents didn't have to come home early to cook for Mike. They went and had dinner at a restaurant. Mike enjoyed his life so much more when his family was home. He was also jollier at work and brought happier days for his patients. He was loved by all.

It was in mid-November that Mike was just getting home and settling down to dinner when the doorbell rang.

"I will get it," said Mike as he got up and went to the door. He opened the door and was thrilled at who he saw.

"Hi Kathy," said Mike and hugged her. Mike's mother heard the commotion and realizing that it was Kathy she ran to the door and hugged Kathy.

"Sweetheart," said Nicola, their mother. "When I talked with you yesterday you said you couldn't make it for thanksgiving this year. So, thank God you are here, but what happened?"

"The people I was supposed to meet canceled the meeting," said Kathy. "They had some kind of death in their family. However, I will only be here for about two days. I want to save my vacation time for Christmas and New Year."

"That is great," said her mother. "I think we have enough food for all of us. I hope you have not eaten and are very hungry.

"I have not eaten," said Kathy, "and I am very hungry. Even if I wasn't hungry, your special dinner will make me hungry." Mike's mother brought food to the table. Mike's father said a prayer and they all ate the delicious food their mother Nicola prepared.

"So how are things in New York?" asked Kathy's father.

"Things are great," said Kathy. "I would also like to mention that I have been seeing a fellow named Ryan for over a year. We are very interested in each other. If things go as I expect and hope, I will bring him here for Christmas, if that is alright with you."

"That would be great," said her mother. "We hope he is the right one for you. We always pray that you find someone who will make you as happy as your father has made me."

"You say that you are interested in each other," said Mike. "What does that mean? What is important is, are you both in love with each other?"

"We are crazy for each other," said Kathy with a smile on her face.

"That sounds better," said Mike.

"I am looking forward to meeting him," said her mother. "I'm sure we will all love him. Is there any chance that he will propose before you come here?" asked her mother.

"I don't think so," said Kathy. "He is going back to school to get his master's degree. Fortunately, it will be here in Cleveland State University. He has a friend that works at the University. He said that if he got a master's degree that he would help him get a job as a professor at Cleveland State University. My company also has a branch here in Cleveland. I will try to get moved there."

"That would be my greatest dream come true," said her mother. "I can't wait for Christmas."

"Well as I said before I am very hungry," said Kathy as she sat at the table. Nicola did not have to be told twice. She got the food and served it to all that was sitting there.

"By the way," said Kathy, "where is dad?"

"He went to the drug store to get a drug that he is taking for his high blood pressure," said her mother. "He should be home any minute." Just then her father just walked in. He had noticed the different auto in the driveway. He rushed and hugged his daughter.

"It is so good to see you," said her father. "I thought that you had an important meeting and couldn't come home for Thanksgiving."

"It was canceled due to a death in his family."

"Listen Joseph," said Nicola, his wife. "We have some great news to tell you about. Kathy has a boyfriend that she may bring here for Christmas."

"Fantastic," said Joseph. "It is about time. You will have to tell me all about him."

"After dinner," said his wife. "I think we should eat first. Kathy just got here from New York and is very hungry. You can talk all night after we eat." They all ate and enjoyed the great dinner that Nicola had prepared. After they ate and they sat in the family room, Kathy told them how she met Ryan.

"We were at a friend's graduation party and we ended up at the same table. We introduced each other and it went on from there. We were attracted to each other. But I remembered what you told me mom, that good looks were not enough. So I dated Ryan for a year. I found that he is very intelligent, very romantic, and thinks of others before he thinks of himself. That is why he wants to be a teacher. He wants to help people."

"That is so wonderful," said her mother. "I can't wait till I meet him."

"I can hardly believe that you may soon have grandchildren," said Mike to his mother.

"Now let's not go overboard," said Kathy. They all had a good laugh. After some small talk they watched TV and after that they all went to bed.

The next few days went by with the joy of all being together. Soon Sunday came and after church they had a fantastic lunch that Nicola made especially for her daughter since she was going to leave after lunch. It happened too fast. After lunch they all said goodbye to Kathy.

"I can't wait until you come home for Christmas," said her

mother. They all hugged and Kathy left. They all had tears in their eyes.

Life for Mike went back to normal. The only good thing he felt was that his parents were home to keep him from being lonely. At the hospital things were slower than usual. Mike only had one surgery for the next two weeks. One day Sophia called Mike into her office.

"Hi Mike," said Sophia, "come in and sit across from me at my desk. I need to discuss something with you."

"What have I done now?" asked Mike with a frown on his face.

"No," said Sophia. "It is nothing like that. As a matter of fact I want you to know that I feel that you are the most important member of this hospital. No, it is not anything like that. It is something that I would like you to do. It is something I hate to ask you to do but unless you have an answer to our problem I have no other course to follow."

"What problem are you talking about?" asked Mike.

"The hospital is losing money," said Sophia. "We are in financial trouble."

"So," said Mike. "What can I do about it?"

"I hate to ask this but could you offer more help to the police department. When you are working for them, they pay your salary. So you see that until we can get out of this problem you can save up some money without us laying-off anyone. I know it is a bad suggestion, but can you offer a better solution? I'm sure it will only last for a little while. We are looking for a financial manager."

"I will do what I can," said Mike. "I don't know how much more I can do for them. However I do have a Financial Manager who helped us in California. She did a fantastic job. She reorganized every department so the hospital made a fantastic income. Her name is Tina Banio. See if you could find her. She worked for a firm that sent her all over America to help organizations that were in financial trouble."

"I'll use all the hospital power to see if I can find her." That said Mike left and continued with his normal routine for the day. The next day Mike called Larry and told him that he wanted to help Larry solve any case that he had. He told Larry that he wanted to do crime investigating as his second job. Larry said he was very happy to hear him say that. He would like Mike's help. From that day on until Thursday the day before Christmas, Mike was available to Larry anytime he was needed. Christmas was on Saturday this year. On Thursday evening after they had dinner the doorbell rang. Mike was the closest to the door so he went and opened it. It was Kathy and her boyfriend.

"Hi Kathy," said Mike and hugged her.

"This is Ryan," said Kathy and then turning to Ryan she continued and this is Mike my brother. Mike and Ryan shook hands.

"It's so nice to finally meet you," said Mike. "Come on in and meet the rest of the family." Mike no longer finished that sentence when his father and mother came up to the door. Both the mother and father hugged Kathy. Kathy's mother Nicola then hugged Ryan but Joseph Kathy's father shook hands with Ryan.

"It is so nice to meet you," said Nicola. "Come on in and relax. You both must be very tired after driving for about eight hours."

"Mom," Said Kathy, "We only drove for about a half hour. "We both live in Cleveland."

"Wow," said Kathy's mother, "when did that all happen?"

"Ryan got a job at a Central Cadillac dealer," said Kathy. "He rented an apartment and moved down here a little over a week ago. I got transferred to the corporate branch here in Ohio last week. I also found a nice little apartment about a ten minute drive from Ryan's apartment."

"Well come in and rest while I cook up a nice dinner for all of us," said Kathy's mother. They all sat at the dinner table waiting for the meal.

"Tell me," said Kathy's father, "what are you doing at the Cadillac dealer?"

"Mostly," said Ryan, "I am a salesman. The reason they hired me was because of my scientific knowledge. I can explain all the functions of the auto engine and other parts of the auto. That is a great selling capability."

"When you receive your master's degree," said Kathy's father, "you will teach auto mechanics?"

"No, I will teach mechanical engineering and some electrical engineering," said Ryan. "That is what I am studying. The auto engine is just a small part of mechanical engineering."

"How about you Kathy," asked her father, "are you doing anything different at this new job?"

"No dad" said Kathy, "It is the same company. "I am still the corporate attorney handling all the firm's legal affairs."

"Well, I still think you are hungry," said Nicola. "I didn't know you were coming this early but I have enough for all of us. She then set the table with a wonderful dinner of lamb Chops. They each had two. They were satisfied especially when they got the apple pie dessert. That evening and most of Friday they spent enjoying each other's company. Friday night was Christmas Eve. The Chrisman's tree was set up a week ago. However, packages began showing up under the tree slowly. For dinner on Christmas Eve Nicola made a small turkey. They all enjoyed it very much. After dinner they sat around and talked.

"You never told us how long you will stay with us," said Nicola Kathy's mother. "I hope you can stay until New Year's."

"Oh Mom," said Kathy. "I wish we could, but we have to get back. Ryan needs the money. I offered to help him but he will not take my money. We will stay till the weekend. After church on Sunday we will have to go back. We also have a New Year's party we were invited to. It is held by the new friends we have met at work. It will give us a chance to get to know the people that we will be working with." Ryan took Mike aside to talk with him.

"Are you the one that will play the part of Santa Clause?" asked Ryan to Mike.

"Yes," said Mike. "I do it every year."

I would like you to do me a favor," said Ryan. He then whispered something in Mike's ear. Mike smiled. Mike and Ryan then joined the others and after enjoying each other's company on Christmas Eve they all went to bed. The next morning they all got up early and had a sweet breakfast. After breakfast they all met in the living room around the Christmas tree. Mike put on his Christmas Santa's hat and went up to the Christmas tree. On the right side there were a group of packages. Mike grabbed one from the group.

"This gift is from Kathy and Ryan together with Mom," said Mike. He then handed the package to his mom. She opened it quickly and pulled out a Christmas card. Inside she found a fifty dollar gift certificate To Red Lobster.

"Thank you so much," said their mom. Mike handed a similar package from Kathy and Ryan to his dad. He also had a fifty dollar gift certificate but this one was to Olive garden.

"Thank you sweet guys," said their dad. Mike then grabbed the last one of the bunch. This was also from Kathy and Ryan and it was addressed to Mike.

"Thank you so much," said Mike as he opened the envelope that was in the package. He took out the envelope and opened it. In it he found fifty dollars in cash. "Thank you. You guys didn't have to do this."

"We didn't know what to buy a doctor," said Kathy. "We thought you could go to a medical supply store and buy something that is from us."

"Thank you guys," said Mike again. "That is so sweet." Mike then moved to the other side of the Christmas tree and grabbed a package. He picked two envelopes. These are from Mom and Dad. He gave one to Kathy and the other to Ryan. They opened the envelopes and found a thousand dollars in each.

"This is way too much," said Ryan. "I don't know how to thank you."

"We know that college today costs a lot," said Joseph, Kathy's father. "I know that you need it and deserve it by loving my daughter."

"I will thank you for both of us," said Kathy. "You and mom are the most wonderful parents any one can ever have." Mike then picked up another package. It was addressed to Mike and it was from Mom and dad. Mike opened it. He pulled out a new cell phone.

"What is this dad?" said Mike.

"It is a new device that has many more things you can do with it than that old fifteen years or older. You need a new, more modern one."

"Thank you so much dad," said Mike with a loving smile on his face. "I have been thinking of buying one but have been too busy. Thank you so much dad." Mike then grabbed a small package. He handed it to Kathy. This is from me." Kathy opened the package and pulled out a very beautiful necklace and matching earrings.

"This is so beautiful," said Kathy. "Thank you so much, wonderful brother." Mike then hands an envelope to Ryan. He took out a bank check for five hundred dollars.

"Thank you so much Mike," said Ryan. "You are already treating me like your brother. Thank you and God bless all of you for treating me like part of your family." Mike then gave a large package to his mother.

"This for you mom from me," said Mike. Nicola opened the package. It was a very nice sweater. "I know that you are always feeling cold. This sweater will keep you warm and the color matches your eyes."

"Thank you so much Mike," said his mother. "I love it."

"Well mom and dad," said Mike. "Do you want to handle it from here or do you want me to continue as with the other gifts?"

"Go ahead and take care of it," said Mike's father. "It is getting late and I am getting hungry." Mike then handed a very large box to his father.

"Dad," said Mike, "this is from mom to you." Joseph then opened the box. It was a beautiful dark blue suit.

"Thank you so much honey," said Joseph. "It is beautiful. I now have a nice suit that I will need to go to a wedding." He then hugged his wife. Mike then handed his mother a small box.

"This is the last gift," said Mike. "It is a gift from my dad to mom. Nicola opened the box. It was a beautiful bracelet that matched the necklace and the earrings that he had bought for her for her birthday.

"This is so beautiful," said Nicola. "It matched the necklace that you gave me for my birthday. Thank you so much." She then hugged her husband.

"Let's go and eat now," said Mike. "I am also very hungry, especially knowing the great dinner mom has cooked." They all put away their gifts and sat around the dining room table. Mike was right. Nicola made the Cavatelli with neck bones that were out of this world. They all enjoyed it very much. After eating they played the card game they called Uno. It was their mother Nicola's favorite. It was her favorite because she won most of the time. At about seven that evening, they sat down to have dinner. They were all so full from the fantastic lunch they had so that no one was very hungry. They each had very little from the lunch leftover. After dinner they sat and watched a romantic movie. After the movie they all went to bed. Ryan was given the guest room at the end of the hall.

The next day was Sunday. They all went to church together. After the service was over they all went home to wait on the great lunch meal that Nicola promised. She had them sit in the family room to wait for her to cook their meal. She told them she wanted it to be a surprise. About an hour later Nicola brought out five large pieces of Prime Beef Tenderloin Filet Mignon Steaks. The stakes were so tender that they didn't need a knife. A fork was all they needed. After they finished the meal they all went back to the family room to let the food settle in their stomach.

"Does anyone want to play Uno?" asked Nicola.

"We can't move," said Kathy. "Let's wait until later."

"I agree," said their father. "If anyone wants to play please go ahead and play." No one spoke up. Later that day around super time Nicola spoke up.

"Does anyone want something to eat for dinner?" she asked.

"Maybe a cup of coffee and a small sandwich," said their father Joseph. They all went up to the kitchen. They all had a cup of coffee. Only the men had a small sandwich. The women only had coffee and a slice of toast. About eight Kathy and Ryan decide to drive home.

"We had such a wonderful time with you," said Kathy. "It has been a great Christmas."

"It was the best Christmas I have ever had," said Ryan. "I will never forget it." They all hugged and said goodbye. Mike and his parents were all very tired so they all went to bed early.

The next day Mike went to work about thirty minutes earlier than he had to, so that he could visit all the patients on the second and third floor like he had done often before. His mission as usual was to cheer up all the hospital patients. After he made his tour, since he had a few minutes before his eight O'clock normal job starting time, he went up to talk to Sophia.

"Hi Sophia," said Mike as he entered her office, "is there any news on the financial problems of the hospital?"

"The police payment for your help has helped a lot," said Sophia. "We also have made some changes which not only gave us a little more hospital income but woke us up to the fact that we need a financial manager."

"Have you checked on the financial advisor I recommended?" asked Mike.

"We searched everywhere for a financial advisor," said Sophia, "but we could not find Tina Banio."

"Well if I can help in any way please let me know," said Mike as he left her office. Mike then went back to his normal job.

The days of December went by quickly. Soon it was Friday. It was New Year's Eve. Mike and his parents did not have anything special planned. They watched TV after dinner and waited for the New York evening festival. Joseph got a bottle of Champagne and three wine glasses. They watched the time go by until the New Year ball came down the building declaring a New Year. The band played the famous song of the New Year and the New Year was declared. Joseph poured the Champaign in each glass and gave one to his wife Nicola and one to Mike.

"Happy New year," yelled Joseph.

"Happy new year," yelled Mike and his mother together. They then touched each glass with each other and drank the Champaign. After they finished drinking they set down the glasses and Mike hugged his mother, and kissed her on the cheek. She kissed him back on his cheek. Mike and his father shook hands and then hugged. Mike was then surprised to see his father and mother having a very romantic kiss on the lips. He didn't remember seeing that before. After watching about fifteen more minutes of the news they all went to bed.

The next morning it was Saturday January one. Mike and his parents overslept. It was about ten thirty when they all got together.

"Are you guys hungry?" asked Nicola.

"I think I could wait," said Joseph, "until noon to have what I believe will be a fantastic luncheon meal.

"I'm not too hungry either," said Mike. As Joseph mentioned they had a fantastic meal for lunch. Nicola grilled twelve Lamb Chops on their indoor grill. They each had four of the tastiest Lamb Chops that had ever had before. They spent the rest of the day watching the news. There was so much exciting news about the events that took place last night that it was a great pleasure watching TV. Finally, the feast was over and they all went to bed.

The next Morning Mike got up early and was walking down to the kitchen for breakfast. As he was walking he passed the master bedroom. He was shocked at what he saw. He saw his parents filling their suitcases with clothes.

"What are you guys doing?" asked Mike. "Are you planning on going on another trip?"

"Yes," said Mike's father. "We don't want to spend winter here with all that snow. We would be bored to death just staying home. We decided to go to Puerto Rico to spend the winter."

"Are you going to travel to all the islands in the Caribbean Sea?" asked Mike.

"No, we are going to spend the complete winter on the warm beach," said Mike's father. We are not going anywhere. We are tired of traveling."

"Well you two have a wonderful time." Mike had breakfast, said his goodbye to his parents and went to his job thinking that he had many lonely days ahead.

The days went by slowly. Soon it was February. Mike had gotten used to being lonely. It was after the first week of February that he got a call early in the morning before he could go to work.

"Hello Mike," said the voice when Mike answered the phone.

"Hello," said Mike, "Is that you Larry?" asked Mike, recognizing the voice. "What is the reason for this call?"

"I need your help," said Larry. "You said that whenever I needed you that all I had to do was ask. I understand that your boss is for it all."

"Yes," said Mike. "I will have to call her and tell her that I am going to help the police department. She likes the idea. Anyway, what is the problem that you want to investigate?"

"A woman has been shot," said Larry. "I would like to find out what happened. We found no weapon so it wasn't suicide. I will pick you up in about ten minutes, if that is OK with you."

"Come pick me up," said Mike, "I will be ready." Larry arrived at Mike's house a few minutes later.

"You better follow me in your own car," suggested Larry. "You may want to leave earlier than me." Five minutes later they arrived at the house of the woman that was shot. The house was surrounded by police cars and police officers that kept any one from entering or leaving the area. Just as they entered the house an ambulance arrived. Inside they found the shot woman near the doorway. Larry and Mike examined her and released her to the fellows in the ambulance.

"Please have the doctor do a complete examination," said Larry to the ambulance fellows. They then took her away. Larry and Mike then walked into the living room. There they found a middle aged man crying loudly.

"I suspect that you are her husband," said Larry. The man could not talk. He only shook his head. Larry turned to the officer who was in charge of the police group. "When did he come and who notified him?"

"As you know the one who called us was the neighbor named Julia who heard the gunshot and called us. She apparently also called her husband. The neighbor woman was here when we got here."

"I think we have everything under control," said Larry to the police officer. I will take over from here. You all can leave now." They did not have to be told twice. A few minutes later the police cars except for Larry's car pulled away. Larry then grabbed the woman's purse that was next to where her body had been. It was obvious that the woman was about to leave the house to go to work when she was attacked. Larry opened the purse and got her identification card. The husband looked but did not disapprove of what Larry was doing. He was too sad to object.

"Her name is Gloria Walker," said Larry. "Her husband's name is Timothy." Larry then walked up to Timothy. "Timothy, are you ready to talk? We want to find out who did this." Timothy started to cry louder.

Let's wait a few minutes," said Mike. "Let's find out more information. I see here in her purse that she has a card with her name as the manager of the woman's clothing store at the mall."

"That is a good place for you to start," said Larry to Mike. "I will try to contact any of her family."

"I'm glad that I came with my own car," said Mike. "It is still early. I think I will go directly to her place of employment." Mike then left and went to the mall. He found the Woman's clothing store and walked in. As soon as he walked in, a young lady walked up to him.

"How can I help you?" said the young lady. "Is there anything special that you are looking for?"

"I am looking for the store manager," said Mike.

"I'm sorry," said the young woman," the manager is Gloria, but she didn't show up this morning. How can I help you?"

"Well who is in charge when she is out," asked Mike?

"I guess I am," said the woman.

"Well then please let's go to the office," said Mike, "My name is Doctor Mike Costello. I assist the police department. I need to talk to each of you separately"

"What is going on?" said the woman.

"Come into the office where we can talk." The woman then took Mike to the office. When they sat down Mike began to speak.

"What is your name?" asked Mike, and how do you fit in this store?"

"My name is Trudy Cordell," said the woman. I am the manager's assistant. Actually, we are distant cousins. I have worked for her for eight years."

"Alright Trudy," said Mike. "Do you know of anyone who would want to harm Gloria?"

"No," said Trudy. "She is the nicest person we know. Many customers ask for her. Why has she been hurt?"

"Yes," said Mike." "She was shot this morning. We are trying to find who hated her enough to shoot her."

"Did she survive?" asked Trudy.

"I'm sorry she didn't survive," said Mike. "Please call in one of the other sales ladies." Trudy waited a while drying her tears, then called one of the sales ladies.

"Do mind if I stay in here with you," asked Trudy. "I love Gloria very much. She is like a sister to me. She taught me all that I know. I don't know how I will get along without her?" One of the other sales girls came in

"Joan," said Trudy, "this is Doctor Mike Costello. He is investigating the shooting of our manager, Gloria. Have a seat." Joan sat down in a state of shock.

"Was she killed?" asked Joan.

"I'm afraid so," said Mike. "I would like to ask you if you have any idea as to who would like to shoot your manager, Gloria."

"I can't believe anyone would want to hurt Gloria," said Joan with tears in her eyes. "She was the most wonderful person I know. She was such a friendly and caring woman. Her heart was made of honey."

"Go out and take care of our customers," said Trudy to Joan, "and please ask Martha to come in." A few moments later Martha came in. She came in with tears in her eyes.

"You heard the bad news I suspect," said Mike.

`Yes," said Martha. "Joan told me about it. I have only been with this store for about a year. But she was very kind and very friendly to me and everyone she met. I think the shooter must have mistaken her for someone else. There is no reason to hurt Gloria."

"Well," said Mike. "I think that I have all the information that you can give me. However, if you can think of anything else or you come up with new information here is my card, please call me. Thank you for the time and information you have given me." Mike then left and drove directly to the police station. As he had hoped Larry was there.

"Hi Larry," said Mike.

"Hi Mike," responded Larry. "What have you come up with?"

"Nothing really," said Mike, "they all loved Gloria and they all had tears when I told them of Gloria being shot. I could tell from the tears that their sorrow was real. They said that they thought that shooting her was a mistake. They feel that the shooter thought that she was someone else. How about you, what have you found out about their family?"

"I found that she has three in her family," said Larry, "she has a father, a mother, and a sister. They are living in Illinois. They will be here for the funeral. They have no Idea who would want to shoot Gloria."

"Well," said Mike, "that leaves us one possibility. Someone was after Tim."

"The neighbor who was the one who called us said that she was out with her dog and heard the pistol shot. She then saw a figure run out of the house. It was totally black. It had a hood over its head. She would guess that it was a man, but she couldn't be sure."

"Then that leaves us one other possibility," said Mike. "Someone wants Time to suffer probably as much as Tim in his action as the acting Attorney made him suffer."

"Let's go and talk to Tim tomorrow morning," said Larry, "I think he should be settled enough to talk with us. I will pick you up at your house at about eight."

"That sounds like the only alternative we have," said Mike. "However, it would be nice if you can get a record of all his past jobs as a lawyer."

"I will see what I can do," said Larry. "I would think that Tim would have a record of all his past lawsuits." Mike then left and went to his home. He was too tired to do anything else.

The next morning Mike went directly to the police station.

"Hi Larry," said Mike as he entered Larry's office. "How are you this morning? Are you ready to go and find Tim? Did you get a list of the cases that Tim had in the last year?"

"I have a list," said Larry, "But it doesn't tell me what each case was about. We have to go over each one with Tim. Let's go. I will take my car. There is little chance that I will want to stay longer than you. The opposite could be the case." About fifteen minutes later they arrived at Tim's house. Fortunately, Tim was home.

"Hi Tim," said Larry. "I hope you are well enough to talk with us this morning.

"I don't know what I could tell you," said Tim. "I have no idea who shot my wife and why."

"Well let me bring you up to date as to what we have accomplished," said Larry, "then you perhaps could understand what we need from you. First, we checked all of the workers and friends of your wife. We found no one who would like to harm her. That leaves us one other possibility. The shooter shoots your wife to get at you."

"If they were mad at me," said Tim, "why didn't he shoot me instead of my wife?"

"Let me answer that," said Mike. "I ran across a similar situation a couple of years ago. When we caught the shoot we asked him that question. His answer was that if he had shot the husband he would have suffered about one minute. If I shoot his loving wife he would suffer for more than a year. That is the thinking that I think your wife's shot had."

"That is very sad and evil thinking," said Tim.

"Therefore," said Larry, "let's start checking your past cases. I got a list of cases you had the past year. So, let's start with the first one a year ago." Larry pulled out his sheet and pointed to the first item on the list.

"I remember that one, said Tim. "That was a case against the company who sold them a refrigerator. The customer claimed that they sent them the wrong refrigerator. It was not the one they paid for. The company checked their records and told them that they had the refrigerator they paid for. That's when I came in. My claiming to sue them, made them come and check the refrigerator they had delivered. The fellow that came was shocked. It was the wrong refrigerator. They quickly replaced it with the right one."

"Explain the story about the next one," asked Larry.

"That was a similar story," said Tim. "The customer had ordered an electric stove but they got a gas stove instead. I made them exchange it for the right one." They then went down the coast and found that most were the same. The company was always the one that made the error. They were half way through the list when Tim interrupted.

"What is your problem?" asked Larry.

"I think from what we are going through, that you are looking for someone who was angry with me and wanted to punish me by killing my wife."

"That is what we are looking for," said Mike "I thought that you understood that."

"I am still hurting from the loss of my wife, so I am not thinking straight. However, what I am trying to tell you is that I think of one case that might be just what we are looking for."

"Which one is that?" asked Larry. Tim went down the list and pointed to the one that he was talking about.

"This case was the strangest case I have ever been associated with," started Tim. "The case is against a woman named Sylvia Mills. She was the manager of a women's Clothing store. The owner gave her full authority of the store operation. She therefore spent most of her time as the financial manager. She handled all the store income, the bank deposits, and handled all the clothing restocking purchasing. She was allowed by the owner to work only six hours a day so that she could spend some time with the homeless children at the Children's Charity House.

"What has this to do," asked Larry, "with the killing of your wife?"

"I'm getting to that," said Tim. "Because of some disease that half of the children caught, and the fact that they had no insurance, and some other expenses that came up, they had not paid the rent of the Charity House for three months. Because they couldn't pay the rent the owner decided to sell the property. He told them if they didn't pay in the next couple of days that they would have to move out. The total of the rent and the other cost amounted to fifty thousand dollars. Sylvia tried to borrow the money from the bank but was turned down. That was when she decided to borrow money from the company she worked for. She placed the house she owned for sale and planned on returning the money after the sale of her house. She then gave the money to the Charity with a signed document that stated that it was a loan. She thought that she would replace the money before anyone would find out what she had done. Unfortunately, a reporter who was planning on writing about the problem the Charity was having, got the news of the money given by Sylvia and reported it in the News Paper. That's when Arthur the store owner hired me. I should have turned it down. But I realized that he would hire someone else. We went to court. I tried to convince him that he would get his money back and that she was only trying to help homeless children. But for some reason the owner was too angry to provide any relief. She was sentenced to two years in jail. She also had to pay the money back plus a large fine to the store owner. The husband Herbert Mills loved her so much that he fell apart at the conclusion of the trial. Herbert lost his job because he was so broken up that he couldn't go to work. He finally got a job cleaning the floors of the local school. I think he planned to get even with me to get his wife in jail."

"It looks like we have to talk with Mr. Miles," said Larry.

If you find out what his car is," said Mike. "Perhaps also his license plate and a Search warrant, we can go directly to the school and check if he has a gun in his car. We can confiscate it and check if it is the murder weapon."

"Sounds like a good Idea," said Larry. "If we can get the murder weapon it will make the job easier. Well Tim," said Larry turning to Tim. "Thank you for your time and information. We promise that we will get the murderer and make him pay. We will talk to you later. Good day for now."

"Goodbye," said Mike. Then they both left for the police station.

Larry got all that was needed and then both headed for the school where Herbert was working. They had no problem finding Herbert's car. Larry used his tool and opened the car. He opened the trunk and searched in it while Mike checked the glove compartment. Larry found nothing in the trunk but Mike found a pistol in the glove compartment. They then both went back to the police station to check to see if the pistol they got from Herbert's car was the murder weapon.

"Look Mike," said Larry when they went to the police station. "I don't see what you can do any more this day. Why don't you go to lunch? I will call you when I have more information."

"Why don't you come to lunch with me?" said Mike. "I would like the company."

"First," said Larry, "I want to stay here to see the results of the gun bullet check, and if it is positive I want to get Herbert arrested. Also, I have a sandwich and a coke here. I will eat it later."

"Alright," said Mike. "I am going back to the hospital to see my patients. I will have lunch there." Mike then left and went to his job at the hospital. It was late in the afternoon that Mike got a call from Larry

"Hi Larry," said Mike upon answering the phone "What is the latest information?"

Hi Mike," said Larry. "The gun we got from Herbert's car was the gun that shot Gloria. I sent officers to arrest him. I will interrogate him tomorrow morning. If you are interested you can view the complete proceedings from the window of the room next to the interrogation room. I will start at about eight. I would like to have you there in case you could be needed. Can we see you then?"

"I would never miss it," said Mike. He then went back to visiting his patients. He was so sure that they had the right man that it showed up to his patients because of his more than usual gleeful nature.

The next morning Mike was there before eight. He was led to the room next to the integration room. The wall between that room and the interrogation room had a window that almost covered the complete wall. Herbert was already there waiting for what was to happen next. It was about five minutes later that Larry walked in.

"Why was I arrested," asked Herbert. "I have not committed and crime"

"You are arrested for the murder of Gloria Mills," said Larry. "Do you deny it?"

"I didn't murder her," said Herbert. "I don't even know that woman. So why would I murder her. I have nothing against her."

"However, you have something against her husband," said Larry.

"I don't even know her husband," said Herbert. "Even if I did, why wouldn't I shoot him instead of his wife? She is not responsible for her husband's actions."

"You were hurt very badly when your wife was arrested and the court found her guilty of robbery, weren't you?" asked Larry.

"She was given only two years," said Herbert, "I was torn apart when she got arrested. I don't remember anything that happened for the next six months. I was out of my mind. But when I found out this morning that she had died in her cell this morning I wanted to die. I was thinking that I had nothing to live for."

"Are you sure she died?" asked Larry as he grabbed his phone and called the jail office.

"Can you tell me the condition of your inmate Sylvia Mills is in." asked Larry when someone answered the phone.

I'm afraid that she is dead," said the officer that answered the phone. "She was found dead in her cell this morning. We called the hospital and they did everything they could to save her, but they did not succeed."

"Did they tell you what was the cause of her death?" asked Larry

"I don't know," said the officer. "They are going to perform an autopsy to find out why." Larry then turned back to Herbert.

"Look Herbert," said Larry. "It will go easier on you if you confess. We understand that you were out of your mind. We have the gun we got from your auto glove compartment and we found that it was the gun that shot Gloria. Your fingerprints were all over it."

"I knew that I should have gotten rid of that gun," said Herbert. "I never dreamt that you would figure out that it was me."

"Tell me," asked Larry, "Why did you kill her?"

"I suffered so much because of the loss of Sylvia for two years that I wanted her husband, the lawyer that convicted her, to feel the same sadness that I felt."

"Why did you hate her husband so much?" asked Larry. "Didn't you know that Tim tried everything he could to change Gloria's boss through the whole case."

"I'm sorry," said Herbert. "I was not thinking straight." Larry then had Herbert return to his cell and went to talk with Mike.

"You know," said Larry, "that we have recorded all that was said. I believe the case is closed. It is all up to the judge now. Thank you for coming. I will see you in my next case."

"Goodbye Larry," said Mike. "I hope it isn't too soon."

The next couple of weeks were extremely busy. The weather had turned very cold with inches of snow that caused many accidents. Although most of these were handled on the second floor, it caused Mike to make many visits to victims who were very depressed. Mike made it his job to enlighten them with his favorite tactic of making them realize how lucky they were to be alive and soon would be back to normal. He told them about the ones that didn't make it. He also told them about the two patients that he brought back to life. His happy disposition and his Jolly nature made them believe him. March went by slowly. The weather was more tolerable. It was at the beginning of April when Mike got a phone call from Larry.

"What now Larry?" said Mike realizing that Larry wanted help in another murder case.

"I need your help in another murder case," said Larry. "Are you available?"

"What is this case about?" asked Mike, thinking and hoping that it would be very different from the one's he had helped Larry on before.

"It's a case where a woman was shot early this morning," said Larry. "She was getting ready to go to work."

"It sounds like this crime is like the one we just finished solving a month ago?" said Mike, being a little disappointed. "Why are the one's getting shot are always women?"

"It just happens," said Larry. "Will you support me?"

"Give me the address and I will meet you there," said Mike. "I want my car there in case I have to go somewhere without you." Larry then gave him the address and hung up. Fifteen minutes later Mike showed up at the crime scene.

"I have searched the entire house and have found only that her name is Sara Pickett and her husband's name is Dennis Pickett. He is a Corporate Business Organizer. She was the manager of a woman's clothing store."

"I guess," said Mike, "that the woman's clothing store is the next place I am going."

"Here is her card with the address of the store," said Larry as he handed Mike the card. "You know what to do." Mike left and went directly to the woman's clothing store. When he got there he went up to the first sales lady on the floor.

"I would like to talk to the store manager," said Mike. "I am a representative of the police department."

"The store manager and owner is Sara," said the young woman. "She is not here today."

"Who," asked Mike "is in charge when she is not here?"

"That will be Karla," said the young woman, "She is the assistant manager. Her office is in the back. Her name will be on the door."

"Thank you," said Mike and walked to the rear of the store. Mike walked to the rear of the store and soon found the door with Karla's name on it. He knocked on the door.

"Who is it?" said Karla, "come on in." Mike walked in and sat down on the chair opposite her desk.

"My name is Doctor Mike Costello. I would like to ask you questions about the owner and the company in general. I would like to speak to all the employees."

"I'm sorry," said Karla. "I don't think it is proper for me to answer questions about the company without Sara being here."

"That is what I want to talk about, because Sara can't be here," said Mike. "I am hired by the police department to find out how you all felt about Sara and who would want to shoot her."

"She was shot?" said Karla in a state of shock. "Is she OK?"

"I'm afraid she didn't make it," said Mike. "I thought you knew."

"No, I have not heard of it," said Karla. "Give me a minute to recover and I will answer whatever question I can." After a minute she looked up at Mike. "How can I help you?"

"Tell me whatever you can tell me about her," said Mike. "How did she treat all of you that work here? How did she handle customers?"

"I will tell you all that I would have held back if Sara was alive," said Karla. Now I guess it will only help find her killer. First, I must tell you that Sara, most of the time, was here only once a week and sometimes twice. It was when her husband was out of town, which was most of the time. Her husband worked for a Corporate Organizer Company." He was gone two or three months at a time. The important thing is that I believe that she was cheating on him. A couple of times I saw her get into a car when a fellow picked her up at work. I know it wasn't her husband because her husband had black hair. The fellow that picked her up had light reddish hair."

"Can you think of any reason," asked Mike, "that someone would want to kill Sara?"

"No, I can't think of any reason anyone would want to kill her," said Karla. "Besides I didn't know her that well. She was very nice and friendly with me."

"How many sales ladies," asked Mike, "Do you have any?"

"Besides me there are two other sales girls," said Karla.

"Can you send them in here?" asked Mike, "one and a time. Karla then called the two sales ladies one at a time. They both repeated almost the same as Karla. They both said they hardly knew her. Mike then thanked them and left for the police station.

"Hi Mike," said Larry. "What did you find out?"

"HI, they hardly knew her. Sara only showed up once a week and then didn't stay very long. She just took care of the books and then left the rest to the head sales woman Karla," said Mike. "What have you found out?"

"I found out nothing," said Larry. "I talked to the neighbor. She said that she thought that Sara was cheating on her husband. She said that she did see her get into a car with a young man with red hair. As for their families, both of her family and his family live in another state. They claimed that they were not close. I also checked and they were all at work when Sara was shot. Let's go back to their house and search every inch of the house to see if we can find anything that will lead us to the killer." They go to the house about twenty minutes later. As they pulled to the driveway they saw the neighbor in her front yard. When she saw them, she recognized them and went up to speak with them.

"I don't think Mr. Pickett has returned home yet," said the neighbor.

"I know," said Larry. "We have contacted him and he is on the way home. They are keeping his wife in the hospital cooler until the burial. Anyway, since we have you here can you answer some questions we have?

"I think I have told you everything I know. What is it that you need to know?" Can you tell us of any activities that have taken place at this house? I mean like carpenters or plumbers that work here. Is there any activity that you can remember that brought people here? We are trying to find the company that first brought the young red headed man here to meet Sara."

"I don't remember any work that was done here. It has been

pretty quiet since Dennis got that job that has taken him away from home for so long a time." She started to walk away when she stopped and looked back. "There was a strange thing that happened one morning. I found Sara walking around her front yard like she was looking for something. I asked her what she was looking for and she told me that they were thinking of selling the house. She said that since Dennis got the new job she had to take care of the whole house. They considered selling this house and buying a small ranch house. I don't know what happened after that. I did not see any salesmen."

"I think that gives us a possibility," said Larry. "Thank you very much." He then turned to Mike. "What do you think Mike?"

"I think that is a possibility," said Mike. "I would like to recommend that you get a warrant to search the car of a suspect. We will then go to the local real-estate company and see if a red headed young man works there. If he does we can search his car before he has a chance in getting rid of his gun.

"That is a good start," said Larry as he got on his phone to get the warrant. They then thanked the neighbor lady and headed for the police station to get the warrant. They then went to the real-estate agency that was just off of Market Street. When they went there they were met by a young lady.

"How can I help you?" she asked, looking surprised seeing that one of the men was a police officer. "I'm Maryanne."

"We have some real-estate business we want to talk to," He hesitated, pretending he had forgotten his name. "I'm sorry I forgot his name. He is a young man with red hair."

"That is Jeffery," said Maryanne. "He is not here. He is on a job.

"Is he selling a house," said Mike. "We can probably meet him there."

"No," said Maryanne. "He has a part-time job as a truck driver. He is currently driving a truck to help someone move some furniture. I'm sorry I can't tell you more."

"Is he driving his truck or your company truck?" asked Mike.

"It is the company's truck. He drives a blue car. It is parked out back in our parking lot."

"Thank you very much," said Larry realizing that they had all they needed for the present time. That said they left and went to the back of the building where they found Jeffery's car. Larry took out his door opening device and opened the car door. It didn't take long when they found a pistol in the glove compartment.

"Well Mike," said Larry. "Let's go directly to the police station. We may have solved this case." When they got there Larry turned to Mike. Listen Mike, you do not have to wait until I check the pistol as to whether it is the murder weapon. I will have an officer go and watch the car. When Andy comes home he will arrest him and bring him to the police station. Even if the gun isn't the murder weapon he is our best suspect. I will interrogate him in the morning. I Came here at about eight. I would like you to sit with me during the interrogation. You can read so much from a person's actions."

"Sounds like a good plan," said Mike. He then left. It was too late to go to the hospital so he just went home.

The next day Mike showed up to the police station at eight in the morning as Larry had requested. Andy was in the interrogation room. Larry was at our side of the room waiting for Mike.

"Good morning Mike," said Larry. "I put our suspect in the interrogation room about fifteen minutes ago. I wanted him to sit there alone for a while."

"Hi Larry," said Mike. "That's a good Idea. Let him worry a bit. If he is guilty it will show up in his actions." Larry then opened the door to the interrogation room and he and Mike walked in and sat down at the table opposite Jeffery. No one said a word. When Larry looked up to Jeffery, Jeffery responded.

"What am I doing here?" said Jeffery. "I don't know anything about any crime. I didn't witness anything illegal."

"You are here charged with the murder of a woman named Sara Pickett," said Larry.

"Who is Sara Pickett," said Jeffery, acting like he didn't know what Larry was talking about. "I don't even know her."

"We have two witnesses that have seen her get into your car. We also retrieved the murder weapon from your car. Can you tell us what happened?"

"May I cut in here," said Mike.

"Go ahead," said Larry. "I have said all I have to say for now."

"Listen Jeffery," Mike started. "My name is Mike Costello. I am a medical doctor. One of the main things I have studied is the mind's activities. What causes the mind to make people react the way they do. Why do they do what they do? I'm sure that you have heard that once in a while a person who has committed a crime does not go to jail but to a special hospital. Their action was considered temporary insanity. What I am saying is that the reason you did what you did, could be, in your mind, justified, if the person you shot did some terrible things to you so that you felt you had to stop him or her. What I am saying is that it is important for us to know the purpose of your action in shooting Sara. If it looked like you had a good reason it may shorten the time you would have in jail. Do you understand what I am saying?"

"I think I understand a little," said Jeff. "What do you suggest I do?"

"I suggest you start from the beginning of all that has affected you to do what you did," said Mike.

"I guess I should start as to when I met my wife," started Jeff. Suddenly Jeff felt a strong desire to empty his mind. For over a year he had felt lonely and unloved. "I met her at a distant cousin's wedding in Cleveland. Her parents were deceased and my father had died of cancer and my mother was in a nursing home. We were both there alone. We managed to sit at a table next to each other. Up until then she seemed very controlled. When she noticed me at the table she became very nervous.

That told me that she was attracted to me. I introduced myself and she told me that her name was Evelyn. We decided since we were alone that we would pretend to be partners. Although she was very pretty, all I wanted was a partner for the wedding. It became a different story when I found out that she lived in Montrose. I told her that I lived in Fairlawn. I told her that we were sort of neighbors. From that day on we dated for about a month. She did not try to hide that she was in love with me. I liked her very much but I didn't have butterflies in my stomach like people in love felt."

"Why are you telling us about your love life," said Larry. "What has this to do with your action?"

"I am telling you," said Jeff, "Because she is the one that was behind my mind problem. Anyway, it was a month later that I met Fred, a friend of mine at a restaurant. Evelyn was not with me that day. She had a meeting about a job she wanted. Fred came up to me all excited. He had seen me with Evelyn the day before.

"Wow," said Fred. "How did you get so lucky to have a girlfriend like Evelyn?"

"She is a very pretty girl," I told him. "Why are you making such a fuss?"

"Don't you know who that is," said Fred. "That is Evelyn Bond. Her parents were killed in an auto accident. Your date inherited sixteen million dollars."

"That made up my mind. We got married the next May. However, there was a written agreement that I had to sign. It said that if I ever divorced her I would lose any right to her money. It also said that if I cheated on her she would divorce me and I would lose any rights to her money. It was obvious that she was worried that I was marrying her for her money. Part of that was true. She is such a sweet person that in time I did fall in love with her. The trouble began when Evelyn accepted the job of checking and analyzing and possibly reorganizing shelters and organizations of homeless children. Some Shelters and children charities were having financial problems. Evelyn would reorganize them and sometimes used her own money to get it going. That was great; except she was sent to places all over the country. Most of the time, she would be gone for more than a month. I became very lonely. I tried to fill my time with work. But there was never enough to kill my loneliness. That is when I met Sara. She had called to get an estimate on selling their house and buying a smaller one in the same area. I notice a strange look on her face and on her voice. It was very different from the voice I hear over the phone. I could tell she was attracted to me. I was also very attracted to her. I took her around the area to see smaller houses. We got to know each other. I took her to lunch several days in a row. I learned that she had the same problem I had. Her husband was out of town some times for several months at a time. He was a Corporate Organizer. He was great at bringing companies that were losing money back to earning a good income. Anyway, we forgot about selling her house and buying another. After three days of being together I told her how attracted I was to her. I told her I had the same problem she had. We decided to see each other when we were left alone by our mates. We both agreed that divorce was not in the plans. With me it was that I didn't want to lose the checkbook money I had. I was impressing Sara with all the money I spent on our entertainment. She said that divorce and any kind of love making was out of the question. She was a Born-Again Christian. So if I had any other plans they had better stop seeing each other right now. I assured her that I would never divorce my wife. The only thing that could occur between us is an occasional kiss now and then. She laughed and asked if one of the occasional times is now? I didn't hesitate. Every day we had a pong joy of hugging and kissing. It never got farther than that. I found a restaurant in Cleveland that had a dance band. Sara just loved to dance. That restaurant saw us for many days. The most important thing, I told her, was that they had to keep their time together very secretly. I told her I didn't want to lose the money. We dated for over a year until one day when I called her she asked me to come to the house. She wanted to talk with me. I told her that it was a great risk that someone would see us. She still insisted. So I went there early the next morning. She let me in and then told me that she was going to divorce her husband. She was tired of all this hiding the truth. She told me that she was crazy in love with you. She said that she wanted to spend the rest of her life with you. She said that she didn't care if I lost the money my wife had. She said that we will have enough to live on. That is all that matters to her. She said that she was going to her lawyer and she asked me to go with her. I told her that I didn't want to lose all that money. I told her that I didn't want to do this yet. Perhaps if our relationship gets accidently discovered we can consider that. She said that she was going to let their relationship out into the world. She said that she loved me with all her heart and she wanted the whole world to know it.

That is when I thought I could scare her into changing her mind. It was a stupid thing but I could not think of anything else. I went to my car and got the pistol I carried in my car. I needed it for protection when I was shipping valuable items for a client. I told Sara that I had a choice between her and the millions of dollars that I chose. I pointed the gun at her. I asked her to promise me that she would keep our relationship private for now or I would shoot her. I don't know what Sara was doing but she happened to have a fireplace poker in her hand. She laughed with a great smile. She told me that she knew that I would not hurt her. She then swung the poker stick at me with the intent to knock the gun out of my hand. Unfortunately when the poker hit the gun it went off. She was shot in the chest. I reached for her purse and called 911. I told them that a woman had been shot and gave them the address. I then, like a fool, grabbed my gun and ran away. I thought that they would take her to the hospital and save her. I left because I didn't want our relationship to become public."

"Thank you for all the information. We did find a white paint mark on your pistol. That assures me that you are telling the truth."

"That will make the charge against you much lighter," said Mike. "I also would guess that telling us the story has made you feel a bit relieved."

"I feel terrible, perhaps a little relieved to get the information off my chest, but I have lost the two women I love with all my heart. I have lost some of the money I had with my wife, and I have lost my freedom. I don't see how I can have any feeling other than the desire to die."

"Don't worry," said Mike. "We will be on your side. I think you could get away with a lenient charge. You don't know what your wife will do. So I suggest you think positively."

"I will have to hold you until I can arrange a court hearing," said Larry. "And Mike I will call you when it is arranged." Mike then said goodbye to both and left. It was too late to go to the hospital so he went home. He felt a little tired. He should have felt happy that the case was solved, but he just felt tired of the whole deal. Mike went home feeling that he didn't want any police work anymore.

A few Happier Days

The next morning Mike went to work at the hospital. He had a great desire to make the patients feel better as he had done before. He didn't go to his office to see if he had a surgery planned for that day. He wanted to feel better before he went there. It wasn't until he had a couple of patients feeling better, which also brought some happy feeling to him, that he ran into Sophia.

"Hi Mike," said Sophia. "It is so nice to have you back for a little while. How do you like to be a police detective?" It was then that Mike realized what it was that was bothering mime.

"I don't like it too much," said Mike. "You see, I want to spend my life helping people. A patient's smile, when I have helped them back to their regular life is a very great gift to my heart. As a detective after solving a case all you see is tears. If it isn't needed I would rather work here in the hospital.

"I'm so glad to hear that," said Sophia. "I hated to send patients that needed surgery to the Akron General Hospital. Alright then, I will stop the police from using you unless it is an absolute necessity." That made the day for Mike.

"How about the hospital's financial problems," asked Mike? "Do I have to take large vacations?"

"Very funny," said Sophia with a great smile on her face. "You have helped in the past. However, we are making changes that have our hospital breaking even, even with paying you your salary. Besides, we are looking for the financial Adviser you recommended. We need one badly." Mike then went back to work and finally went into his office. He saw several patients and enlightened their day as well as his own. This was the work he liked he thought that day. The next two days he also had two surgeries that saved the life of an elderly man and a middle aged woman.

Several days went by before Mike heard from Larry. Mike had just gotten home from a successful day.

"Hi Larry, " said Mike, recognizing Larry's phone number being displayed on his cell phone showing who was calling. "What is new he said hoping it wasn't another case?"

"We got a date for the final hearing at the courthouse," said Larry. "You are invited if you want to come, however I don't think you have to. We talked to the judge and the prosecuting attorney and they both agree with our judgment of the case; however, they have to hear the tape Larry made and all the testimony of any witness."

"I will try to be there," said Mike. He then wrote down the time and date. After a few comments they hung up. Mike went back to work. He couldn't wait until it was all over. It was about three days before the hearing that a woman presented herself at the front counter of the police station.

"I would like to see the man you have in prison. His name is Jeffery Ross."

"And who are you?" asked Ron the officer that was at the entrance counter

"I am his wife Evelyn Ross," said Evelyn.

"Just wait here I will get the arresting officer," said Ron. He got on the phone and called Larry who was in his office.

"Larry," said Ron, "there is a woman here who wants to see your prisoner. She says that she is his wife." Larry showed up less than a minute later.

"Hi Mrs. Ross, " said Larry, trying to be friendly. "What can I do for you?"

"I would like to see my husband."

"He is in very bad condition," said Larry. "He feels that he has lost a very good friend, his wife and he has nothing left. I feel it would kill him to see you and hear you telling him that he has lost you."

"You don't understand," said Evelyn, now sounding like she was hurting more than Jeff. "He is not losing me. I'm afraid that I am losing him. This whole thing was my fault. Please let me see him"

"Alright," said Larry, "follow me." He then led her to the prison cell. When they got there Jeff was sitting on the bed with his eyes closed. Larry opened the cell door and let Evelyn in. He stood on the outside looking through the bars. As Evelyn walked in Jeff opened his eyes. Suddenly his face showed the pain he felt.

"Oh no," he yelled out with great sadness. Haven't I had enough pain today that I have to hear that I am going to lose my wife from her own mouth?"

"Oh, Jeffery darling," said Evelyn with a painful voice. "I love you. I will never leave you."

"But you said that if I cheated on you, you would divorce me," said Jeff. "

I put that in our marriage certificate to check if you were marrying me for my money," said Evelyn. "If you remember I am a Born-Again Christian. I will never divorce."

"Are you saying that you forgive me?" said Jeff.

"No," said Evelyn. "I am asking you to forgive me."

I don't understand," said Jeff. "What did you do that I should forgive?"

"I know you like the back of my hand. I love you with all my heart. You have a sweet and loving heart that does not like to be alone. You went with Sara only to have a companion. I should have thought of you before I thought of helping homeless children. I'm sorry. Forgive me. I quit the job and if I can help homeless children it will be here in the Fairlawn area, but only if we get you out of this and you come home and decide to go to work to keep busy." Larry who had left then for a second was just returning.

"You are being released on bond, so you can go home," said

Larry. "We will meet at the Courthouse at eight in the morning the day after tomorrow."

"Don't I have to pay some money to be released on bail?

"That is no problem," said Larry. "Your attorney has taken care of everything." Less than one hour later Jeff and Evelyn were settled in their sweet home. Later that day Larry called Mike. He explained to Mike all that occurred at the jail. He told Mike that he was still invited but didn't have to come. Mile decided to be there. He was sure there would be good news. Mike also knew the attorney who was handling the case. He had a fantastic good reputation. Mike was sure that Jeff would get off with a small price.

The next day went by very quickly. Mike met Larry at the courthouse. The session went by sooner than Mike expected. Evelyn's lawyer gave a fantastic speech. After every one testified to what they knew, the judge listed the death of Sara as an accident. Jeff was then released. Mike was glad it was all over. He then went back to the hospital. He was glad that this session with the police turned out with some smiles. That was what Mike wanted. He became a doctor to help people and see the happiness of the patients and their family when he helped them. As he entered the hospital he stopped off at the first floor first. He wanted to create some happy faces. As he entered he heard a woman crying. He entered the patient's room where he heard the crying. He found a man in bed and a woman with her head on the man's chest crying.

"Can I help you?" asked Mike, being surprised at what he saw.

"My husband is dying," said the woman with her voice full of tears. "He is my whole life. I don't know what I will do without him." Mike then walked up to the man in bed.

"My name is Dr. Costello," said Mike. "Can you tell me what your problem is?"

"My name is Todd, said the man. "I had a growth in my chest the size of a plum," They said that it was precancerous. Then after it was removed the ex-rays found that the bad infected fluid was spreading all over my chest and it was cancerous.

"They said that it was spreading so fast that I had only a few days to live."

"I would like to pray for you," said Mike. "I am a born-Again-Christian. Are you a Christian?"

"My wife Lena is a Born-Again-Christian," said Todd. "Me, I'm not sure what I am. "I have not seen any evidence of a supreme being. I wondered if it was made up so that the government could control people."

"How can you say that," said Mike. "You look around the world and see all the life that exists here. Do you think that by accident all the dirt that was here on earth was blown by a wind into a few living organs that accidently got together to become a living human or animal? God created us and set us free on this earth. We turned our backs on him. Since he is perfect he could not accept a sinner in heaven. That is why he sent Jesus to pay for our sins. Therefore, if you accept Jesus as your savior you will have a home in heaven."

"I never thought of that," said Todd. "Living bodies are too complicated to exist by accident. So, if I accept Jesus as my savior all my sins will be paid by him. But what sign would I get that I was accepted?"

"The Lord may answer one of your prayers before he takes you home with him."

"You are so right," said Todd with tears in his eyes. "I accept Jesus as my savior with all my heart. My greatest prayer is that he helps my wife get through all that may occur in the next few days." Mike then knelt down by the bed and said a prayer that mainly asked God to accept Todd and help him and his wife through whatever God now plans. After he finished he turned to Todd. "I promise you that God will give you a sigh that will tell you that you are saved. He always gives a message to anyone who just accepted Jesus." Mike then looked at the medical papers that were there on the wall. After viewing them he asked if it would be OK with them if he would do a final check on Todd.

"Of course," said Todd and his wife at the same time. Mike then ordered the nurse to take him directly to his operation room. Mike had seen something that interested him. He had seen that the bad cancerous fluid was spreading but so far had not left the chest cavity. Mike put Todd to sleep and then inserted into the cut that was there from the operation, a tool he had just obtained due to a problem he had earlier that year with another patient that had a similar problem. He then turned on the tool and it started to suck all the fluid out of Todd's chest. It only took twenty minutes until all the fluid in Todd's chest was removed. As fluid started to come back in he would suck it out. Soon the fluid that started in was clean like fresh water. Mike waited about fifteen minutes and seeing that the fluid that was coming into his chest was very little and it was clean, he then closed the cut he had opened. He then took him back to the hospital room where his wife was still waiting.

"What did you find?" asked his wife.

"I found something I had seen before," said Mike. "I have a drug that has a small chance of helping. Let's pray that his life is the gift that God gives him for accepting Jesus as his savior." Mike then went up to his office area to check on some of his patients. The next morning Mike stopped at Todd's hospital room. As he walked in Todd's wife Lena ran up to Mike and gave him a great hug.

"Thank you so much," said Lena. "You are an angel. You have saved my husband's life. How can we ever thank you?"

"You got this all wrong," said Mike. "It was a gift for Todd's accepting Jesus as his savior. I was just a tool. God did this as a sign of Todd's acceptance of Jesus. Why are you saying that Todd is saved?"

"The nurse came in here and said she was amazed how much Todd had recovered," said Lena. "She checked all his vital signs and said that he was back to normal. He probably could go home in a few days." Mike then left to check on his other patients. He felt very happy. This is what he wanted. It was to see people smile, not solving crimes that made people sad. Several days went by. Todd was soon well enough to go home.

The days went by slowly. The winter months were worse than normal. Mike had difficulty going to work. Soon April came. The days became more normal. Mike went back to his normal happy days. Larry called once to say that he may want him to help him. There was a problem where a young girl had disappeared. To Mike's joy they found her alive and well. It was on a beautiful Sunday that Mike went to church as usual. As he pulled in to park he saw a young man on the corner of the church walkway, looking one way and then turning the other way. Mike parked his car and walked up to him.

"Are you having a problem?" said Mike, "can I help you?"

"Yes," said the man. "I am looking for the entrance to the church. The door on my right is locked and the one on my left says it is for disabled members."

"You are not from this area are you?" asked Mike.

"No, I am not," said the man. "I am here in Fairlawn Ohio for a few days for a short job. I am a Christian and want to go to church, but I can't find the front door."

"On the right past the closed door is the main entrance way," said Mike. "The closed door is the door to the sports room. Come with me. I can use the company. I usually go with my parents but they are currently out of town. Come and sit with me. We will go in the closet door. My name is Mike Costello. I am a medical surgeon for University Hospital."

"My name is Joel Brendon. I am an Inspector. I graduated as a detective. I work for the Crime Investigation Department for the Orlando Detective Agency. I have been solving crimes for six years. I have been solving crimes for small town police stations all over America. I am so sick and tired of traveling and being alone for those years." Mike led Joel through the side door, then down the hallway and into the church main room and they went to the fourth aisle row of seats where Mike usually sat when he attended the church service. Mike went into the second seat and let Joel sit on the end seat. Mike then introduced Joel to the two members that always sat in front of him. After some small talk he introduced Mike to the two that sat behind him. After they settled down Mike got an Idea.

"Joel," said Mike. "How long do you think you will be on the job you have here in Ohio?"

"Oh, that job got canceled," said Joel. "I was going home today but I decided to go to church and then leave tomorrow morning. What do you have in mind?"

"I was wondering," said Mike, "if you would like a permanent job here in Ohio."

"I would love that," said Joel. "However, most small police departments just need an investigator for a short time."

"I think I can talk to a friend of mine to consider an investigator for a full time job," said Mike. The Fairlawn police department is not that small. The last I heard they need a police man. Maybe with your background and education you could do both. Let's get together tomorrow morning. I will call my friend Lieutenant Larry Benten and see what he thinks." Mike stopped talking because the service started with the music played by the church band. Every 0ne joined in singing the song. The words to the song were displayed on the screen in the rear of the church altar. Five different songs were played. After the band stopped playing the pastor came up to the stand that was in the center of the altar and preached the sermon he had prepared for that day. After the sermon a final prayer was said and the people were released. Mike and Joel walked out to where their cars were parked.

"I will pick you up at your hotel room at about nine O'clock tomorrow morning," said Mike. "I will tell you what information I will have for the job I think you can have." Mike got his room number and his cell phone number. "Before we part, how about having lunch with me? I know a restaurant that has wonderful food. It's on me."

"How can I refuse that," said Joel. Mike then took Joel to Bravo Cucina Italiana. They had a great lunch. While eating, they each learned more of each other. After lunch Mike took Joel to his car at the church parking lot and said goodbye.

The next morning, at approximately eight O'clock Mike called Larry.

"Hi Larry," said Mike when Larry answered the phone. "Are you busy today?"

"No," said Larry, "what can I do for you today?"

"I ran across a gentleman who has several years' experience in crime investigation. He works for a company in Orlando that solves crime for small police departments all over the country. He is tired of traveling. He would like to have a job in one location. I think you can use one like him. He told me one of his important subjects in college was to learn what to look for and how to recognize good evidence. I think that with his experience and education he could be one of your officers when not checking a Crime Scene."

"I would like to talk with him," said Larry. "How soon can you get him here?"

"I can have him in your office in less than an hour," said Mike. "I am going to pick him up at nine O'clock."

"See you then," said Larry. After they hung up Mike went to the hotel where Joel was staying. It was still early so he decided to wait in the lobby until nine. He was surprised to see Joel in the lobby.

"Hay," said Mike. "You are up early."

"I couldn't sleep with the anticipation of this morning's activity," said Joel."

"Come and follow me in your car. I don't know how long either one of us will be at the police station," said Mike.

"Let's go out and show me your car that I must follow," said Joel. "My car is a light gray Cadillac." Mike took Joel to his own car and he drove him to his car. Ten minutes later they were at the police station. Mike took Joel to Larry's office.

"Larry," said Mike starting the introductions, "this is Joel Brendon, and Joel this is Lieutenant Larry Benten.

"So nice to meet you," said Larry. "Please come into my office. Mike, please excuse us, I would like to talk to Joel in private. I would like his information to be private. I will promise him that whatever he tells me will stay private.""

"That's fine with me," said Mike. "I have a lot to do at the hospital." Mike then left.

"Come and sit down Joel," said Larry. "You can just call me Larry. "Mike has been a great help to us. He has a fantastic sense when it comes to getting evidence especially at the crime scene. He knows exactly where to look and has a fantastic ability to recognize evidence. Now, tell me about your experience in this field."

"First of all I graduated with a degree in Criminal investigation," started Joel. "I had a course on what to look for in a crime scene. Some evidence is unrecognized as being important by an untrained officer." Joel then related to Larry five of his latest crime investigations emphasizing the evidence he found in each that helped close the cases. After Joel related all his history in crime solving, Larry told him what would be expected of him as an employee. After a short discussion Larry went to the final thing that had to be addressed.

"I would like to hire you," said Larry, "but we have to discuss salary. Since I think you want a full time job that makes it a little harder. Mike only works with us a week or so each month. However, since we paid Mike a pretty high salary when he worked for us being a surgical doctor, here is what I am going to do. Have a little patience while I do it." Larry then went onto his computer and came up with a figure. "I have added all the money we paid to Mike in one year. Since you will also be a part time police officer I will add this much. Now I will divide this by 26 and this will be what we will pay you every two weeks. Is this acceptable?"

"I will accept that for now," said Joel, "considering the fact that I will be in line to get a raise when I prove that I am better than you expect." Joel did not tell him that the amount that they were talking about was about ten percent greater than what he was currently making.

"That sounds fine to me," said Larry. "When can you start?"

"I have to find a place to live," said Joel. "How will next Monday do?"

"That is perfect," said Larry. Joel then left and went directly to the real-estate agency he had seen on Market Street. It only took two days for Joel to find a nice three bedroom ranch to rent.

Mike lost track of what was happening at the police station. He also decided not to ask. It was none of his business. Although he had heard that they had hired a detective to work with Larry. He was extremely busy at the hospital. He had two surgeries each week. He also spent any free time he had on the second floor bringing some cheerful moments to badly injured patients. It was several months later in the last week of April that Mike got a call from Larry.

"Hi Larry," said Mike as he answered the phone, "are you in trouble again. Didn't the fellow I recommended to you do a good job?"

He is doing a fantastic job," said Larry. "But that is not the reason I am calling you. Didn't you get the invitation to David and Vanessa's wedding?"

"I haven't checked my mail for a couple of days," said Mike. "There is so much trash being mailed. I will check my mail as soon as we hang up."

"I'm sure you were invited," said Larry. "I called to ask you if you want to go with us. You know that it is in South Bend Indiana."

I would love to go with you," said Mike. "I'm sure that if they invited you they would invite me too. We were the couple that saved her life."

"Sounds great," said Larry. "I will pick you up at eight on Wednesday morning, May seven. The wedding is on May tenth. That will give us a day to visit every one and ready for the rehearsal dinner on Friday"

"I will be ready," said Mike. "By the way, how is Joel doing?"

"I will tell you all about it on our way to Indiana," said Larry.

May seventh came up faster than Mike expected. He was ready when Larry came to pick him up. His wife was with him.

"Hi Sylvia," said Mike as soon as he entered the car. "It's so nice to see you. It's been too long."

"Yes, it has been too long," said Sylvia. "If you find yourself a wife we could double date."

"Someday perhaps," said Mike. "I understand that you still keep in touch with my sister Cathy."

"Yes," said Sylvia, "we text each other all the time. However, she is very busy so we don't speak over the phone often."

"Tell me about it," said Mike. "I have a hard time speaking to her. She is always busy with her boyfriend." Soon they were on the road to Indiana. Sylvia related the times she actually talked with her.

"By the way Larry," said Mike. "Tell me how Joel is doing"

"He turned out ten times better than what you thought of him. The first two cases we had he immediately went into the crime scene and looked around. Somehow, he knew exactly where to look. He found the evidence that put the criminals in jail. We only spent two days on each crime. He is fantastic. The other crime took a little longer, but it probably would not have been solved without him."

"I'm glad it worked out," said Mike. "I hated to see sadness like you see around a crime scene. I became a doctor so that I could make people smile and not cry."

"That's enough of this crime talk," said Sylvia. "Tell me about some of these patients that you helped smile at." Mike then told of the most interesting patients he had. Larry told them of the most interesting crimes he investigated. They enjoyed the discussions so much that they didn't notice the time that went by. They did stop for a sandwich for lunch and then return on the trip. Because they enjoyed the time together so much they arrived at the hotel in South Bend Indiana not feeling tired from the long trip. After parking the car they walked into the hotel and headed toward the registration counter. They never got there. Dave, Vanessa and a young woman were in the lounge and when they saw Mike, Larry and his wife they got up and called out to them.

"Hey you guys," said David, "We are so glad to see you. We were hoping you would be here today."

"Hello Dave, Vanessa," said Mike. "Is this all a coincidence? I can't believe you are here waiting for us."

"We knew you were leaving today and we knew you would get here about this time," said Dave. "We didn't want you to be here in a strange place by yourself. Anyway, I want you to meet my sister Regina. Regina this is Mike the doctor that saved Vanessa and this is Officer Larry and his wife Sylvia." They all shook hands and the females hugged each other. Mike was shocked at how beautiful Regina was. "Mike, "continued Dave. "Regina will be your partner during this wedding."

"Well it is nice to meet you Regina," said Mike, "but what does Dave mean that I will be your partner? Is there some kind of game we are going to play?"

"Well since Regina is Maid Of Honor," said Dave, "and you are going to be the Best man, you will have to stick together and get to know each other."

"I'm the best man?" said Mike, being extremely surprised. "How can that be? I didn't know that. I don't have a Tuxedo to attend as a Best Man.

"I think if you don't have a good enough suit to attend we will go and rent one," said Dave. "What did you bring with you?"

"I brought a dark blue suit," said Mike.

"If you have a matching tie," said Dave, "that will be fine. We are not wearing tuxedos, at least I am not. That is old fashion to me."

"If that is OK with you," said Mike, "so let it be"

"We had better go and check in," said Larry. "We don't want to lose our rooms."

"Vanessa and I are going to the main office," said Dave. "We have to do some checking of the facilities we are going to use here in this hotel. We will see you here at the hotel cafeteria at six. Diner is on me." That said they left. Regina walked up to mike.

"I will stick with you," said Regina. "We have to get to know each other. After you check in we can sit in the cafeteria and have a drink while we talk."

"I have to bring my suitcase to my room and wash up a little." said Mike.

"I will wait right here for you," said Regina." I would like to spend time with you and have dinner with you." Mike didn't know how to say no to her under the circumstances of being her wedding partner. Mike then left and went to the room assigned to him. After putting his suitcase on the bed Mike went into the bathroom, washed his face, combed his hair and then he went down to meet Regina.

"I think it is too early to have dinner," said Mike.

"Let's go into the cafeteria and have a drink and get to know each other," said Regina. "When we feel hungry we can order dinner. Dinner is on me."

"No way," said Mike. This was one place he would say no. "I have never in my life let a woman pay for my dinner. I will not start now. If you insist I will get up right now and leave."

"You win," said Regina. "I will not be the one to break your record." After that they ordered a drink and Mike started the conversation.

"Please tell me about your life as a lawyer," said Mike. "Tell me what you do and some interesting experiences you have had." Regina told Mike about some unusual and interesting cases she covered. She explained that much of her time was spent protecting children. She told Mike about a few that ended up in the hospital beaten up near to death. It was my desire to find out and punish the ones who did it and the ones who let that happen. She told Mike how some cases left the children in the dark. She said that she made sure that they were treated with justice. I am also a Born-Again Christian and am spending my life to promote Christianity. Mike was very impressed with all that she told him. He felt she had a big loving heart.

"Now tell me about your experience helping police find a criminal," said Regina. Tell me about some of the cases you worked on."

"Incidentally I am also a Born-Again Christian," started Mike. "Anyway I am a surgical doctor. Most of my experience is with sick patients. Some need special treatment." Mike then told Regina about the few persons who arrived dead or had a problem that was leading to death. Mike then explained what drastic measures he had to take to save their lives.

"I understand, " said Regina, "that by pretending that a victim died when it was really alive, to trap a criminal in what he intended to achieve after the person had died."

"Yes, that worked for a couple of cases," said Mike and then continued to talk about strange hospital cases. Regina would not let him get away without talking about some police cases Mike had worked on. Mike decided that they had talked enough about their lives. "I am getting hungry and tired from the long trip," said Mike, "let's order and let me get some sleep. I'm tired of talking about our past lives. Then they ordered their dinner and ate quietly. They spoke only of what they expected for the future and they also spoke of the failure of our government. After dinner Mike excused himself and went to bed. The next morning Mike showered change into clean clothes and went down to the hotel cafeteria. To his surprise Regina was there holding a seat for him at a table. She had a soft drink she was drinking. Obviously, she had the drink waiting for Mike to come down from his room.

"What are you doing here so early," said Mike when he saw Regina.

"I was waiting for you," said Regina. "We have most of the day available before the rehearsal dinner which is at five this afternoon. I feel we can visit a few of the interesting places to see. I was born here but I have not reviewed South Bent since I was twelve. I would like to visit my favorite places.

"Well let's eat first," said Mike. They both ordered breakfast. Mike paid the bill and Regina then led Mike to her car. Regina drove through the town and was soon at the western part of the city. Mike was about to ask her where they were going when he saw a sign ahead of them. It was the direction to the city Zoo. Regina also saw the sign.

"I guess you now know where we are going," said Regina.

"I have not been to a zoo since I was a teenager," said Mike. "However, I feel we are out of line going here for a friend's wedding. We should be spending time with them"

"They will not be available until this evening," said Regina. "You would only be spending time in your hotel room or at the hotel cafeteria." One minute later they reached the zoo. Regina already had tickets. They were soon viewing the Zoo animals. After a while Mike relaxed and enjoyed the view of the different Animals. Mike was surprised how big some of the animals were. He was especially surprised at the size of the Antelopes. Mike was also surprised at the knowledge that Regina had of the animals. She gave a small dissertation for each animal they viewed. It took about two hours for them to see the complete zoo. After they left the zoo Regina started to drive back towards the hotel. It didn't surprise Mike when she stopped at a restaurant. It was almost noon.

"I guess you are getting hungry," said Mike. "Is this one of your favorite restaurants?"

"I have not been here for a long time," said Regina. "However,

I remember that I had a fantastic dinner here once. I have no idea what they will have for lunch. We need to have a very light lunch. We are going to have a large dinner this evening." Mike agreed and at the restaurant they each had only a light sandwich. After Mike paid the bill they left and headed back toward the hotel. To Mike's surprise Regina pulled over on a small side road and stopped in front of a building. Mike saw the sign at the top of the doorway which said, "South Bend Art Museum."

"I guess you are not ready to go back to the hotel," said Mike.

"It's only around One o'clock," said Regina. "I want to spend time with you here in the city where I can see your reaction to what we see. I want to get to know you better. That will be done better when we are alone together. I will explain it all later."

"Is there a lot to explain?" asked Mike.

"There is something about me you have to know," said Regina. "It is very important that we discuss this after dinner tonight."

"I can hardly wait," said Mike, thinking that she was kidding or had something she expected of him. The tour through the museum was very delightful to Mike. He had never been through an art Museum. Mike was starting to feel that going on this tour with Regina was great. He was not only happy to spend time with Regina he also was thrilled with all that he saw that morning. It was about three thirty when Regina finally returned to the hotel.

"Go get cleaned up and I will meet you at five at the restaurant," said Regina when they entered the hotel lobby.

"See you later," said Mike as he went to his hotel room. After a quick shower and a change of clothes Mike went down to the restaurant. It was five minutes to five. Sitting at the center of the longer side of the table was Regina. When she saw Mike she waved for him to come and sit beside her.

"Hi Mike," said Regina, "come and sit here besides me." Mike did as asked.

"How are you this morning?" asked Mike.

"I'm fine," said Regina. "I am looking forward to the marriage rehearsal. It normally is before the rehearsal dinner but it was changed because one of Vanessa's important relatives couldn't make it on time."

"I understand," said Mike. "I was wondering about that." The dinner was great. Vanessa's father gave a loving speech. A couple of other female relatives also gave a romantic speech. Soon they were at the rehearsal. It was over quickly and as they were leaving, Regina grabbed Mike by the arm.

"We have to talk," said Regina. "Let's go to a private area."

"I agree," said Mike. "I feel like I'm up in the air about our relationship.My room will be the best place during this time of day."

"Great Idea," said Regina. "We can be alone the rest of the evening." A few minutes later they entered Mike's room.

"Before I start telling you about myself," started Regina. "I want to know what you think about our relationship. What you are thinking may change what I will tell you. It may be that I don't have to tell you anything. If you have no feelings for me there would be no reason for me to say anything."

"I'm not sure I understand but I will be honest with you about my feelings for you," said Mike. "I am very attracted to you. "I have great feelings for you. However, I wonder if you really have any feelings for me."

"You wonder if I have feelings for you," said Regina. "I have great feelings for you. I am in love with you. I have never felt this way for anyone else. That said, I must tell you how we must continue our relationship. We must continue our relationship like the two days I had in Paris. I went to Paris with the intention to enjoy it with all of my ability. I enjoyed it with all of my heart. I did not hold back anything. I spent the time there being in love with Paris. I enjoyed it completely ever knowing that I would have to leave and come home. I was looking for a great memory. Our relationship must be the same. We must spend the time we have like two people madly in love. We must hold back no romantic action as long as it was within acceptable Christian actions."

"You lost me," said Mike. "Are you saying that we should act like two people madly in love but are planning to separate in two days with only memories?"

"You have it right," said Regina.

"I don't understand," said Mike. "If two people are madly in love why would they not want to spend the rest of their lives together?"

"I'm sorry," said Regina, "I hoped I would not have to explain this to you."

"Well I'm sorry but I need an explanation," said Mike. "I don't want to spend romantic time with you then end up with a broken heart."

"I'm sorry, Mike," said Regina. "I was hoping you would accept this as a trip to Paris or a trip to lover's lane."

"I'm sorry but I don't understand that if you love someone with all your heart you would not want to spend the rest of your life with him," said Mike with a big question look in his eyes.

"I'm sorry," said Regina. "I was hoping I would not have to tell you this to you. "A few people that I told of my position in this world thought that I was crazy or mentally sick."

"Well, said Mike. "I am all ears. Since I've known you I have seen no sign of ether."

"Well here it is," started Regina. "I understand that you are a Born-again-Christian. It means that you have accepted Jesus Christ as your savior. It also says that you gave your soul to Jesus. I did a little more. I gave my soul, my heart and my whole body to Jesus. My body is only a tool to be used to do God's job here on earth. I gave my word to God that my body was his to be used to do whatever he wanted it to do. I became a lawyer so that I could have some respect from the people. I do not go to court to fight criminals. I go to court to save Christians from non-believers. Most of my time is spent as a children's teacher teaching Christian values to the youth of this country. My job is to do what I can to bring this country back as a Christian country."

"I am shocked at what you have told me," said Mike. "So is it alright to have a short term romance?"

"God is Love," said Regina. "Love is the only thing that my body desires. My body is now part of God. Love is God's greatest asset. The reason that you are saved is because of God's infinite love."

"I think I understand," said Mike. "You are like a priest. You dedicate your whole life to God."

"I guess that is a way to put it," said Regina. "So now can we start our two day romance?"

"I'm ready," said Mike. "How do we start?"

"Like this," said Regina. She threw herself into Mike's arm and put her lips against his. Mike at first wanted to pull away, but then the soft sweetness of her lips made him react with a loving response. They then sat on his bed and continued hugging and kissing. Soon Mike felt her tongue try to force itself into her mouth. Mike opened his mouth and let her tongue play with his. This went on until early in the morning. When it was around three Regina pulled away.

"We had better go to bed," said Regina. We have a wedding to go to tomorrow. We don't want to go looking tired." They both then walked to the door. Regina was about to kiss him goodbye when Mike pulled away.

"We had better not kiss goodbye," said Mike. "I probably would not let you go." Regina smiled and left.

The next morning Mike went down to the hotel cafeteria for breakfast. When he walked into the cafeteria he saw Regina sitting at a table by herself. He joined her.

"Good Morning sweetheart," said Mike as he sat down. "How are you this morning?"

"I am a little tired," said Regina. "As I'm sure you are also."

"A little," said Mike. "I didn't get much sleep last night. Not only because we went to bed late but I enjoyed reliving the time we spent together."

"I know," said Regina "wasn't it great?"

"It was the best time I have had my whole life," said Mike. "Do you want to go up to my room after breakfast? We have all morning before the wedding starts."

"I think we had better not," said Regina. "I think we are already too tired. We have to be up and bright during the wedding. Besides, I have several phone calls I have to make." Regina finished her breakfast first. Mike insisted that he pay for the meal. Regina then got up and as she left she said, "See you at the wedding." Mike then went up to his room, turned on the TV to listen to the news. He didn't hear much. He had fallen asleep after the first minutes of the news. When he woke up it was noon. He dressed in his dark suit with a black tie and went down to the cafeteria. No one he knew was there. Regina was not in sight. He had a hamburger and left. He was a little later than he wanted to be. He entered the church and headed for the isle leading to the Altar. The pastor was in the middle of the altar. Dave was standing on the right side, and Regina was standing on the left side of the altar. Mike walked down the aisle and headed for the right side of the altar. As he walked up he smiled at the pastor, Regina, and David. He softly said "Hi." Once settled in his place he looked at Regina. He couldn't believe how beautiful she was in that fantastic dress she was wearing. It seemed like a long time but it was only a few minutes when the music started and soon Vanessa, led by her father, came down the aisle. Vanessa looked so beautiful that even Mike who spent most of the time since he got there looking at Regina could keep his eyes off of her. The ceremony was so very beautiful. It soon was over and they all went to the church hall. At the hall Mike and Regina sat together next to the bride and groom. The dinner was fantastic. During the dinner Vanessa's father gave a very loving speech. After the dinner the music started to play. Dave and his bride started to dance first. No one interrupted them during the first song. When the second song came on a few people started to dance. One by one they interrupted Dave and Vanessa to dance with them. Mike and Regina started to dance. Mike was pleased that Regina held him close and tightly. After a few dances they also had a dance with the newly wedded. Mike and Regina wanted to dance all the songs that evening. They were in each other's arms most of the time. However, they were interrupted several times by people who wanted to dance with Mike. They had learned that Mike was the doctor who had saved Vanessa's life. When not dancing many of the relatives of Regina, Dave, and Vanessa went up to Mike and introduced each other. They all knew who Mike was. The evening went by too quickly. Mike was hoping it would last longer, however soon it was midnight. After visiting all the other tables, Dave and Vanessa approached Mike and Regina.

It was so nice for you guys to come to our wedding," said Dave. "I also thank you and was very happy that you accepted being my best man. After all there would not be a wedding if not for you. We will never forget you. We pray that you will find the happiness you gave us. God bless you." That said they left. Mike, Regina as well as Larry and Sylvia started to leave.

"Mike," said Larry as they were walking out the door. "We are leaving at eight o'clock tomorrow morning. Please be ready. If you want to stay there is a train that could take you home. Don't spend too much time with Regina tonight. Get up early and have breakfast so that you are ready by eight."

"I'll be there," said Mike. "I will meet you at the hotel cafeteria." After they parted Regina turned to Mike.

"Are we going to my room or yours?" asked Regina.

"Let's go to my room," said Mike. "Didn't you hear? I have to be ready to leave at eight tomorrow morning." They soon were at Mike's room and back to their romantic activity. They were in each other's arms all the time. Their lips and tongues were together all night. It was around three in the morning when Mike's lips parted from Regina's mouth.

"Have you had enough," asked Regina.

"I will never have enough," said Mike. "But I have to be ready by eight or I will have to take a train home."

"I guess all good things come to an end eventually," said Regina as she got up and headed for the door. At the door she turned around and asked Mike. "Kiss me goodnight and goodbye." Mike bent over to kiss her and then stopped. "I had better not," said Mike, "There is too good of a chance that I would not let you leave." Regina smiled and left. Mike went directly to bed.

Mike woke up in the morning and looked at the clock. He was still half asleep. Suddenly he realized that it was seven thirty. He realized that if he wasn't down stairs by eight he would have to take a train home. He quickly showered, got dressed, closed his suitcase and quickly went down stairs. He checked the cafeteria and saw no one. He then quickly went to the front entrance. He was happy to see Sylvia at the doorway with all their suitcases.

"Hi Sylvia," said Mike as he walked to the doorway. "I guess I made it in time."

"Larry went to get the car," said Sylvia, "so that we would not have to carry these suitcases halfway across the parking lot."

"I'm glad I made it in time," said Mike. "I don't think I could take the train home. I'm so tired that I can't think straight." Just then Larry dove up next to the door. He opened the trunk and put all the suitcases in the trunk.

"Hi Mike," said Larry when he grabbed Mike's suitcase. "Glad you made it in time. Did you eat breakfast before us this morning?"

"No," said Mike, "I got up at seven thirty. I just made it down here in time."

"I'm not surprised," said Sylvia. "We hardly saw you for the past two days. You spent them with Regina. What is going on with you two?"

"Let's get in the car and head for home," said Mike. "We have a long time to talk on the way home. Once we get moving

I'll answer all your questions." Once they got on the road Larry started to ask questions about Mike's time at the wedding for two days.

"Mike," started Larry. "We hardly saw you for the two wedding days we were here. Where were you most of the time? I know that you were with Regina, but were you two most of the time?"

"Well," said Mike. "Regina grew up in South bend. However, she has not been here for years. She wanted to see it while she had a chance."

"Where did you guys go?" asked Sylvia.

"First we went to the city Zoo. After reviewing all the animals there we went to one of Regina's favorite restaurants for lunch. After a great lunch she took us to the South Bend Art Museum. That was a very interesting trip. They had some very interesting paintings."

"All right," said Larry. "Let's get down to the more important times. You were gone Friday night and last night. You must have gone to bed very late at night. Were you and Regina fooling around?"

"I don't know what you mean by fooling around," said Mike. "If you are talking about sex, forget it. We are both born-again Christians. The thought never entered our minds."

"So what did you do all this time?" asked Sylvia.

"I admit that we love each other," said Mike. "We hugged and kissed like loving brother and sister."

"Do you guys have any plans on seeing each other again?" asked Larry.

"I don't think so," said Mike. "Don't you understand her? She has given her soul, her heart and her complete self to God. Her life is serving God.

"I would think that you have a broken heart," said Sylvia.

"I knew what to expect when we first met," said Mike. "She explained everything to me. We were to love each other and while we could we would enjoy each other's company. A few hugs and kisses were OK."

"Why don't you lay back and get some sleep while we travel," said Larry. "I can see that you can hardly talk. We will wake you when we stop for lunch." It was about twelve thirty when Larry stopped at the restaurant in a small town. When he parked the car and he and Sylvia got out, Larry called Mike. Mike was fast asleep comfortably in the back seat. He called twice and then shook his shoulder. Mike gave out a short mown and then went back to sleep.

"Let him sleep," said Sylvia. "We have no idea how long they stayed together last night. He could have just left Regina this morning."

"All right," said Larry. "We could get him a sandwich he can have when he wakes up."

"Good Idea," said Sylvia. "I'm sure that he will be very hungry when he wakes up. I would guess he didn't have breakfast." They went in and had a quick lunch. They got a nice Roast Beef sandwich and a cola for Mike. Mike had not moved since they went into the restaurant. Mike did not move during the rest of the trip. It was about five when Larry pulled up to Mike's house front door. He then opened the rear door and shook Mike till he opened his eyes.

"Wake up Mike," said Larry. "You are home."

"Are we home already," said Mike, still sort of in a trance. "That was quick."

"It was not quick," said Larry. "It seems short because you slept most of the way. It is a little after five. It is time for dinner. We bought you a Roast Beef sandwich. You can eat it for dinner. Then I suggest you go to bed."

"Thank you so much for all you have done for me," said Mike, getting up and stepping out of the car. After Larry handed Mike the food bag, Mike checked his pocket and brought out his house key. "I'm sorry to be such a burden on you. I enjoy being with you two. Good night."

"Good night," said Larry and Sylvia together. Larry then started his car and drove away. Mike entered his house and went directly to the kitchen. He realized that he was very hungry. He ate the sandwich and went directly to bed. The next morning Mike got up at eight O'clock. He was later than he normally was. He didn't have time to visit the second floor so he went directly to his office. He noticed that he had two possible operations to perform. When he went out into the hallway he heard a person sobbing. He went into the room that he thought the sound came from. He noticed that the person was a young girl named Caroline.

"Caroline sweetheart," said Mike. "You should be happy, not sad. You could be a lot worse. I will fix you so that you will forget you had a problem" Mike was looking at the chart to find out what her problem was. Then he remembered about her problem. He had been away from his job for too long. The hospital was waiting for Mike to remove the cancerous growth she had in her body. Mike then opened her folder and looked at the x-rays.

"I was going to get married next month. Now, I don't know if I will live until then," said Carolina, starting to cry again.

"Who gave you that idea," asked Mike. "I think I need to remove the cancerous growth before it can spread."

"The doctor who first checked me said that it was very bad and possibly fatal.

"That is the standard for doctors who only examine a patient," said Mike. "The reason is that if they say you are in good shape and they find that you are in bad shape he is looked at as a poor doctor. However, if he says that the patient is in poor condition and the patient survives no one questions him. Don't worry. I will take care of you. Let's get you into surgery. One thing is correct. We have to take care of it before it spreads." Mike and Vera then took her into the surgery room. After putting her to sleep he opened her stomach up to half of her chest. He wanted to make sure he got everything. Vera helped keep her opening wide so that Mike could see inside. The cancer tumor was about the size of a golf ball. He removed it and spent the next few minutes cleaning the area in her stomach where the tumor had grown. Mike cleaned the complete area so that nothing was left that could start the cancer again. After he felt sure that he cleaned everything, he closed and stitched the opening very tightly. He then covered her and had her moved to the recovery room. He felt very satisfied with his work to save Caroline. He then went into the rooms of his other patients. He began to feel back to normal. In the patient's rooms he acted back like he used to be. His jolly attitude brought a little relief to the patients. Feeling that he had helped them he went down again to the second floor back to jeering the patients. Three hours later Mike heard from Vera.

"Mike," said Vera, "I think you should know that your patient Carolina is awake and would like to talk to you."

"Tell her that I will be right there," said Mike. "Mike then went directly to the room that Vera had moved Caroline to. When Mike entered the room he went to the side of the bed.

"Hi Doc," said Caroline. "I couldn't wait to find out how I was doing. What did you do?"

"I found and removed all the cancerous cells. You are now completely free of any cancerous cells in your body. I also fixed it so that a cancerous cell could not exist in your body. I think when your surgery heals in about a week that you will be back to a healthy pretty lady. I think you will be well enough to go ahead with your wedding."

"How can I ever thank you?" said Caroline

"You have to thank God. I was only the tool that he used," said Mike. It was a week later that Caroline left the hospital as healthy as any other young woman.

On the way home that evening Mike thought of Regina. He felt a very strong affection for her, but as he was thinking he remembered his greatest love. He thought of Tina. He realized that he had never felt for anyone else what he felt for Tina

She gave his stomach something he had never felt before. It was a stomach movement like what they called butterflies in the stomach. When he was with her his thinking was hard to control. The thought made him realize that he didn't feel this way for Regina or anyone else. At that moment he told himself that he would not settle for any romance where he didn't feel for a girl the way he felt for Tina. With that in mind he drove home feeling a little relieved. After all, he decided that Regina was not the right one for him. At home he went directly to the kitchen for dinner. After dinner he sat in his family room to watch a movie. He never saw the movie. He fell asleep after the first ten minutes. When he woke up he noticed that it was nine thirty. He decided to go to bed.

The next morning Mike woke up ten minutes before his alarm went off. He got up and after a shower and new clean clothes he went downstairs to the kitchen. He was eating breakfast when Mike got a phone call.

"Hi Mike, " said Larry as Mike answered the phone.

"Hello Larry," said Mike. "You have another murder mystery to take care of?"

"Very funny," said Larry, thinking that Mike was trying to be funny. Mike however was serious. He could think of no other reason for the call. "I'm calling to see if you want me to pick you up Friday."

"What are you talking about?" asked Mike, puzzled by Larry's question.

"Oh no," said Larry. "Didn't you get the invitation? I'm guessing that you have not checked your mail since we got home from David and Vanessa's wedding."

"I just haven't had the time," said Mike. "I had so much to catch up on at work. It is always mostly trash. Hold up for just a minute and let me get the mail."

"Don't take too long," said Larry. "I am at work." It took two minutes for Mike to get the mail.

"I got the mail," said Mike. "I have the invitation to my sister's wedding. I also have a note from my father telling me that they left for Cleveland two days ago."

"Of course," said Larry. Your mother had to help set up the wedding. That is the duty of a mother. I will pick you up about two after lunch on Friday. I will also get a hotel room for both of us. I hope that is alright with you."

"That would be great," said Mike "See you then." Mike then hung up. The joyful feeling he had overcame his thoughts of Tina.

CHAPTER SEVEN

An Unexpected Turn of Events

During the four days before Friday, Mike found himself to be back with the joyful personality he had before Dave and Vanessa's marriage. The thought of his sister Katharine's marriage enlightened him completely. At the hospital he was a joyful and happy doctor. Friday finally came. Larry picked him up at two O'clock.

"Hi Mike," said Larry when he first saw Mike. "I got us two rooms at a hotel that is one block from the church where your sister will be married."

"That is great," said Mike as he got into the car with his suitcase. He then turned to Sylvia. "How are you doing, Sylvia? You look fantastic."

"I am doing great," said Sylvia, "and you look a lot better than you did the last time I saw you."

"This time I had eight hours of sleep," said Mike. "I also decided to forget Regina. That alone helped a lot."

"I'm glad your back to the Mike we know and loved," said Sylvia

"Thank you," said Mike. "This is very kind of you." It was around an hour later that they arrived at the hotel Larry had chosen. They got their suitcases and entered the hotel. They walked up to the desk. The desk clerk looked up at them as they entered.

"How may I help you?" said the clerk.

"We would like to get the rooms we have reservations for", said Larry. "We have one room for Mike Costello and one room for   Larry and Sylvia Benten.

"Yes," said the clerk. "I see it here. How long will you need the rooms?"

"We are here for the wedding that will take place tomorrow. We will probably leave on Sunday afternoon after a church service."

That will be fine" said the clerk. "Here are your keys. The rooms are next to each other on the second floor." Larry then turned to Mike.

"Look Mike," said Larry. "It is a little after three. They are probably doing the rehearsal right now. I don't want to go to the actual rehearsal. I'm suggesting that we leave at about four thirty and go to the church to be there for the rehearsal dinner."

"I think that is a good choice. I want some time to get ready for the rehearsal dinner and prepare for the great day tomorrow," said Mike.

"Alright," said Larry. "I will meet you here at four thirty."

Great," said Mike. "I will see you at four thirty." Mike then went to his room. He unpacked his suitcase and set aside the clothes he was going to wear that evening. He then hung up the dark blue suit he was going to wear the next day. After that, he sat down and watched the news on the TV that was provided in the room. At about four he cleaned up, put on the clothes he was to wear for that evening and headed down stairs. Down stairs he met Larry and Sylvia that were waiting for him.

"Just on time," said Larry. "I think we will walk to the church."

"It is nice outside now but would it be like late tonight when we come back to the hotel," said Mike. "Why don't you want to drive?"

"I went out and checked the distance," said Larry. "There are only three buildings on this block. The hotel is on one end and there is a small bookstore next to the hotel and the church takes up the rest of the block at the other end. I check the parking lot. It will depend on the place we would park as the distance to the church entrance. It could end up that we would have to walk farther from the parking place to the church than to walk from the hotel to the church."

"I don't have a car so I have to follow your direction," said Mike smiling to show that he was kidding. They then started to walk to the church. It was a shorter distance than Larry had said. They soon walked into the church hall that was used for the rehearsal dinner. As soon as they walked in Katherine got up and ran to her brother. She hugged him.

"Oh Mike," said Katherine. "I was worried that you could not make it. Mom said that you were on another trip. It is so good to see you."

"You remember Larry and Sylvia," said Mike, turning to them.

"Of course, I remember them," said Katherine as she hugged Sylvia and then shook hands with Larry. Ryan was right behind Katherine. He went up to Mike and hugged him.

How are you doing dad," said Ryan. "I hope you don't mind my calling you dad. After all, you will be there tomorrow night."

"That's fine son," said Mike following Ryan's line of thinking. "It is so nice to see you son."

Great," said Ryan. "I will let Kathy introduce you to the other members of this family."

"Come and follow me," said Kathy. "I want to introduce you to everyone."

"Is everyone here?" asked Mike.

"Yes," said Katherine, "we were waiting for you," she said, kissing her brother. She then led him to all the others sitting at the table that she knew were strange to him. She introduced her brother, as well as Larry and His wife to them all. The last one she introduced to Mike was her best friend Tammy. "I want you to meet my best friend Tammy. She is here by herself. You can't feel like you are a part of the celebration if you are alone. You will feel like you are outside looking in on the activity. So Tammy, how would you feel if Mike would be your partner for this wedding? You can attend everything together."

"Are you kidding," said Tammy. "I would be thrilled and feel honored to be his partner. Would he want to be my partner?"

"I would love that," said Mike. "I would love to go through the wedding day as a member of a young couple attending the wedding. I would be proud to have people think we are a young couple and see me with a beautiful young lady."

"That is settled then, said Kathy. After Mike sat down next to Tammy she went back to her future husband. Mike then took the opportunity to wave to his parents that sat across the table from him. They waved back.

"I will love to hear of some of the exciting experiences you have had," said Tammy. "I understand that you have saved several lives."

"First let's talk about you," said Mike. "You know a lot about me and I don't know anything about you."

"There isn't much to say about me," said Tammy. "I am attending Ohio State University. I am working towards getting a doctor's degree in teaching. I want to be a history teacher. As you know my brother is a teacher. We both love children. We want to do our best to teach the new members of America to know how to run it for its best future. Right now, as you know it, the future of America doesn't look that good."

"I know," said Mike. "Let's not talk about that. It will make this beautiful occasion less wonderful."

"I agree," said Tammy. "Now you tell me about your experience." Before Mike could start talking they began delivering the food. It looked so good and smelled wonderful.

"Let's wait until later," said Mike. "We have two days to talk about our lives." Just then Mike's father got up and gave a prayer.

"I thank you lord for this occasion," started Joseph Mike's father. "I pray that you bless all that are at this table. I also thank you lord for the food you have provided and I ask that you bless it. In Jesus name I pray." He then sat down and we all started to eat. When they were all almost done the waitress brought in the desert. It was a Strawberry cake. It was as delicious as the main meal. While we were eating the desert Carl Picket, Ryan's father, got up and gave a short speech on the wonderful lives Ryan and Katherine have and what a wonderful future they will have. He said he knew this because of the great love he knew they had for each other.

"That is the truth," said Mike.

"It is pretty obvious if you notice how they look at each other," said Tammy.

"I know," said Mike. "I have known it since I have spent some time with them. There are many other things that tell me how much they love each other." After the cake was all gone, Mike's father got up to address the group.

"Well everyone," said Mike's father. "The church will be open this evening until nine. You can go to the counter and get more coffee if you want. You can also stick around and spend time with your relatives or good friends. You all have to leave at nine. See you all tomorrow." He and Nicola, his wife, left for another room down the hall. They still had some preparations to do for the wedding tomorrow.

"We are going to the Hotel," said Larry. "We would like some drinks stronger than coffee. That said they left. Mike turned to Tammy.

"Tammy honey," said Mike. "I would like to spend more time with you. I would like to know you better. We only have a little more than an hour till the church closes."

"I agree with you. I would like to hear about your experiences. Why don't we go to the hotel," suggested Tammy. "I think I could use a beer or stronger drink."

"Do you want to go to my hotel room?" asked Mike, concerned at what she had in mind.

No," said Tammy. "I am a strong Born-Again-Christian. I just have friendship in mind."

"Thank God," said Mike. "You had me worried there for a while. I am a born-Again-Christian also. So, let's go to the hotel cafeteria. I think it is open till midnight." A few minutes later they settled at the Hotel cafeteria. The waitress came quickly

"What can I do for you?" asked the waitress.

"I would like a cold drink," said Tammy, "maybe just a Coke.

"We have a new drink that I recommend," said the waitress. "It is not only very tasty, but very healthy. They are only available online but I bought several for my favorite guests. It is called Boost. It has many vitamins in it. Would you like to try one?

"Sounds very interesting," said tammy. "OK, let's try one."

"How about you sir?" asked the waitress.

"I'll just have a beer," said Mike. A few minutes later the waitress brought them their drinks.

"Wow," said Tammy. "This is fantastic."

"Well maybe I will try one tomorrow," said Mike.

"Now maybe we should start talking about our lives," said Tammy, "I am dying to hear how you have saved lives."

"Are you sure you want to hear this boring information?" asked Mike.

"I would want to hear every little detail of what it took to save a life," said Tammy. Please start as if you were doing it now."

"I will if you promise to do the same thing about your past experience," said Mike.

"I promise," said Tammy. "If we will have time, after you tell your story."

"You are not an undercover newspaper agent," said Mike. "Are you planning to write an article about what I tell you?"

"That is a good Idea," said Tammy with a smile. "I have thought of writing a novel. Maybe what you tell me will help my imagination."

"Don't do it without showing it to me," said Mike.

"I promise," said Tammy. "So, let's get started."

"You know that I will be looking at your face as I tell you my story," said Mike.

"Why will looking at my face make a difference?" asked Tammy.

"There are three reasons," responded Mike. "First you are beautiful and I love looking at your face. Secondly, if you are bored it will show up on your face. No one could hide boredom. And third, I will see if you fall asleep. I will not awaken you."

"You are wrong on all three accounts," said Tammy.

"Alright then," started Mike. "I will tell you about a young lady. She was at a restaurant to get some breakfast, when suddenly she fell down on the floor. A waitress checked her and after noticing that she wasn't breading she called 911. Ten minutes later the ambulance came and brought her to the hospital. At the hospital they found that she wasn't breathing and that her temperature was very low. They called for a doctor to pronounce her dead. Fortunately, I was the only one available that early in the morning. I went down to the hospital emergency entrance. I quickly examined her and found that her body was still warm and that her skin was still soft and possibly alive. I then asked them to take her to my surgical room. On the way I met Sophia, the head of the hospital. Where are you taking this dead body? She asked me. I told her thatI wanted to try and revive her. Her body was still warm. Let me see what I can do, I answered her. She said that she will give me until tomorrow evening and then the body will be shipped to the undertaker. At my surgical room I hooked her up to the special equipment I had perched."

"You perched Hospital equipment?" asked Tammy.

When I was in college I took a course in possible surgical assistant equipment. I kept in touch and found a few that were very promising. The hospital here has a financial problem and would not let me buy them under the hospital. A couple of the gadgets that I wanted to buy were too expensive, and not yet approved. When I use them, I will describe what they are and do. I will not name them. The names are meaningless and hard to pronounce."

"I'm sorry," said Tammy. "Please continue."

"First I hooked her up to equipment that replaced the heart. It was hooked up to the main heart blood vessel and it replaced the heart. It pumped the blood through the body just as the regular heart did. I also connected a heart monitor to see if the regular heart started to beat. The next thing I connected was the air pump to her mouth. This device pumped air into her lungs and then helped the lung exhale. After I did that I opened her chest and replaced the heart veins that were blocked. If I remember right there were three blocked veins. I then brought her out to a second floor room. The next day Sofia came by and criticized me. He said that I was tying up equipment that could be used on live patients. She said that she would give me until tomorrow when she will get rid of the dead body. Can you imagine that? She had no idea that the equipment she was referring to was my equipment. I bought it with my own money. I was not using any hospital equipment. I was only using a hospital room.

"So, what happened that allowed you to keep her hooked up?" asked Tammy.

"She came by the next day," continued Mike. "I showed her that the patient's temperature was up a little. She said that I was wasting time and equipment. However, she gave me another day, the next day she came and was about to send the body down to the morgue. I told her that I was the doctor and if she took away my patient I would quit the job and charge her with interfering with a doctor. I will give you two more days only because I will not be here she said. Then I have several witnesses that will testify that she was dead when brought here and has been dead for three days. Fortunately, the next day her heart started to beat. Her temperature rose to near normal. I cut back the heart equipment twenty five per cent to see if her heart was ready to take over. It took two weeks for her to come back to normal. Are you bored to death?

"Not in the least. That is the most interesting experience I have ever heard," said Tammy. "Did you look at my face like you said you would?"

"Yes," said Mike. "You can hide your thoughts very well."

"Well what did your boss have to say about the results of your job saving the lady's life?" asked Tammy.

"Do you really want to hear more?" asked Mike.

"Someday," said Tammy. "I would like to hear your experience when you saved another person's life. By the way, thank you for giving me the fine details. The fine details made me feel like I was living it with you."

"All right," said Mike. "About two weeks later Sophia called me into her office. I thought that she would fire me for taking a chance that could hurt the hospital's reputation. However, she asked me to forgive her for interfering with his doctoral work. She gave me a salary raise and a raise in the doctoral position. Now it is your turn. Tell me about your experiences."

"After hearing your story," said Tammy, "I don't think I have anything to tell you. I don't have anything to tell you that will be close to what you have told me."

"Well, let's start with what you wanted to be as a teenager," asked Mike. What did you go to school for? And what is your dream of the future and why? And how far have you gotten toward what you want to do?"

"Well let me start from the first time I felt like doing something to solve a problem that bothered me," started Tammy. "I was around ten and in middle school, when a young boy was kicked out of school because he came to class wearing a tee shirt that had, Jesus is my king. The school I was in didn't believe in the constitution that gave us freedom of speech and freedom of religion. It bothered me because I had a thing for that young boy. I was only around ten but I think I was in love. I never saw him again. Since then I have wanted to stop that kind of action which happens in a lot of schools and organizations. So I always wanted to be a teacher so I went to college and became a teacher in our city high school. I had forgotten what had happened in my teenage romance. However, it happened in my present school. A kid said a quick prayer so that God would help him pass a test. Everything came back to me. When I complained they told me that if I insisted they would fire me. They said you are not a lawyer. So now I am going to school during the summer months to become a lawyer. That's my story."

"That is a pretty wonderful story," said Mike. "I have gained a great respect for you."

"Well I have enjoyed the time together," said Tammy. "I think it is time to go home. See you at the wedding tomorrow."

"Your car is at the church isn't it?" asked Mike.

"Yes," said Tammy. "It is near the church exit."

"Let me walk you there," said Mike. "I don't trust the city at night."

"You don't have to do that," said Tammy. "You have your room just a step away."

"I still will not let you walk back alone," said Mike.

"Alright," said Tammy. "I will let you walk me back if you will let me drive you back to the hotel after we get to my car."

"Well if that is all it will take to make us both happy," said Mike, "let's go."

"I can't wait to watch that wedding," said Tammy as they were walking to the church. "I never saw two other people that are so much in love."

"I know," said Mike. "I just loved to see that loving look in their eyes." They soon were in the car. Tammy drove Mike back to the hotel. When they got there Mike got out of the car and as he left he said. "Thank you and see you tomorrow."

"Listen," said Tammy as he walked away. "I will see you at the hotel at lunch time, about one. The wedding will not start until two. I will eat breakfast at home, but I feel that it would be so nice if we walked in as a couple."

"As you wish," yelled Mike back.

The next morning Mike stayed in bed until ten O'clock. He was not very hungry and realizing that he would be up until late tomorrow, he decided to get as much rest as he could. At about twelve thirty he went down to the hotel cafeteria. He was only there about five minutes when Tammy showed up.

"Hello," said Tammy as she walked and sat across from Mike. "Or should I say, good afternoon."

"Good afternoon," said Mike. "I just got here so I have not ordered yet."

"I think we should order something light," said Tammy. "We are going to have a fabulous dinner."

"Do you know what we are having for dinner tonight?" asked Mike.

"No," answered Tammy, "but I know the supplier."

"Then what do you suggest?" asked Mike.

"How about some Mother's Oats and coffee," said Tammy?

"Sounds good to me," said Mike. They both ordered the smallest order and were soon eating their lunch. It was a quarter to two when they finished eating and left the hotel.

"I am so excited, I find it hard to walk," said Tammy. On their way to the church Mike turned to Tammy.

"I was wondering," said Mike. "Why is it so important for you to go to the wedding with a companion? I know that it is nice, but it seems a little more important to you than normal."

"I hate that when I'm alone that those young eggheads think that I am available. The last time I went to a party one of the young fellows wanted to hug me and acted romantically. I told him that I had a boyfriend but that he couldn't make it today. Do you know what he said? He said, "I won't tell you if you don't.""

"All right, we will be a loving couple," said Mike. "I kind of like the idea. However, I understand your problem. For one you are very beautiful and secondly you are a very joyful person."

"That was very sweet of you to say," said Tammy, "You lie so sweetly." Before he could answer they arrived at the church. Tammy put her arm under Mike's arm and they walked into the church. Inside they started to walk down the church aisle towards the church stage. There were people sitting on both sides of the Isle. Mike did not recognize most of them. On the stage, the pastor stood in the center of the stage, Ryan stood on the right side of the stage, behind Ryan, stood his best man, and on the left side of the stage stood the maid of honor. Mike noticed that the first two seat rows were mostly empty. Mike's mother was in the first row and Larry and his wife were in the second row. Mike led Tammy down the aisle. Mike felt very strange. He felt that someday a father will be leading the love of his life down the aisle just as he was leading Tammy. When they got to the second row Larry and Sylvia moved over and let Mike and Tammy have the end seats. A few minutes later Ryan's mother and father came and sat in the front row with Mike's mother. They were there only a few minutes when the music started. It was obvious that they were waiting on Ryan's family. Because of the music, everyone stood up and looked towards the rear of the room. Sure, enough there was His father leading Katherine down the aisle. Mike was amazed at how beautiful his sister Katherine looked in her wedding dress. He felt so happy for her. Mike noticed that his father was walking slower than he had to and looked very tired. Mike figured that his dad must be very tired from all that they did the last three days. When they finally got to the first aisle Mike's father kissed Katherine on the cheek and after a big hug he went and sat with his wife in the front row. Katherine then walked the three steps onto the stage and walked up to Ryan. The pastor started a speech. It was a long speech like it was a Sunday day sermon. It was about love, how when married that they were one person and that no one could separate what God had put together. He brought up a few other Biblical commandments. It was about a half hour or more long. Finally, he turned to Ryan and Katherine.

"Ryan," he said, "will you take Katherine as your lawful wife?"

"Yes," said Ryan. "I promise that I will love her with all my heart and take care of her the rest of my life." Ryan then put the ring on her finger.

""Katherine," the pastor said, "will you take Ryan as your lawful husband and love and obey him the rest of your life?"

Mike was shocked. He thought that they had eliminated, to obey, from the church requirement. Although he realized that the bible mentioned it several times.

"Yes," said Katherine, "I promise to be true to him, love him and obey him the rest of my life." She then put the wedding ring on his finger.

"With the power given me by the Lord I now pronounce you husband and wife. You may now kiss your bride." Ryan gave Katherine a great kiss and as soon as they parted the music started. Arm in arm Ryan and Katherine started to walk down the aisle. At the other end they stopped and turned to face the stage. A church member was leading the people one row at a time. Each person then stopped hugging and wished Ryan and Katherine a good life. It took about fifteen minutes before all the people had passed Ryan and Katherine. After Mike, Tammy and most of the people congratulated Ryan and Katherine, they walked across the hallway into the celebration room. After looking around inside and seeing brackets on the far wall he realized that the celebration room was really the church's Sports Room, probably the basketball Court. At the end of the room under the windows was a narrow table with chairs on the wall side only. Obviously, thought Mike, it was the area for the bride and groom and the other members of his wedding group. On the left side was the band. On the left before the band were two tables with four chairs on each side. On the right there were five tables. Larry had gone there ahead of them. He was standing by the table that was next to the band. Larry was waving at them. Mike, Tammy, and Sylvia went to the table where Larry stood. He had found the table with our name on it. Mike, Tammy, Larry, and Sylvia were on the wall side of the table. Mike's mother and father were on the aisle side of the table. Ryan's parents were next to Mike's parents. It was about fifteen minutes later when the bride and groom came into the room. The bride and groom sat in the center of the narrow table by the windows. The best man sat next to Ryan and the maid of honor sat next to Katherine. Four other friends also sat at the table, two on each side. A few minutes later, Mike's mother came in and sat down across from Mike.

"Hi, mom," said Mike, "where is dad?"

"He had to go to the bathroom, said Mike's mother. "This has been too great of a job for him. He has been very quiet and very slow in walking or any motion all day today. I have never seen him so quiet. I can't wait until this is over and I can take him home."

"Let's not let Kathy know that dad is not feeling well," suggested Mike. "We don't want to spoil her honeymoon."

"I'm sure your dad wants to dance one dance with his daughter," said Mike's mother.

"It will be up to him to act like he is well," said Mike. A few minutes later the dinner was distributed to everyone. A little time went by. Everyone had not finished their dinner when the band started to play. Ryan and Katherine got up to dance. Apparently, they did not overeat. No one disturbed them during the first dance. However, after the first song finished and the second song started you could see the audience moving up to get the chance to dance with Ryan or Katherine. They delayed a little knowing that the family would want to go first. It surprised Mike that he saw his father go up first. When he had interrupted the dance he waved for his wife to come and dance with Ryan while he danced with Katherine. Mike could tell that his dad was having a hard time. When the song was over Mike and Tammy moved in.

"Sorry to interrupt your dance," said Mike, "but I thought that I had better got my turn in before you got tired."

"I will not get tired," said Katherine. "This is my day. I will dance until I fall over." After that song Ryan's family moved it. After they were done the rest of the people moved it. Mike danced the rest of the night with Tammy. No one cut in on them. It is amazing how time flies by when you are having fun. It was almost midnight when Ryan and Katherine started to make the final rounds. They went to all the tables, one at a time, going to the table where Mike Tammy and their parents were last. They all hugged and all wished them a great Honeymoon. After that they left. Mike's father never stood up like the others had done. Fortunately, Katherine was too excited to notice. Larry turned to Mike and Tammy.'

"Listen," said Larry, "we decided to stay at the hotel tonight and go to church tomorrow morning. After the service we will go to lunch and go home late in the afternoon."

"I was thinking the same thing," said Mike. "What do you think about Tammy?"

"I would love to expand the party as long as we can," said Tammy. "I'm with you."

"How about you mom and dad," asked Mike. Are you with us?"

"I would love that," said Mike's mom, "but is your father able to stay awake another day?"

"We will see how he feels tomorrow morning," said Mike's mother. I'm glad we parked the car here at the church. I can drive your father to the hotel."

"I think Tammy and I will go with you," said Mike. "I will drive your car to the hotel. You may have trouble getting dad up to his room. Tammy's car is at the hotel"

"I thought you would never offer," said Mike's mother. "What about your car, where do you have it parked?"

"I didn't drive," said Mike "I came with Larry. I will go home in your car and if dad is not well enough to drive, I will drive." Mike then got his father's car keys. Tammy, Mike, and Mike's mother, then got Mike's father in the back seat. There Mike's mother would hold him. They soon got to the hotel. They carried Mike's father into the hotel's waiting area. Mike went up to the gentleman at the front desk. He expanded what had happened and checked out for himself and his mom and dad. While Tammy stayed in the lobby to watch over Mike's dad, Mike and Mike's mother went upstairs to pack up their belongings. They came down just as Larry and Sylvia walked in. They walked there from the church. His car was parked at the hotel,

"Hi Mike," said Larry. "How is your dad?"

"I'm afraid he is not well," said Mike. "I don't think we can stay here tonight and go to church with you tomorrow. Tammy, why don't you go with Larry and Sylvia? I don't think you want to go alone. I also feel you should go as originally planned."

"We would love to have you come with us," said Sylvia.

"Thank you," said Tammy. "I don't like to go anywhere alone."

"Please help me get my father in his car," said Mike. Before he lifted his father Mike turned to Tammy. "I wish I could have spent more time with you Tammy. Perhaps we will meet again someday. We are not that far apart and we are now relatives."

"It was nice spending these two days with you," said Tammy. "However, I will spend a great amount of time out of town at college. "Take care," she said as she left for the elevator. Larry grabbed Mike's dad by his feet and Mike grabbed him under his armpit. Mike's mother had left to bring the car up to the front door. Slowly they placed Mike's father in the back seat with his wife.

"Are you going to need help getting him in his house," asked Larry.

"Thank you Larry, but it is already past midnight. Mother and I will do fine." Mike then got into the front seat and started to drive home. It was almost two O'clock when they got home. With great struggle getting Mike's father out of the car, they got Mike's dad in the family room.

"Let's leave him here on the couch," said Mike. "I will get all the equipment that I need to see what his problem is." They laid him on the couch and Mike got the equipment. He first checked his temperature. It was higher than Mike had hoped. He then checked his blood. He couldn't check very much but he could tell that it showed some problem. He then checked his blood pressure and it was high.

"What did you find?" asked Mike's mother.

"I think dad has a very serious infection somewhere," said Mike. "I wanted to wait until tomorrow but I don't think I can. Let me call the hospital ambulance. I think I need to get him to the hospital where I can give him medication and have instruments to get a better picture of what his problem is. I think you should stay home. You will only be in the way. You can't go to every place we put dad."

"Never in my life," said Mike's mother. "I am going to be on his side day or night until he comes home." She put it so strongly that Mike stopped trying anymore. Ten minutes later the ambulance arrived. They did some testing and agreed with Mike to bring him to the hospital. Fifteen minutes later they had Mike's father in Mike's operation room. He placed his mother in a waiting room. He hooked up the equipment like the heart monitor, the blood pressure monitor, and the body temperature thermometer. His initial indication pointed to his father having a very serious infection in his body somewhere. He suspected that it was on the left side of his stomach. He could not prove it until morning when the lab was open, so that he could get an ex-ray of his stomach area. Vera, his nurse, was with him most of the time helping him with all that had to be done. She did give Mike's father a shot in the arm that would fight any infection. Mike then got a room and made sure he had a soft pilled chair there for his mother. He moved his dad there and then got his mother to sit next to her husband. The night went by very slowly. It was eight in the morning when Mike moved his dad to the lab for the Ex-rays. When he got back, he went in to talk to his mother. She was awake sitting in the soft chair.

"Mom," he said. "I have taken dad to get an ex-ray of his body. That will tell us where his infection is. It is eight O'clock. Do you want some breakfast?"

"No, said his mother. I'm not hungry. I don't think I could eat anything until I know what your father's problem is, and how soon it can be cured.

"You have to eat," said Mike. "We don't want you sick either."

"After the ex-ray you tell me what your dad's chances are."

"The instrument this morning told us that the infection had settled a little," said Mike. "It shows that our medication is working. I have also sent some of dad's blood for a blood test. I should know everything by noon." That afternoon Mike received the results of the ex-rays. It showed that Mike's father had a very serious infection around his colon However, the ex-ray did not show what the problem was. Mike found a strong drug that was developed for that kind of infection. Now it was a matter of time. Mike's father stayed in bed the next day. The next morning they checked his infection. It seemed like it had not changed. Mike and Vera talked it over and decided to wait another day. The next morning, seeing that the infection had not changed, Mike sent his father back for some ex-rays of the infected aria.

"Mom," said Mike. "I am getting hungry. I'm going down to the cafeteria for something to eat. Do you want me to get you something?"

"No, I wanted to wait until the results came in. Mike then left for the cafeteria. When He got there he noticed a young woman sitting alone on a small table eating her breakfast.

"Tina," yelled Mike walking hurriedly towards her. Tina however, when she saw Mike, she got up and ran out of the cafeteria down the hall. Mike ran out to the hall but couldn't find her. He was shocked that she ran out. He looked at the table where she was eating and found that she had not finished her breakfast. Shocked, he grabbed a doughnut and a cup of coffee and went back to the hospital room. Mike's father came first so Mike did nothing but wait for the ex-ray results. Later that day the result came in. They were so devastating that it made him forget Tina. The result showed that the infection had spread and that it was starting to affect the bladder. This was a very dangerous thing. Mike talked it over with Vera and he decided that the only answer was surgery.

"I can't operate on my father," said Mike to Vera. "What doctor can we ask to help us?"

I know of a doctor on the first floor who is a fantastic sergeant," said Vera. "Let me go and talk with him." Vera left and went directly to Doctor Jesser's office. The doctor was sitting at his desk.

"Doctor," said Vera. "I am Doctor Costello's assistant. We are looking for a doctor to help us with a surgery. Can I talk to you about this?"

"Come on in," said the doctor. "What does the heavenly angel want with me? He has the reputation of having godly power to bring dead people back to life"

"I'm sorry doctor," said Vera. "Do you hate Doctor Costello?"

"No, I don't hate him," said Doctor Jesser. "I admire him. I'm just very jealous. What is the problem?"

"His father has a very bad infection around his colon. It is spreading onto his Blather. He doesn't want to operate on his father," can you do the surgery. I think you have to move the colon. The problem seems to be under the colon. The infection has moved so that it is now at the edge of the bladder.

"I will come over tomorrow afternoon, "said Doctor Jesser.

"Thank you," said Vera and left.

Doctor Jesser came into the hospital room in the early afternoon. Mike's mother was the only one there.

"My name is Doctor Jesser. My office is on the first floor. I was asked to help this patient." He then examined Mike's father. After he had examined him he went into Mike's office.

"Hello Doctor Costello," said Doctor Jesser. "I am here to help you. I have examined all the ex-rays and I have examined your patient. I think surgery needs to be performed as soon as possible."

"Please call me Mike. I will be available as soon as you are."

"I have a surgery scheduled for tomorrow morning but I will cancel it and be ready at eight tomorrow morning. We can do the surgery in your surgical room. We don't want your patient to lose his Bladder."

"That will be great," said Mike. "See you then."

"OK, I will see you tomorrow morning," said Doctor Jesser. "By the way, you can call me Harry." Next morning Doctor Jesser was there with his assistant. Vera was also there. The surgery took only one hour. After the surgery was complete doctor Jesser went into Mike's office. Mike was there waiting patiently.

"Well," said Doctor Jesser as he walked in. "The surgery was very successful. I found that under the colon between the colon and the bladder was a tumor. It was surrounded by an infection. The infection had already started on the Bladder. We got there just in time. It was no problem removing the infection which was caused by the Tumor. I cleaned the whole area and washed it with an infection killing drug. I think he will be able to go home in about six days. We should check him every three days at least twice to see that no infection returned. However, since I removed the tumor it is unlikely that it will return."

"Thank you so much," said Mike. "How can I ever repay you for what you have done for me?"

"Well if I need help maybe you could help me," said Doctor Jesser. "OK then, you can take it from here. Keep in touch."

"Thanks again," said Mike. There are no words in the English language that can tell you how grateful I am. You are welcome to come and check on my father any time."

"Take care," said Doctor Jesser and then left. Mike moved his dad to the recovery room where he made sure he was recovering as expected. After an hour he moved him into the hospital room that was his. He then got his mother and explained to her only what she really needed to know. Mainly that he will be fine in three days. Mike's father was just beginning to wake up. Mike's mother hugged him and kissed him on his cheek. Seeing that things were all looking good, he thought of Tina. It was only a little past ten. He decided to go and see Sophia. She was in her office.

"Do you have a few minutes?" said Mike. "I need to talk with you."

"Sure," said Sophia. "Come and sit by my desk. How is your dad doing?"

"He is fine. Doctor Lesser removed a tumor and some infection." said Mike. However, I didn't come in here to talk about my job. I came to talk to you about the suggestion I made for a financial advisor."

"Yes," said Sophia. "I have already hired one.

"Yes," said Mike. "I saw Tina in the cafeteria.

"Who did you say you saw?" asked Sophia.

"I saw the girl I recommended," said Mike.

"What did you say her name was?" asked Sophia.

"Her name is Tina Bano," said Mike.

"I never heard of her," said Sophia. "I hired a young girl named Catina Banozano, " said Sophia. "She did such a great job. She also impressed me with her wonderful personality. I was so impressed that I hired her as my assistant. I am getting old and I could use the help."

"But I saw Tina in the building," said Mike, being confused. "Can she have two names?"

"Of course," said Sophia. "That is why we couldn't find her. Can't you see? They are the same one. The one I hired is named Catina Banozano. Catina is the Italian name for the American name Catherine. Because she was traveling around the country every few months she shortened her first name from Catania to just Tina. And her last name from Banozano to just Bano."

"Why did she change her name back to her full name?" asked Mike.

"She hated to use her full name every few months," said Sophia. "Now she does not have to."

"Why is it different now?" asked Mike.

"She worked here for two weeks at the beginning. She said that she no longer wanted to move around. She was asking for a full time job in one place. After seeing the great job she did and I was impressed by her personality, I hired her not just as our financial adviser but as my assistant. I'm getting old and could use some help running the Hospital."

"So now she is a full time employee?" asked Mike.

"Yes," said Sophia, "she is a full time assistant manager."

"Does she have her office here?" asked Mike.

Yes," said Sophia. It is in room 223, down the hall from here. However, she will not be there. She is working on the third shift. She goes home at eight in the morning just when you come in."

"Why is she working that shift?" asked Mike.

"A lot of the redesign is easier if the regular workers were not there. She doesn't want to interfere with the normal worker. Not only that they would get into each other's way.

"How is she doing?" asked Mike, being impressed.

"In the first two weeks she has increased the hospital income so that even after her income we are still earning twice that we were earning before she got here."

"I had heard that when I told you about her," said Mike. "It is a coincidence that you hired her anyway."

"It was a gift from God," said Sophia.

"If she goes home at eight in the morning," said Mike, "she must come in about midnight. I will have to come in early to see her."

"She said that she will be working the third shift for about three more weeks." said Sophia. "After that she could make financial changes with people there. But most importantly, she also needed to train the workers to use the new equipment."

"Thank you very much," said Mike and left.

The next morning Mike tried to get up early but he was too tired and could only make it by seven thirty. He went directly to her office. It was almost eight. As he got off the elevator he saw Tina walking down the hall towards the elevator.

"Tina," yelled Mike down the hall towards her. She walked right past him yelling back at him.

"What don't you understand," said Tina. "I don't want anything to do with you." She got into the elevator and left Mike in a state of shock. When he came too, he rushed down to the cafeteria thinking that she would be there. She was not there. Mike could not find her. Mike was not going to give up. He remembered his father telling him about the power of the heart. He remembered that his father said that if you desire it in your mind you could give up what you wanted. But if you place what you want in your heart, the power of the heart will never let you quit going after what you wanted. Mike decided he was going to fight for her. First he had to find out why she was angry with him. What did he do that made her angry? He then went directly to his father's hospital room. His dad was just waking up.

"Hi dad," said Mike. "How are you feeling?"

"He is just waking up," said Mike's mother. Mike was hoping she was still asleep.

"Hi mom," said Mike. "Why are you not asleep? It is only around eight in the morning."

"I have been awake most of the morning. I am waiting to see how your father is."

"I told you that it was a simple surgery," said Mike.

"I want to hear it from him," said Mike's mother.

What are you two arguing about?" said Mike's dad, now wide awake.

"How are you feeling honey," said Mike's mother. She then got up and kissed him. "How do you feel?"

"I feel like I'm still half asleep," said Mike's father. "Mike, you tell me how I should feel," said his father.

"Joseph honey," said Mike's mother. "Please tell us what you are feeling."

"Sweet Nicola," said Mike's father. "I just told you. I feel like my whole body is asleep."

"Dad," started Mike, "you will be back to normal in a few days. You had a minor surgery." Mike then explained in detail what was done to him.

"Thanks to the Lord," said Mike's dad. Mike examined his

dad and after he finished he turned to his mom. How long are you going to stay here? Dad will not leave for a few days. We have to watch the cut on his side heal."

"I will stay as long as he does," said Mike's mother.

"You can't stay here all day," said Mike. "You are going to need some rest, some food and a little while away from here."

"I told you what I am going to do," said Mike's mother. "Go out into the hospital and take care of your other patients." Mike thought that he should leave them alone for a while. He left and headed to his office. He had postponed all his other jobs. So, he headed out to see some of the patients that were recovering on the second floor of the hospital. He was about to enter one of the rooms when he was encountered with his nurse Vera.

Hi doc," said Vera. She only called him Mike when they were alone. In the hallway she didn't want to take the chance of anyone hearing her. "How is your dad?"

"He is doing fine," said Mike.

"What are you doing down here," said Vera. "Did you run out of patients on the third floor?"

"I canceled all my calls thinking I was going to stay with my father," said Mike "However I feel like he and my mother would like to be alone. I don't know why. She is going to be stuck there for at least three days. What are you doing down here?" asked Mike.

"Sometimes I come down here to help," said Vera. "You do also sometimes."

"I'm deep in worry about my dad," said Mike, "so I didn't want any of the third floor patients to see me in a dull mood."

"If you don't have anything to do," said Vera. "I have a favor to ask you."

"How can I help you?" asked Mike.

"I have a patient with Doctor Jesser, said Vera. I think Doctor Jesser is ready to give up on him. I think the patient heard Doc telling me that he didn't think he had a chance. He is now in his room crying. If I know you, I think you can save him." Vera showed Mike all the records she had of the patient including an Ex-ay. Mike checked the room number and the name of the patient.

"I will see what I can do," said Mike. I need a distraction anyway."

"I hope you can help him," said Vera. Mike went directly to the patient's room.

"Hello Todd," said Mike as he entered the room. "I hear that you are worried about your health. I think I can help you."

"Who are you?" asked Todd. "I don't know you."

"I'm Doctor Mike Costello. "I specialize in sickness like you have."

"I have cancer in my stomach area," said Todd, "and it is spreading like crazy."

"What religion do you believe in," asked Mike. "Do you have faith in your beliefs?"

"I don't believe in things like Gods and especially angels." said Todd. "I think it is all a spam to have control of the people."

"What is your education like?" asked Mike.

"Before I got sick I was in college," said Todd. "I was studying corporate Management."

"Apparently you are pretty intelligent," said Mike. "Let me ask you a few questions. Where do you think people came from?'' Do you think that two pieces of dirt got together and decided to join other pieces of dirt and become a living thing? You know man has many parts in the body that we don't even understand. Do you think they all just happened by chance?"

"I never thought of that," said Todd. "I never thought of where life or even the planet came from. You have given me something to think about."

"Well think of this," said Mike. "Let's say that there is an unexplained existence of a power that is not material. And that power can design and create fantastic things and can create life and all material things."

"Do you think it designs and set up things like trees?" asked Todd

I'm glad you asked," said Mike. "Let's take the seed of an apple. If you plant it in a good ground with water it grows into an apple tree. Do you ever wonder how that happens?

"No," said Todd. "I just know it happens."

"Well let me tell you how." said Mike. "Inside the seed is software that tells the seed what to do. It also has a little battery-like thing that gives it a little energy to start the process. The software tells it how to get water out of the ground and how to get some material from the ground to start the process of growing the tree. It follows the software and until the little branch sprouts out of the ground. It then tells it how to grow small leaves. The battery is about out when it gets energy from the leaves which get it from the sun. Then the seed reads the software and makes the tree."

"This is all very interesting but what has this to do with me," asked Todd.

"I am trying to get you to accept that nothing you see or have could have come to being by itself. It all had a designer and builder," said Mike. "I want you to accept the builder who sent his son to earth to pay for our sins. What I want you to do is accept the son, Jesus, as your savior. If you accept him he will make you a son of God. When you accept all this he will love you and help you in your problem. He will surprise you with his help. Do you accept him?"

"What you say makes a lot of sense," said Todd. "I would be a fool if I didn't accept Christ as my savior."

"Great," said Mike. "I know you have a little doubt but that is normal." He then called Vera who came in and gave Todd a shot which put him to sleep and they brought him to Mike's surgery room. Mike quickly set everything up and when he was sure Todd was asleep he started the surgery. He eliminated the tumor that was the cause of it all and then he spent everything he had and knew to wipe out the cancerous cells around the area the tumor was in. He spread a certain chemical that he knew would eliminate any cancer that would want to recur. He then closed the surgical cut and moved him to the recovery room.

"I think you did a great job," said Vera. "Doctor Jesser was sure he was going to die."

"I understand his reasoning," said Mike, "he doesn't want to be known as the doctor whose patient died in his surgery room. I trust in the lord so I don't care what people think. Will you take over and keep me informed."

"I will keep a close eye on him," said Vera. That said Mike left and went to his father's room.

"Hi dad, how are you doing," said Mike. "You look like you want to get up."

"I want to get up and go home," said Mike's father.

"I promise that you will go home," said Mike. "We have to keep you for three days. It will go quickly." Mike then turned to his mother. "Have you been eating OK?"

"I have been getting a small meal three times a day from the cafeteria," said Mike's mother. "It is too much."

"I would have you throw some away rather than starve." After some small talk Mike went back to his visiting and encouraged some of his patients.

Mike visited his dad at least twice a day. Finally, on the third day Mike walked into His dad's room.

"Dad," said Mike. "I have good news. The ex-rays you took this morning show that you are free of any infections. I have permission to let you go home. So mom, if you will help him dress, I will get a nurse that will take you to your car so that you can go home. I will be back with a nurse and a wheel chair. Both are necessary. Five minutes later Mike came with Vera and a wheel chair. Mike's father was all dressed and to Mike's surprise he didn't complain about the wheelchair. When Mike's father was settled in the wheelchair he was pushed out of the room and down the hall. "Goodbye Dad and mom. See you tonight. Mom, I expect a fantastic dinner. Mike's mother smiles as they leave. Mike was ready to go to his office when he got a call from the second floor nurse.

"Hello," said the nurse. "Is this Doctor Costello?"

"Yes," said Mike. "This is he."

"Our patient Todd Marten would like to see you," said the nurse. Can you take a moment to speak to him?"

"I will be right down," said Mike. Five minutes later Mike walked into Todd's room. Todd was all dressed up and ready to go home.

"Hi Doc," said Todd. "I didn't want to leave without telling you how much I appreciated that you have given me my life. All the nurses and doctors tell me that you are a special doctor with fantastic medical abilities. "I can now see what they see."

Oh Todd. They don't know what they are saying. I am a human just like you. I don't have any more intelligence that they all have. What they don't see is that I am a shovel and God is the farmer. I am just a tool that God uses. I am no one special except that I have given myself as a tool to God."

"Then I not only thank you, I also thank God," said Todd

"Are you going back to be a Corporate Manager?" asked Mike.

"No," said Todd. "I am changing to be a teacher. At home we have a Christian city but our schools are directing our children away from Christ. "I am going to stop that and teach the children what I have learned these last few days."

"God Bless you and May God help you." Todd the hugged Mike and said Goodbye. Mike headed back to his office. He was so happy that his father and Todd, a new Christian man, we're going home. As Mike walked down the third floor he saw Catina's office. Mike decided that he was not going to give up. He wanted to know what happened between them. Mike remembered his father telling him about the power of the heart. Mike therefore decided that in his heart he wanted Tina. He then decided that he would go home and come back around midnight. He had to find out what Tina had against him. It was now Friday. Mike decided to wait until Monday. That gave him the whole week to get what he wanted. He also decided to go in the second shift. The second shift started at four in the afternoon and ended at midnight. Mike decided that he could stay a little longer and catch Tina at work, hopefully in her office. He had notified Sophia that he had some special work and would be working the second shift. Sophia agreed.

Monday Mike stayed in bed most of the morning. He wanted to be alert that late at night. Mike got to work at four in the afternoon that Monday. At about twelve thirty Monday night Mike went to Tina's office. She was there preparing to go to one of the departments she was working on.

"Hi Tina," said Mike as he walked into her office. "How are you doing this morning?"

"What are you doing here," said Tina. "Why can't you understand that I don't want anything to do with you? Now I'm out of my office. I have something important to do right now."

"I just want to know why you have changed your mind so quickly," said Mike. You owe me that explanation. The last time we were together you were the love of my life."

"I found out that you were a womanizer," said Tina. "I am a born-again Christian. I am looking for a lifetime partner who does not go after other girls."

"What makes you think I go after other girls?" asked Mike.

"I saw you on your knees telling another girl how much you loved her," said Tina. "Go away; I have to go to work." With that Tina left. Mike stood there completely shocked. What was she talking about? He never told another woman that he loved her. Then the thought came suddenly to his memory. He realized that she may have seen him when he was telling his sister Katherine, when she was getting over her car accident, how much he loved her. Mike decided he had a full day to answer her,

The next day about fifteen minutes after midnight, Mike went back to Tina's office. As he expected she was there getting ready to go to one of the departments that she was reorganizing.

"Tina," said Mike as he entered her office. He never got to continue when Tina jelled out.

"What will it take to get rid of you," she said. "Do I have to call the police and charge you with harassment?"

"I just have three things to say to you and then I promise that you will never see me again," said Mike.

"All right," said Tina, "what are your excuses?"

"First I want to tell you," started Mike. "I have never dated another girl since I dated you. In God's name I am telling you these facts. Secondly, I am not interested in you anymore. I do not accept a woman with your personality. You could have fought for me and asked me to explain my actions. And, thirdly I admit that I love Katherine with all of my heart. I will love her until I die. She is a wonderful sister. Have a great life," said Mike and left the room. It took Tina a few minutes for all to sink into her mind. Suddenly she sank into her chair with a very shocked look that soon turned into tears. She realized that in spite of everything even before this morning that she still loved Mike. She realized that her stupid action was due to her heart break feeling and her loss of mental control which started in California. She remembered that when she was with him, back in California, that she lost control of her mind. Due to the different hours they worked it was hard for them to get together.

Two months later, Tina went back to the first shift. It was now easy for Tina to go and see Mike. Mike had no plans on seeing Tina. Tina however was going crazy and wanted to get Mike back. She had to build up courage. It took a week when she decided to go to Mike's office in the morning. It was about eight in the morning when Tina went into Mike's office. Mike was there on his computer.

"Hello Mike," said Tina as she walked into Mike's office, "can I see you for a few minutes?"

"Is this hospital business?" asked Mike.

"No," said Tina. "I know that you can't forgive me. I just want to remind you of something."

"What's on your mind?" said Mike with a not too friendly voice.

"I just want you to think back to when we first met," said Tina. "It was love at first sight. If you remember our stomachs had fireflies in them and our brain found it hard to think clearly. At least mine was like I was drunk. I had no idea of what to do or say. That is why I reacted the way I did. I wasn't thinking straight. I was heartbroken and could never be sadder than I was seeing you tell another woman how much you loved her. How would you have reacted if you saw me telling another fellow how much I loved him? I just wanted you to know why I acted so stupidly. Have a great day."

"I will think about it," said Mike. "You have a great day." As she left Mike was stunned. He wasn't thinking straight. Mike started to remember how he felt back when he first met Tina. He was in a state of mind he had never been in before. He didn't know what to say or do. She was right. They were not in a very stable state of mind. In fact he felt that at present he was not in a good state of mind. He needed some time to settle his mind. One thing he was sure of. He loved the girl he knew in California. Mike went to bed that night with only one thing on his mind.

The next day, Mike went to Tina's office.

"Tina," said Mike, "we need to talk. I have been thinking of what you said. You were right. We were not in our right mind. However we do have a problem. We don't see each other as the person we really are. We don't know our real personality. You think I am after girls. I think you are an arrogant girl who always wants your way. We have to get to know each other as we really are."

"I agree heartily," said Tina. "What do you suggest?"

"I think we have to go back like we were in California. We have to date until we learn who we really are. Let's start tonight. We can go to a movie which I would like to do some time but not now. We can't get to know each other in a movie. I think we should go to a restaurant and have dinner together and we can stay there for a long time or we can find a club or bar that had music we could dance to. I would like to get my arms around you.

"I would love that," said Tina. "Will you let me go home and clean up? You can pick me up at six."

"Of course," said Mike, "that would be perfect."

They followed that routine every day except on Sunday. Sunday Mike went to church with his parents. The rest of the days they had dinner together and often they went to a club or restaurant that had music they could dance to. Sometimes they had to go out of town to get what they wanted. What Mike liked the best was the good night kiss. Every night it lasted longer. Days went by quickly. Soon winter came. They canceled a few dates because of bad weather. It didn't hurt because they had found out what they wanted to know. Mike found out that Tina had a very sweet personality. Her heart was very sweet and caring. He found out that he loved her twice as much as he did before. Tina found that Mike had a very joyful personality. He was exactly what she wanted. Soon it was Christmas. Mike had informed his parents about his time with Tina. Mike's parents invited Tina for the Christmas dinner. On Christmas day when Tina arrived at Mike's house she was very shy. However, as she entered Mike's mother hugged her and brought her inside.

"It's so nice to meet you," said Mike's mother. "Mike has not stopped talking about you.

"We are so glad you could come," said Mike's father. "We want to thank you for making Mike such a happy person. We thank you also because since you have been dating Mike we have saved several dinners. Tina knew that Mike's father was kidding.

"Well if I have my way you will save three meals," said Tina following Mike's father's joking.

"Dinner is ready," said Mike's Mother. "Are you all ready to eat?"

"Just wait a little while," said Mike. "I have something I have to say. Mike then went over to Tina's chair and went down on his knees. "Tina, will you marry me?" said Mike, showing her a lovely ring. Tina was shocked. She never expected that to happen. However, she could not hold back the word, yes. Mike then put the ring on her finger and hugged and kissed her. Mike's parents followed Mike's action and hugged and kissed Tina. The evening went by as jolly as an evening could. They declared their love for each other and finally the evening was soon over. All parted with love and joy in their hearts.

Mike and Tina spent New Year's with Mike's parents. It was during this period that Mike's parents wanted to know more about Tina. She first explained about her education and Job.

"Where are your parents," asked Mike's father.

"My father passed away several years ago. They only had me in their old age. My mom is at a nursing home. She has a mental problem. She doesn't recognize me or anyone.

"Sorry," said Mike's mother. "Well you are going to have parents soon. Have you guys planned your wedding jet?

"No," said Tina. "We are going to need your help setting it all up."

"I would be thrilled to help you," said Mike's mother. "Let me know when you want to start the planning."

It was about a month later that they started planning the marriage. Unfortunately, there were many weddings taking place that year so the soonest they could get the hall and all the other things that had to be planned was May 6. Therefore, they had four months to get everything ready. The time went by too quickly. Mike and Tina invited Vera and most of the nurses and doctors at the hospital. Tina asked Vera, Mike's nurse, to be her Maid of honor. Mike asked Todd to be his best man. About two days before the wedding Mike and Tina's minds became unaware of the time. They were both in a trance. They were hardly aware of the rehearsal and rehearsal dinner. The only thing that stuck in Mike's mind was Tina walking down the path being led by Mike's father. She was so beautiful in her wedding dress. During the wedding he remembered his lines of promise to Tina. He remembered hearing her promise to love and obey. And most of all he remembered the pastor saying,

"I now pronounce you husband and wife. You may kiss the bride"

The rest of the evening he remembered vaguely. He was like being in a trace. Everything from that moment was vague. The next thing he remembered, like he just snapped out of his trance, he was driving down the highway going on his honeymoon.

"Sweet heart," said Mike. "Are we dreaming, or is this really happening? All I know for sure is that I   love you very much."

"Shut up and take us to Florida," said Tina trying to be funny. "I want to feel your love, not just hear it."

"We are married and you are my wife right?" said Mike grabbing her hand. He had finally snapped out of his trance.

"And you know what is funny," said Tina. "During the day I am your boss and during the night you are my boss.

"You are still dreaming," said Mike with a large smile on his face.

The End